Redemption Ridge

The Taliaferro Chronicles

Volume II

Reneé Porter

Roet Press   Plantation, FL

DEDICATION

For Rob, who does hear the piano most nights.

ACKNOWLEDGMENTS

It's strange how life takes twists sometimes. This book was one of those twists. I never intended to write another book about the Taliaferro sisters. But, as wiser writers than I have said, sometimes characters will not leave. They're there, knocking around on the inside of your brain, saying, "We have more to tell you. Listen." And so, The Taliaferro Chronicles were born.

If you have a first edition of *The 13th Victim* in paper, you'll notice that the Taliaferro Chronicles aren't mentioned. That's because they didn't exist and I had already started my next novel, *Bell Park*. The second edition of *The 13th Victim* does mention the Chronicles.

So first, I must acknowledge my readers who responded far beyond my expectations with my other books. The world becomes a bigger place when readers become as involved in your characters' lives as the characters became involved in your life as a writer.

That my books, published by a small independent press in Florida, managed to reach a wider audience completely surprised me. I will never take those readers for granted. And, to those who asked for this book, I hope you enjoy it and the two more to follow. (Yes, those characters still have more to tell about their story.)

I have to thank P.J., my editor, and the staff at Roet Press. I know I can be hard-headed sometimes – remember I was an editor once myself. So forgive my grouchy phone calls. You know it's been a tough year and your patience is much appreciated.

As always, I have to acknowledge the support of my love, Rob, who gives me strength, forgives my absence from daily life when I'm writing, and who remembers the real anniversaries. To my friends and family who were always there – my sister, Janie, and my brother, Robbie, Tami, Pam, Erna, Bobbie & Jim Jackson, and Jamie Parker. I cannot thank you enough for your friendship.

Reneé Porter

Chapter One

1975

Their first kill was accidental. If the old man hadn't been walking the ridge alone. If he hadn't been wearing a brown plaid flannel coat. If their dads had come with them or had made them obey the hunting laws, for that matter. If Sandy at the Beer Bell had asked them for ID (though they decided later that that one didn't count because Sandy had a crush on Doug and would have given them the beer free.) A lot of ifs Doug called it or the old man might not have died that glorious October afternoon.

At first they decided that no matter how they looked at it, they agreed that it was the old man's fault. Years later when they were still killing, his death was the one they remembered most. They laughed about walking across the ridge to where he lay gasping for breath. That was when they found that they liked killing people more than deer.

Although deer hunting season was almost six weeks away, that Sunday afternoon deer hunt was their own reward to themselves for having played what they considered an excellent football game the night before – one where they had trounced Clay County 35-0.

They had decided to go hunting the night before while driving home from the game and playing their favorite game of busting mail boxes. As they took turns driving and swinging a baseball bat at the mailboxes, they were also finishing off the case of beer that Doug's dad had just given them.

Doug's dad was proud of his quarterback son and rewarded the boys with a case of Schlitz every time they won a game. The reward wasn't as good when they lost like when they had failed to beat Woodrow Wilson last year in the Regionals. Doug's dad had beaten the shit out him. Doug took the beating without saying a word. Doug accepted it as the way things were supposed to be and knew he just had to do better the next time.

When Doug was little, he had asked his mother to keep his dad from hitting him, but his mother, Helen, told him to take it like a man and to stop being a whiny baby like his older brother, Sammy. Not that Doug's dad had spared her or his brother in his rages either. He had been harder on them. But Doug was determined to show his dad what a man he could be, so he was as merciless on the football field as he was off. He was a bully hero of his high school. If he were beaten at home, some poor jerk would get beaten at school the next day just for being in the hall or the bathroom or the locker room at the wrong time.

But the Sunday afternoon the boys shot the old man, they discovered so much more about themselves than their families or church or school or football or sex or even drinking had ever taught them. It had taught them that watching a person die was the best high they could get.

The day was warm enough to shed their jackets, but they kept them on anyway. They were the varsity stars of Gladstone High and they wore their letter jackets everywhere. They kept their hair just a little bit shorter than most kids in their school, especially the hippie band students or even the shop boys who stayed away from them most of the time. The slightly shorter hair was a symbol of whom they believed they were in the social order of the school. They believed they had their choice of any girl at the school, although they weren't really liked by many of their fellow students. But they were feared and because they associated being liked with being feared, they never knew what most people thought of them.

Doug was stupidly unaware of what the girls in the school had to say about him. At 5'9", his shortcomings were more than just his height and more than a few girls had giggled over that. With light brown hair and a constant smirk, he was not handsome, but he was muscular. He never understood the difference between the two. One of the cheerleaders, who had spent a few too many hours watching the *Gong Show*, always called him the Unknown Comic - someone with muscles but who needed a bag on his head before she would go near him.

Tim was handsome and tall, but not very bright. When Doug wasn't with him, he could be kind. But Doug was almost always with him and that tainted his reputation. It was only after Doug went off to college that Tim began to make other friends.

That day in the mountains above the New River Valley where the seemingly benign, but actually deadly river meandered below them, the leaves had turned bright red and orange, almost glowing against the brilliance of the clear turquoise blue sky. The river looked small and peaceful from where they sat, but one of the earlier lessons they had learned in life was that the river killed and it killed fast.

Tim told Doug once that he had heard a legend that the river was called New in English because the Indian word for the river sounded the same as the word new, but that the Indian word actually meant death. Doug told him he was stupid to believe those old stories.

But that legend, whether true or not, was one they came to believe because of their own young stupidity.

When they were twelve years old, they dragged the rusted and abandoned car top of a 1950s Dodge and decided to use it to float down the river. They pushed the car top into the water and then jumped on, each of them grabbing a long metal arm at the front of the car top, thinking they could use it to steer the top through the water.

They had gone about a quarter of a mile when they realized they were in real trouble. The car top kept hitting hidden rocks that tossed the top and them with it up into the air, causing it to spin wildly. They finally both jumped from the car top in what looked to be a place close to the bank. As they crawled up over the bank they watched as the car top was thrown high in the air and landed in the river right side up. It had overturned and sank as it bashed itself against one large rock. After that day, they watched the river from above. Tim was thoroughly convinced that the river was cursed, but Doug came to believe that just like most rivers, it could kill the stupid and foolish and decided to stay away from most rivers, choosing to swim at the swimming pool at the state park instead.

They had almost finished off the case of Schlitz when they saw a movement in the tree line across from them. The old man's brown plaid jacket had just enough cream in it to fool Tim's drunken eyesight into thinking that he was looking at a doe.

Tim picked up his shotgun believing a doe would be an easy shot, but he was too drunk to see the old man's human face and thinning white hair. He just saw a brown movement in the trees and fired. He missed and the shot went wide and far in front of the man, but not wide enough for the old man to realize some idiot had shot at him. The old man took off running, but in his confusion came running towards the boys instead of down the opposite hillside away from them. Tim, still thinking it was a deer, started giggling and tried to aim and shoot, but missed again.

The old man was Bill Harrison. He had left his home at the base of the other side of the mountain earlier that Sunday, thinking about his dead wife, Sarah Jane, and how much she would have loved this beautiful autumn afternoon.

He was 72 and the black lung was slowly killing him after spending his life working in the black dust of the Seneca Sycamore Mines. Although he had tried to get disability, the people at the disability place had denied it every time so he just had to keep working until he was old enough to collect his Social Security.

He had never expected to live to see 72 or outlive Sarah Jane, but he had. Of course, his Social Security wasn't much and certainly not enough to pay the hospital bills when Sarah Jane got sick.

He tried not to think of her in that hospital. She had cancer in her female parts, at least that's what the doctors had told him. She had spent most of the last year of her life taking that chemo-poison, as he called it, strapped first to a chair in the hospital and then at the end unable to move in the bed they had put her in to die. He never left her side those last weeks except when the Black Lung made him cough so hard that he was afraid he would wake her. She had been in a lot of pain that even the drugs the doctor gave didn't seem to help. She would moan as she slept and would clench the sheet in her fist with every pain that tore through her tired body.

She had passed one morning at four a.m. He had been holding her fragile hand when she squeezed it one last time and then she was gone. Just like that.

That's why the hike up the hill had been so important. It was about a year ago that he had lost her and he felt the need to see the mountains from the ridge one last time.

The climb had left him wheezing and at one point his breathing hurt so much that he thought he would be seeing Sarah Jane sooner that he had thought, but once he was up there and breathing normally again, or at least what passed for normal for him, he was glad he had done it.

The view from the ridge had been magical for him since he had first gone there as a child with his parents. He had grown up on that mountain, chased through the woods as a wild boy, had kissed his Sarah Jane there the first time, and had conceived the first of his kids there one starlit summer night.

His kids had long since moved away from Gladstone Gap, and while he missed them and his grandchildren something fierce, he was glad that they had found jobs in Detroit where they wouldn't end their lives coughing up black tar just to keep breathing. It had been his dream to send them off to college, but every time he would get some money put back, it seemed that a strike would stop work or the company would do lay-offs and the money he had saved would be spent just trying to keep his family fed.

He was thinking of his new baby great-grandson when the first shot came whistling by him. He got turned around and didn't see the boys over on the ridge with the guns. He just started running in a circle, completely confused at the sounds of the gunshots whistling around him.

By that time Tim was so drunk that he dropped his gun and slid off the rock he had been sitting on, holding his sides as he laughed uncontrollably. He was way too drunk to realize that he had been shooting at a person and not a deer.

But Doug saw from the first shot that it was no deer. He saw the old man's face and waited until after Tim had taken the second shot. When he saw that Tim was too far gone to do anything else, he took his rifle and carefully aimed at the old man, leading him just a bit before firing. The old man went down with one shot.

"You got it!" Tim said and picked up his shotgun and began heading across the top of the mountain where he thought he had seen a deer fall.

Doug didn't say a word. He knew what was waiting and felt a little bit of excitement building in his gut as he followed his friend through the woods. He wondered what Tim would say when he realized what had really happened.

Tim stopped about 20 feet from the old man and turned back toward Doug and started to puke. Doug carefully avoided his friend's vomiting and walked up to the old man. The only surprise he found was that the old man was still alive, blood pouring from the wound in his belly. By that time, Tim had sobered up enough to join Doug next to the old man.

"Shit, Doug, you shot a person. Shit. Ah, shit, what're we gonna do? Your dad's gonna kill us if he finds out."

Doug looked over at his friend and saw that he was starting to turn a little green again.

"Well, I guess we can't let daddy know about this," he said.

Tim stared at him, his eyes wide with fear.

"We can't leave him here. He's still breathing. Shit, shit, shit. We are in so much trouble."

Doug grabbed Tim's shotgun and pushed it into his hands.

"Shoot him. Where ever you want. Just don't kill him yet. Let's watch what he does."

Tim stared at Doug in horror and then the beer buzz kicked in again and he began to giggle.

"Anywhere?" he asked.

"Sure, why not? We can throw his body down one of the old caves after. Anyway, no one knows we're up here. We'll clean up good and no one would think it was us up here if someone does find him."

Tim giggled again and aimed the shot gun at the old man's knees and shot.

The old man screamed and tried to get up to get away from them. Between the gut shot and the buckshot in his knees, he couldn't move much at all, but he did open his eyes and saw the two boys standing over him. His eyes showed his terror, confusion, but also some hope that he could reason with the two boys into helping him.

But before he could utter a word, Doug casually took his rifle and shot the old man in the hand. Instead of words begging for help, the old man screamed again, the sound echoing down into the valley below. Tim started giggling again.

"My turn now. It's my turn now," he said and pushed Doug to the side. This time he shot at the old man's feet, but the buckshot almost severed one of the old man's feet and Doug put his hand on the shotgun to stop Tim.

"Don't do too much. We gotta find a way to carry him to get rid of him and I don't wanna be carrying his feet around after we throw him in a hole," Doug said.

"You're right. Sure. Damn, do you think he's still alive?" Tim asked.

Doug walked over to the old man's head and gently prodded it with his boot. The old man groaned and clutched his gut with one hand

"Hey, old fuck, still breathing?" Doug asked.

The old man was quietly weeping and by his shallow breathing, Doug thought he might be bleeding out.

Tim had stumbled closer to examine the damage they had inflicted on the old man's body.

"I ain't ever seen a person die 'cept in the movies," Tim said as he tried to focus on the wounds they had inflicted on the old man.

Doug looked at Tim and wondered if he was just drunk or was really that stupid.

"They don't really die in the movies, asshole."

Doug walked back to the feet of the man near where Tim now stood.

"Stand back. We don't want his blood to get on our jackets. My dad would kill me if he had to buy me a new one," Doug said to Tim.

Both boys moved back about 20 feet and Doug took careful aim at the man's crotch and fired. That was a scream that the boys would never forget. Later that night, they would both go to their separate homes and close their eyes tightly as they jerked off to the memory of the old man's last scream.

Neither of them realized that nothing would satisfy them sexually after that moment except for the memories of the torture they would inflict on their victims. And, that first time, that first death, nothing would be a sweet as that.

"Take your clothes off except for your underwear," Doug said.

"What the hell are you talking about?" Tim said.

Doug threw his varsity jacket in Tim's face. What a moron, he thought.

"If we go home with bloody clothes, somebody's gonna figure out we did do something so get your fucking clothes off. I ain't carrying that old man to that cave by myself."

Tim blushed. "Oh, ok. I just . . ."

"Oh shut the fuck up and help me," Doug said.

Doug thought that by the time both of them had undressed and walked back to the body that the old man would be dead, but the old bastard was still breathing.

"Shit. Tim, go back and get my knife. This old fucker just won't die."

Tim ran across the hilltop in his white briefs and he forgot to put his shoes back on and his feet hurt on the rough rocks on the trail. Tim's dancing among the rocks made Doug laugh and as he laughed, the old man opened his eyes and surprised Doug by speaking.

"Why, son? Why? You're gonna go to hell for this. Why? I don't even know you," he said.

Doug jumped back from the old man so fast that he landed in a dead blackberry bush. How was the man still able to talk? The thorns scratched his arms and back and felt like bee stings. By the time he had crawled out of the bush, Tim was back with the knife.

Doug walked over to the old man. He didn't want to hear anything else from the man's mouth and he intended to cut his throat, but as he leaned in to make the cut, he realized the old man was dead and put the knife back in its sheath.

For a moment he wondered if the old man had spoken to him at all.

"Grab his feet. I'll get his shoulders. And try not to get blood on yourself," Doug said.

Tim picked up one foot, but the other was hanging by shreds where the buckshot had torn into the ankle. He reached above the dangling foot and grasped the man's shin instead.

Both boys were surprised by how light the old man was. They had expected his dead weight to be heavy, but the man was skinnier than either of them had thought.

The afternoon sun was beginning to fade and they hurried to cram the old man's body into a small cave mouth down from where they had shot him. They pushed his body into the hole and then covered the hole with some brush and pieces of deadfall from the maples on the hilltop.

By the time they had cleaned up the mess, dressed, and gathered their guns and beer, they saw it was close to dark as they climbed down the mountain to where Doug had parked his pick-up. Neither of them spoke as they performed this ritual, though Tim stopped once more to puke as they headed down the hill.

It was only when Doug was pulling in front of Tim's house that Tim finally spoke.

"What do you think his name was? I ain't never seen him around here before."

Doug looked up the street at the old coal camp houses built almost on top of the road. When the old mine companies had first built the houses, they had left just enough room between the two mountains for the railroad, a regular road, the houses and a tiny back alley next to Gladstone Creek where the mine run-off and sewage poured into it.

Doug turned to Tim and just shrugged. "Does it matter?"

Tim didn't respond and started getting his gear out of the back of the truck.

"Guess I'll see you at practice tomorrow. We got that Oak Hill game coming up," he said.

Doug smiled and said "Sure thing. We'll kick their asses," and drove on down the road toward his dad's farm.

He felt good and he would be getting home early for a Sunday night. His mom would be happy to see him there when she got home from evening church.

As he pulled up to his folk's old farmhouse that sat a couple miles from the coal camp, he was smiling as he whistled *Bringing in the Sheaves*.

Chapter Two

June 2011

Mary Taliaferro was sitting in her childhood bedroom trying to figure out what exactly she was doing sitting there in a wedding dress. She looked down at her hands and they were shaking so hard that she clasped them together to try to calm herself down.

Downstairs, in the same garden where Pea had married Manley, Joseph was waiting for her with over 50 people, including his New York family. She loved him so much, but she was so scared and she couldn't understand why. She wanted to marry him. She wanted to walk down that aisle to him. She knew he loved her as much as she loved him and that neither one of them was afraid of marriage or their future.

So why was she so afraid right now?

She was on the verge of tears when Pea came into the room to see if she was ready. Pea saw the fear in her sister's blue eyes and went immediately to her, kneeling in the blue violet chiffon sheath in front of her sister.

"Tell me, Ree. Tell me what's wrong. Do you not want to do this because I'll go get Joseph and tell everyone else to go home," Pea said, holding her sister's trembling hands in hers.

Mary shook her head.

After everything that had happened last year, they still called each other by their childhood nicknames. And, although Pea was stubbornly "Pea" to everyone instead of her real name, Pearl, Mary was Ree only to Pea.

Mary reached out and stroked her sister's shoulder length blonde hair and smiled. Since their trauma last year, they had grown closer than either of them could have thought they could be.

"No, I don't know what's wrong. I want to marry him. I love him. I do want to spend my life with him."

She paused and smiled. "I haven't even told him about the baby, yet. I'm saving that for tonight. I am so happy and I love him so much . . . but there's something about going down there that scares the hell out of me."

Pea stood and went to the window. She was Mary's only attendant and she saw Joseph standing there with Thomas next to him. Joseph was quietly and nervously waiting for them to appear. What could the problem be? Joseph's family? They had been cool, but polite. No, Pea thought, Ree wouldn't let that stop her. And that was when Pea realized what was frightening Mary so much.

Oh good lord, Pea thought. How stupid could she be? The garden. It was where she had married Manley and whether Ree realized it or not, that was the problem. So many bad memories of that day, that time, that decade all rolled into the form of one place. Ree had been her lifeline when she had prepared to marry Manley and Ree had seen Manley's deception even that day. So many bad associations were connected with having a wedding there, from Manley to the loss of their parents. How could either of them have missed it? Pea wondered.

Pea hurriedly went back to Mary.

"Ree, can you give me about 15 or 20 minutes? I can fix this," she said.

Mary looked at her sister with complete confusion. How could Pea know what the problem was when she didn't know? She wanted to cry. Joseph would never forgive her for this. She could just hear his family saying "I told you it was a mistake" and seeing him being finally unable to forgive her. Her hands started shaking again.

Pea took Mary's hands in her own and smiled at her sister's beautiful face. They had shared so much together – frustration, pain, love, strength – that Pea felt anything could be solved as long as they had one another.

"Ree, it's the garden. It's the garden. We're just going to move everything to the front of the house. Trust me. You won't be afraid then."

Mary shook her head.

"Pea, that's stupid. Everything looks beautiful, just like . . . oh, shit." She looked up at her sister's smiling face. Pea was right. It was the garden. It did look as it did the day Pea and Manley had married. And Mary had never told Pea that she had thought that their wedding was so, so sad. She had just wanted Pea to be happy, but even then she knew deep in her heart that Manley would never make Pea happy.

It was the garden. She felt so stupid.

"Oh, Pea, you are my hero," she said. "Should I talk to Joseph first?"

This time Pea shook her head and said "absolutely not." She told her sister to just wait there until everything was ready and then Pea ran from the room to the waiting crowd at the back of the house.

It took Mary more than a few minutes to get the courage to go to the window and see what was happening in the garden.

When she saw Joseph and Pea leading everyone to the front of the house, she covered her mouth with her white gloved hand and did start to cry and laugh as she watched their family and friends folding their chairs and moving around the house, laughing and joking with one another as they moved the wedding to the front of the house. She could see a broad smile on Joseph's face and she felt calm for the first time in days. She placed her hand on her white chiffon covered belly and whispered softly, "You are going to have the best daddy in the world. The best."

By the time Mary had returned for her, she had repaired her make-up and was waiting quietly, holding the small bouquet of violets and lilies of the valley, her hands no longer trembling. She took a single violet from the bouquet and placed it in her sister's blonde hair.

"If I forget to say it later, I love you and thank you for this," she said.

Pea smiled and grabbed the tiny bouquet of lilies of the valley she was to carry and took her sister by the arm and led her to the front door. As Pea walked down the makeshift aisle between the crowded chairs filled with smiling faces, she bowed her head and smiled, thinking how lucky both she and Mary were. She glanced about the crowd and saw their local friends, saw Thomas standing next to Joseph, and best of all, saw Trey sitting in the front row.

The pale pink old fashioned roses that her great-grandmother had planted along the front fence filled the air with a sweet perfume. As she reached the end of the aisle and stood back and across from Joseph, she turned to watch Mary begin her own walk down the aisle. As Pea watched Joseph's face, she saw that his focus never left Mary. She almost cried herself then, remembering her own walk down the aisle, how bad it had been and turned her face to Trey whose smile vanquished Manley's ghost immediately.

Joseph and Mary exchanged their own vows and Pea felt so happy for both of them. She couldn't wait for Mary to tell Joseph about the baby, but she had kept Mary's secret. Even Trey didn't know. She was going to tell Trey tonight and Pea knew he would share her joy for her sister and Joseph.

Thomas stood next to Joseph and felt a bittersweet pang as he handed the ring to Joseph to place on Mary's finger. They had all forged a bond last year, but in the hospital Joseph and Thomas had formed a strong friendship that was further bound by Thomas's loss of Shawnette and Joseph's near loss of Mary at Manley's hands.

As Thomas watched the ceremony, he felt a calmness descend and he realized that Shawnette would always be with him, even now. Pea and Mary had not been able to save Shawnette, but they had released him from his self-imposed hell. He looked into the crowd and saw his own date sitting behind Joseph's family on the groom's side.

She was Diana, Shawnette's former roommate, whom he had been seeing for a few months now. She flashed a quick smile at him, but then looked down, her shyness overwhelming her. She was a petite dark beauty and she made him feel like a giant when he stood next to her, but she never made him feel guilty or less a man for failing to save Shawnette.

Diana was so different from Shawnette. Diana was a botany student and had filled his apartment with plants, from scarlet dragon wing begonias to petite African violets. Sometimes that was how he saw the differences between Shawnette and Diana. Shawnette had been brash and bright, a flower that no one could ignore like the scarlet begonia and its cascades of blooms. But Diana was a tiny African beauty who bloomed in all seasons and was there for him from the day he had been wounded and began his long recuperation from Manley's almost fatal shots.

When he had waked up in the hospital to find her sitting across from him, he was stunned. He had tried to speak, but found his voice and throat painfully coarse. Diana had held her finger to his lips and then lifted a straw to his dry lips for him to slowly sip water from. She had stayed with him as much as her schedule allowed and she had been the one who had been there standing next to him as he began the long and arduous ordeal of physical therapy.

At first, he had thought he would never find anyone after Shawnette, but Diana had filled a void that he hadn't seen in his life. After he left the hospital she was there for him in his grief and had grieved with him. Her gentle shyness belied a strength he hadn't seen at first and she had waited for him to stop blaming himself and allow himself to learn to live again.

No, he thought, she was nothing like Shawnette, but she made him happy and that surprised him. He had never thought he would be able to be happy again. Diana had given him that gift.

After the vows were said, everyone headed around to the side pasture to the tent where the reception was to be held. There was much laughter and joy that night and for some of them, more than a few ghosts were finally laid to rest.

As best man, Thomas was given the task of the initial toast. Had it not been for Diana, he would never had been able to find the right words, but Diana had helped him by giving him the gift of a single sonnet by Shakespeare that was more appropriate for Mary and Joseph than any words he could have tried to write.

As he finished the last line, "and no man ever loved," Pea then stood and made her toast for Mary and Joseph, also a simple poem from Emily Dickinson that both summarized their life to this point and celebrated the strength of their love for one for another.

Thomas noticed that Joseph's family had said little either before or after the ceremony and that Joseph's father had kept looking at his Rolex as if the wedding were such a bother. Joseph was such a contrast to his patrician father, who was tall and thin. He was a man who seemed to control every aspect of his life and he looked very uncomfortable sitting in a farm pasture, no matter how beautiful the farm was.

With the exception of his coloring, Joseph took after his mother's Italian family. Joseph's mother was a beauty and Thomas could see that she answered to her husband in every way. Beautiful and smart, but so different from her husband and yet probably completely controlled by his beliefs and opinions. And that was most likely why Thomas had failed to see a smile on her face since the wedding had begun.

Ah, but when Thomas looked to Joseph's tiny grandmother, he saw a different story. She was a woman as happy as anyone there. He hoped that she would help Joseph's family accept Mary, but he didn't think it would be an easy task. It was a fear he shared with Pea and Trey. People outside their small group did not understand what had occurred in any of their lives. They would never understand, but Thomas didn't care. He was there for Joseph and Mary and that was all that was important.

Joseph's family would make it difficult for Mary, Thomas thought, with the exception of Joseph's Nana Giordano who took Mary in as if she were already Joseph's wife. He just hoped that eventually the rest of the family would not fault her role in the events of the past year. Joseph's parents had blamed his heart attack on Mary and on Pea for involving Joseph in a drama that they did not believe concerned him. They could not see the love in Joseph's eyes for Mary. So they sat there stiffly, offering only tight smiles during the reception.

Mary's first visit to Joseph's home had been an "unreal" experience as she described it to her sister. A monster of a house on acres of unused land. Servants everywhere. Formal dinners each night which often were just Joseph and Mary as his parents still worked in the city late most nights. His Nana Giordano still lived in her small house that she and her husband had built over 60 years ago.

Mary had told Pea that they spent most of the time in the city themselves, but were back to his home every night just in case his parents decided to be there. They were none too happy with Mary's presence and often made sarcastic remarks about her home. It had taken all her willpower not to lose her temper with them she had told Pea. She said that had it not been for Joseph, she would have said something, but she had kept silent for him.

Pea was amazed that Mary had held her tongue for anyone. Too often her sister's temper and sharp wit had gotten her in trouble. Those had who dared to insult her or her home in the past had often found themselves verbally fencing and losing to a master intellect.

"Ree, why? You've never backed down from anyone," Pea had asked.

"I love him. It was out of respect for him," Mary had replied. "I tried to keep it from being a disaster so I kept my mouth shut."

His parents had wanted the couple to move to New York after the wedding, but Mary had politely told Joseph "No" in private and Joseph had agreed without question.

He had no idea that she had said "No" because of the baby. Mary simply told him that she needed some time "off" and that she wanted to stay at the farm. And he really didn't care as long as he was with her. His heart attack had taught him to take better care of himself and to slow down. The farm had been perfect for both reasons.

Pea had taken her dogs to Staunton to Trey's family place and had been living there for the past year. Neither of them mentioned marriage or children, although Trey wanted both. But he knew she was not ready. Instead, she threw herself into redoing the Staunton house and he let her make whatever decisions about it she wanted without interfering. It was a task that took her away from the grief of what Manley had done and how he had killed her precious Alicia. She never spoke of what took place at the farmhouse in Goshen that night or even much of her life before Trey.

Instead of just going through the house throwing things out, she had started first by organizing everything into things to be kept, trash, and things to be donated to a local thrift store. After tackling most of the house, she knew it almost as well as she did her parents' home. She kept all family correspondence and photographs and set them aside for the next winter when she could sit down and organize them as well as digitizing some of the priceless archival pieces. Shoved in a box at the bottom of a drawer in one of the servant's rooms were items that stunned even her.

She had been raised with a healthy respect for the importance of historical documents and had often read her own family's history through their documents and correspondence. But what she found at Trey's was a treasure trove of pre-Revolutionary and later civil war papers. The most important piece was the original land grant on thick velum parchment. With that, she found letters from Washington, Jefferson, and several presidents who had come from Virginia. In addition to those letters, she found more correspondence from the various members of the Lewis family, including John Lewis, who was considered the father of Augusta County.

After sorting through the contents of the rooms and purging far more than she wanted to, she approached Trey's mother's beloved solarium. Pea had filled the room with local plants and rare tropical blooms and had used furnishings and other decorating items from throughout the house.

She wanted the room to meld Trey's family history and his mother's love into that one room. She had not necessarily restored the room, but had made a room that reflected the history of the house and his family to show Trey her love for him.

One day, as he watched the glass and solar panels being placed into the roof, he was overwhelmed with the loss of his mother. For the first time in decades, he had walked down to the family plot and stood at his parents' grave and wept. Pea had seen him walking down there and had given him some time alone there before she followed him and walked up behind him, leaned her head against his back and wrapped her arms around his waist.

They stood that way for several minutes before he turned and placed his arm around her waist and led her back to the house. They never spoke during the walk, but they had made love that night with an urgency that promised that they would never let the dark days behind them overshadow the sunlit days they hoped to see in their future.

Sometimes they would stay in Lexington when Trey had business, but they spent most of their time now in Staunton. While Pea's main concern was the restoration of

Trey's home, she also proved to be a valuable asset in his business dealings and he often turned to her for her advice in various business affairs.

They never formed attachments to other people in either Staunton or Lexington other than Joseph, Mary and Thomas. The last year had changed them forever and very few people realized just how much. The initial, and what seemed unending, media coverage of what had happened and whispers from Staunton to Lewisburg about the murders, including Pea's killing of Manley, all served to tighten their small group even more so.

It was only when Thomas brought Diana into their small group that some of the darkness truly began to lift. They were so happy to see him smiling again that his happiness had helped shaped theirs.

Joseph and Mary were leaving that evening for Washington, D.C., and then to Italy for two weeks. Pea, Trey, Thomas and Diana had decided to spend the rest of the weekend at the farm. Joseph and Mary's honeymoon would actually provide a much needed break from work for them as well. Thomas had opened his own metal shop and had become quite successful in the past six months while Diana traveled each day to work on her Ph.D. in Botany at

Washington and Lee. The wedding and the long weekend in Greenbrier County had given them all an excuse to leave the pressures of work for a few days.

Pea had not been to the farm much in the past year and she was surprised by how much Mary had done to keep it going. Her first steps when she arrived at the farm led her to Alicia's grave and she cried when she saw that Mary had made sure that Alicia's grave, as well as those of their parents and other family members, had been carefully maintained, with fresh daisies laid at the foot of Alicia's grave. She no longer felt guilty for her daughter's death, but she did feel a pang of remorse that she had stayed away from the farm and her daughter's resting place for so long.

As for the farm, in some instances, Mary had gone beyond Pea in her attention to it. While Mary did not buy more horses, she did buy out the leases from the cattle farmers and had brought in her own small herd of cattle to graze. She had also bought lambs to keep in several pastures.

One day Mary had been taken with the idea of raising the woolly lambs and learning not only how to care for them, but how to shear their wool, clean it, dye it, and spin and weave it. She had taken more than a few classes at

Carnegie Hall, as the local arts center was well known in the state for their support of the arts and for bringing the arts to school children who might never have experienced them otherwise. She eventually became a supporter of it and volunteered there when she could.

Mary had even joined a local weaver's guild and had bought an antique barn loom and had installed it in the barn where she practiced the early indigo and cream patterns that had existed in Greenbrier County since her family had first came there so long ago.

It had all left Joseph and Pea feeling confused at times. It was as if she and her sister had suddenly changed places. Pea was busy working with Trey and his business and her sister was back at the farm running it better than Pea had when she had lived there.

It had left Pea confused until Mary told her about the baby one afternoon as they sat in Trey's Lexington kitchen and Pea had realized that Mary had been nesting without realizing that she was doing it. Pea asked Mary about taking the West Virginia or Virginia bar exam and Mary had just shrugged her shoulders. Maybe, she said, but not now.

Pea had teasingly called her sister "Green Acres" as Mary had used to call her. When Pea had said that, both sisters had laughed so hard that they were in tears when Trey and Joseph had joined them back in the kitchen. It was a week later that Mary had accepted Joseph's proposal of marriage, much to his surprise, and had extracted a promise from Pea that she would tell no one, including Trey, about the baby and only then on the night after Mary and Joseph would wed.

The sisters talked everyday on the phone, which both Joseph and Trey had finally gotten used to. And at least once a month, the couples met in Lexington, sometimes joined by Thomas and later, Diana, and had shared stories and food at the little Italian restaurant where Trey had taken Pea for their first night together.

But secrets between lovers are difficult to keep, Pea discovered the night of the wedding. After she and Thomas had read their poems, Thomas raised his glass of champagne to toast the newlyweds as did everyone else. Just as Mary was about to sip from her glass, she smelled the champagne and stopped. She was supposed to have been served ginger ale and her face flushed with embarrassment when she was forced to set the champagne flute back upon the table.

Joseph noticed immediately her failure to drink and, of course, would not allow her to avoid his questions about her failure to toast their marriage. She looked to Pea pleadingly, but Pea shrugged, having no answer to help her.

It was Joseph's Nana, seated at the bridal party table, who realized before anyone else why Mary had refused to drink. She grinned broadly and she slowly made her way to Mary and reached up to take Mary's face in her hands and said, "Bless you, my new daughter." She hugged Mary tightly.

Joseph, Thomas and Trey watched in the confusion of most men, but Pea noticed that other women there were beginning to realize what was going on.

Nana Giordano turned to Joseph and laid her hand upon his heart. "Now your heart will be strong again. You will be a family," she said and smiled as she walked back to her seat.

Suddenly Joseph realized why Mary had not drunk the champagne and he grabbed Mary by the waist and kissed her.

"Are you . . . are we?" he asked quietly and Mary nodded yes.

Joseph turned to their friends and family. His joy was overwhelming as he raised his glass to Mary this time.

"To my beautiful wife!" he exclaimed.

Everyone applauded as Joseph led Mary to the dance floor. Even Joseph's parents, after a few stiff drinks, were smiling a little more as Joseph's Nana had explained everything to them. Pea felt a small amount of relief flood her heart knowing that her sister's life with Joseph's family might not be as difficult as she or Thomas and Trey had feared.

As Pea watched Joseph and Mary dance their first dance together, she looked over to see Trey, Thomas, and Diana watching them as well, smiling and happy. After a few moments Trey came to her and Thomas went to Diana and led them onto the dance floor to join Joseph and Mary.

"Did you know?" Trey asked her as they began to dance and she nodded yes.

He smiled and held her tightly as she laid her head against his shoulder. She closed her eyes as they swayed to the sound of *Tiny Dancer*, Mary's favorite song that Pea had often played on the piano for Mary when they were growing up.

At one point in the evening, a teary eyed Mary looked to her sister and said, "I miss Mom and Dad so much tonight. I grew up dreaming of a perfect wedding, father-daughter dance and all."

Pea felt her sister's wistful need.

"As bad as the wedding to Manley was, especially with his constant attention to Laura, I felt the same thing then. And it seemed as if he coerced me into that marriage too soon, but I felt so lost then that that's one thing I can't completely blame on him."

Mary frowned and said, "The man was such as monster that someone could blame the hundred years war on him and I wouldn't disagree. But forget him. Look at the man who truly loves you. He won't let you down."

With that said, they did not think of the horrible things that they had endured a year ago except for Pea, who unfortunately thought about it every day. Her husband had killed their beautiful auburn haired daughter and she had killed him after discovering the abominations he had performed upon 12 other women, including Thomas's love, Shawnette. She never spoke of it with Mary or Trey or even Joseph, who had helped her solve the mystery of the dead women, but she never forgot it. And no matter how much she tried to banish those ghosts from her life, she never really could.

She could also not know that grief and terror were about to enter their lives once more. Had she or any of them known, they might have altered the actions they later took. But loss never shows its face until it is too late and the sisters would never have seen it coming as their happiness was so strong that night. Neither of them would have believed that misery was looking for them once more.

It was only later that Thomas said to them that life was never fair or easy, but he said he had learned from Shawnette that love was the one thing that made life bearable, that love made them strong and kept them from sinking down and living mired in fear.

Chapter Three

Joseph had never felt so happy in his entire life. He had thought that when Mary had accepted his proposal that life could not get much better, but here he was in a bridal suite at the Adams in Washington, waiting for his wife and the woman who was about to be the mother of his child to come join him in their bed.

Instead of drinking champagne the rest of the evening, he, too, had refrained, wanting the night to be a perfect memory that was not clouded by alcohol. He wanted a crystalline remembrance of their love that night and how it had grown and changed over the past few years.

Mary emerged from the bathroom nude. He could see clearly the small bump at her belly that he had not noticed before and he moved across the bed to her and watched her, rather than touching her delicate porcelain skin. She kissed the top of his head and looked down at him on the bed and smiled.

"You can touch me. I won't break," she said.

"Is it safe for the baby?" he asked and gently laid his hand upon the small bump.

She laughed and said, "It has been for the past four and a half months."

"Four and a half months? Why didn't you tell me?" He wanted to be cross with her, but he found it impossible. He loved her and needed her so much now.

She lay down on the bed next to him and wrapped her long legs around his hips. He ran his hand down the length of her hip and kissed her shoulder.

"I wanted to wait until tonight. I wanted to surprise you after the wedding, but the caterer mixed up the drinks and I smelled the champagne and had to put the glass down. I was supposed to have ginger ale so no one would know, but . . ."

"Your grandmother figured it out very quickly. For 83, she's a quick study. I can see where you got your profiling skills from," Mary continued.

Joseph laughed and brushed Mary's hair away from her face.

"You have no idea."

"Your parents did not look as happy as your Nana did," she said and looked down.

"My parents never look happy. I've seen my father reduce other doctors to tears and my mother just follows his lead. I think over time she had just come to forget her own family roots, although Nana tries to never let her forget," he replied and laughed.

Mary sighed and touched his mouth with her fingertips.

"I just wanted them to be happy for you. To tell you the truth, I never felt so, so inferior socially until I met them. My family never made a difference in someone because of their background or who they were or where they came from. I grew up without wanting for much and was always taught to appreciate it because others were not as fortunate. I never thought that someone might judge me simply because of where I was from. I guess I naively thought that your parents would feel the same about me."

She sat up and looked around the room.

"I'm sorry. I shouldn't say these things. They're your family. You love them even when you don't agree with them."

Joseph pulled her back down to his side.

"I love you. You and little bump are my family now. All my plans, all my hopes rest with you two now. My parents will get over whatever objections they might have, especially after the baby comes. And if they don't, they lose. All I know is that I love you and always will."

Mary smiled and decided that she wouldn't allow any storm clouds of family dramas to dim her happiness.

"Maybe they think I married you for your money," she said.

Now it was Joseph's turn to smile.

"Now, that is hysterical since you have much more money than I do. I'm just a civil servant who retired very early and who happened to write a book that sold fairly well."

Mary shook her head and pulled back slightly from him.

"No, Joseph, one day you might inherit the Hallett money. That might be what they're thinking about."

He rolled onto his back and sighed. How could she be so insecure and why didn't she see that none of that made any difference to him.

"Mary, it just doesn't matter. If something happened to me, I know that your parents left you enough money to live quite well, not to mention that you have a law degree that could take you wherever you wanted to go."

"Believe me. My parents have never been happy with how I chose to live my life, but I chose my own path. The fact that it led to you tells me that it was the right path."

He rolled back to her and lay still next to her, studying her face.

"Have I told you today how absolutely beautiful you are?" he asked.

Mary laughed out loud and rolled on top of him, sitting up.

"No," she said, "but you can show me. This is our wedding night. Don't ever let me forget how much you love me or when I'm old and grey that you still love me this much."

This time he rolled her onto her back and looked into her eyes.

"I will never forget this night and how much I love you and the wonderful gift you have given me tonight," he said as he began to kiss the small bump of her belly and moving upwards with each soft kiss. He had never been as gentle with her as he was that night, not even after his heart attack and the doctor had told him to take it slowly with sex.

This night was different for them and if they had ever doubted their future together, that night sealed it forever.

Tomorrow they would be arriving in Italy and Joseph stopped his small kisses and looked at her.

"You know, I just realized that I'm can't eat all the wonderful things that you're going to be able to indulge in while we're in Italy. Somehow it doesn't seem fair," he said, giving her the pretense of a frown.

She rolled to face him in the bed and placed her hand over his heart.

"Well, you can drink the wine. I can't do that. But . . . I'm sorry. I can't promise not to eat your share of Tiramisu and fettuccine Bolognese and . . ."

"Oh, you are one evil bitch," he said and they both burst out laughing as they began to spend the rest of the night making love. Life felt right for them as it had never felt before.

Chapter Four

1980

Today, Doug was going to kill his dad. He thought of the last five years of hell his dad had put him through and believed that that had put his dad at the top of his list. Five years had given Doug and Tim five good years of hunting experience and even though the two boys had gone different ways, they still hunted at least once a year along the New River Valley. Doug felt that the fact that this year they had chosen his father this year made it all so much sweeter.

Tim had taken the police course in Institute, West Virginia at the State Police Academy, but had joined the Gladstone County Sheriff's department, aiming for two things: anonymity from suspicions about the murders and eventually being elected sheriff, sealing his protection concerning the deaths that had mostly gone unnoticed by the counties that the New River flowed through.

They had almost been caught one time in Summers County in 1978 when they were throwing a body overboard on Bluestone Lake. The people were high up on the road at the scenic overlook just south of the dam and saw them toss the body overboard, but they were too far away to describe the boat or the boys.

All they could tell the police was that they had seen some white men in a white boat throw something that looked liked a body out of the boat.

The lake patrol had searched the area and had even sent divers down, but the people had sent them in the wrong direction and the body, which the boys had chained to cinder blocks, was never found.

That was also the year that they began to feed a black bear cub they named Rosie. They named her for Rosie Grier because he was one of their favorite football players in the 70s. They learned where she ranged and tried to keep her within a specific locale, feeding her raw meat and never getting very close to her so that she never became tame.

Doug had gone off to college on a football scholarship, but he had blown out his knee his sophomore year and his mother had been unable to pay for his tuition at Morris Harvey College. His father refused to pay his tuition, even if he had changed schools. He told him he was old enough to take care of himself and that he had no home with them. Instead of trying to console his son, he had berated him and had made him feel like a loser.

He thought about joining the army, but dismissed that idea quickly, thinking that they probably wouldn't take him with a bum knee either. He had an assistant coach who took pity on him and found a job for him at a printing plant in Charleston. Doug never gave a second thought as to moving back home to Gladstone County, which his father wouldn't have allowed anyway.

Tim had tried to convince him to take the police exam and join him in the sheriff's department, but Doug was once more struck by how stupid his friend could be. They needed to be as far apart as possible most of the year so that no one would suspect what they had been doing since 1975.

Doug hated his job, but he knew he probably would have hated any job and that it was a necessary evil that kept him from his father and Gladstone Gap. He became adept at making people like him and trust him. Although he did very little at work, most of his co-workers thought of him as one of the hardest working, most valuable employees at the plant.

What only a few of them noticed was that he spent most of his time on the floor talking to buddies and messing around with some of the machinery. He did just enough to keep the job and nothing more. Those people who did notice his act were often sabotaged by Doug and found themselves out of work very quickly.

The thought of killing his father was almost as enjoyable to Doug as their first kill had been. Doug had put a great deal of thought and planning into just how he would kill the bastard. Feeding Rosie at the same spot for the past few years was just part of it. They needed Rosie to find the exact spot where they would put Doug's father and stage it as an accident.

They had taken Doug's father up the mountain to the site of their first kill and had gotten him so drunk that he could barely stand. They had poured bourbon down his throat as fast as he could swallow it and given his love of bourbon, it hadn't taken long to get him drunk.

When his father had finally come out of his drunken stupor, he found himself trussed to a tree. He struggled with the ropes and while Tim stood next to his cruiser in his new uniform and laughed, Doug hadn't said a word. Instead he walked up to his father and began to punch him over and over in the gut with his fists. He knew that after years of drinking that his father had developed a bleeding ulcer and that every blow had been agony for his dad.

His father had drunkenly cursed them both as blood flowed up his throat, filled his mouth and then down his chin with every punch. He had demanded to be freed from the tree. Tim looked at him from beneath his deputy's hat, looked away and just laughed. This time he didn't have much to do, but he still enjoyed the show.

"I ought to kill you myself for what you and my dad did to us in school, but I'm gonna let Doug take care of you. He earned that right. If my dad hadn't hit that tree coming home last winter, he'd be getting the same shit that you're about to get," Tim said. He then smiled at Doug and walked away over to the rock where they had placed a case of beer they had brought with them. He opened one and sat back to watch Doug continue to exact his revenge on his dad.

Doug's dad saw that he might be in real trouble and decided to try to reason with his son. He wasn't going to beg. He believed that his son was an ignorant piece of shit and he thought that he could either talk him out of hurting him or at least scare him out of it.

"Son, you don't want to do this to your mother. Just think how she's going to take it, especially when they catch you and take you off to jail. You know you're not smart enough to get away with this," his dad said.

Tim snickered and almost spewed beer across the space between him and Doug.

"Dad, no one's going know. Don't you realize the sheriff's department will rule your death from driving drunk over the mountainside as an accident? Course, there won't be much of you left to look at after we feed you to Rosie," Doug said and almost growled as he laughed.

His father groaned for a moment and said, "Rosie?"

Tim laughed again and Doug looked from Tim and back to his father.

"Oh, yeah, Rosie is a special surprise we have for you. She's just going to love you to death," he said and giggled.

"You stupid piece of shit," his father said and struggled even harder with the ropes. "I'm gonna beat the crap out of you when I get loose. Now untie these ropes. This isn't funny anymore.

"Dad, it was never funny and it's never going to happen again."

Doug laughed and walked back to retrieve a beer for himself. He shook it up and the explosion of foamy beer from the can spewed all over his dad. He drained the rest of the can and then belched loudly in his dad's face. That made Tim laugh even harder.

Doug said, "Yeah, on second thought, it's funnier than hell, but then I guess you'll be seeing hell real soon."

Doug took a baseball bat to his dad's legs first. He could feel and hear the bones splinter with the first blow.

"Oh, a homerun! Listen to the crowd cheer!" and he swung the bat in the air over his head. The sound made him excited and he wanted to hear what other bones and parts of his father's body would sound like so he went after his dad's feet, then hands, arms, and finally shoulders. He laughed with every scream that came from his father's mouth.

"Did you think I could ever forgive you for what you did to me and Mom? You never cared or gave a shit about anything but yourself and getting drunk."

Doug's father had soiled himself while Doug had broken his bones with the bat. The only part Doug avoided was his dad's trunk and head. He knew that Rosie would take care of that.

"Uh-oh, I think your Daddy's pooped his pants, Doug. Wow that stinks worse than my patrol car after I've had to transport a drunk."

By the time Doug had finished his batting practice and he and Tim had finished off more of the beer, his father was slumped and unconscious, the ropes the only thing holding his body up. Doug watched his father and remembered every time his father had beat him.

Tim helped Doug untie Doug's father and drag him down the hill and load him into the pickup that they had already pushed down the hill where it crashed into a tree.

After throwing a little raw meat at Rosie's den, Doug walked back up the hill a bit and waited and watched as Rosie followed the small trail of raw meat and ambled over to where they had placed Doug's father half hanging out of the open door of the old pick-up. They had covered his beer gut with a couple of pounds of raw hamburger.

Cheap bastard, Doug thought. Too cheap to even buy a new truck for his mom to drive to church,

Doug squatted on the hillside and watched as the bear began to tear at his dad. The bear's claws brought his father back awake and he thrashed about uselessly, his limbs impossible to move. Doug's dad's screams for help should have been heard all the way down to the river, but because it was just far enough from the river, there was no one in the woods to hear him. The bear tore one of his arms off first and then went after the big gut that promised the bear a feast of soft, tasty meat.

Tim walked down to where Doug squatted.

"You want me to stay or come back later?" he asked.

Doug shook his head and said, "Come back in a little bit. I wanna watch the whole thing. Rosie's havin' a good meal and I like watching her enjoy her food."

Doug sat there till dusk waiting for Tim to return. By the time Tim's cruiser climbed up the hillside, Rosie had long since left and the buzzards were having their own little feast on what the bear had left behind. Doug's father had died slowly enough to feel the birds ripping at his face long after the bear had had his fill of him. And Doug had enjoyed every scream, pleading cry, and moan.

Tim watched as Doug walked back up to the cruiser and wished he'd stayed to watch the old bastard get eaten, but it was really Doug's choice and next year he'd get to choose. He realized that they had been hunting for five years now and no one had thought that any of the deaths were connected.

Doug jumped in the cruiser and told Tim to take him back to his car over at his mom's. He wanted to be there when his Mom reported that his dad hadn't come home. He figured that by the time that someone found his dad's truck that Rosie would be long gone and that there wouldn't be much left of his dad. And if they did track the bear and kill it, it would just secure his dad's "accidental" death even more firmly.

He thought that he'd have to buy a new suit for his dad's funeral and then thought about wearing it out to dinner with one of the girls from work. The suit could do double duty. That really made him smile.

Chapter Five

2011

After the guests had left, Pea, Trey, Thomas and Diana sat on the front steps of the farm house and watched the catering people and the grounds keeping crew clean away the debris of the wedding. The four of them were for the most part silent, each alone in their thoughts that shared the same theme.

Their minds were all entangled in the land of If, with each of them looking at a different landscape, from Trey's worries if Pea would ever make a commitment to him to Pea's landscape of what their lives had might have been like if she had not brought Manley into their lives.

She had tried to talk to Thomas one time about her guilt over Shawnette's death, but he had refused to even talk to her about it. She had driven to his apartment from Trey's place just outside of Staunton and he had greeted her with a great hug that made her think of the first time she had climbed those steps to his apartment and forcing her way past him, leaving him surprised at her bravado.

She remembered being surprised that Thomas had made changes in the apartment since her first visit, mostly superficialities such as new paint, a new TV, house plants everywhere and a few new pieces of furniture. The one thing that struck her the most was not the removal of Shawnette's photograph, but the physical change in him.

It had taken months of physical therapy to recover from being shot twice and while his body had regained most of its muscular build, it was no longer tense. He seemed more relaxed now and for the first time she noticed small strands of gray in his closely cropped hair.

They sat and drank coffee together as they had so many months ago, but this time Pea finally broke her silence about Shawnette and the other lost women. She couldn't look at Thomas's face as she said Shawnette's name as she was about to apologize to him for what she considered her role in his love's death. But he stopped her before she could continue,

"Stop it, Pea. You're as much a victim as any of us are. You did nothing wrong. You have to leave it and let us all move on."

He paused and waited until she looked at him. He wanted her to understand what he was trying to say. He knew deep within himself that she was holding so much back.

"Pea, you're one of only a few people I trust in this world. That should tell you something. You are not to blame. Manley killed them, not you," he had said.

She had looked into his deep brown eyes and searched for blame or questions, but had seen nothing there but a need to move on with his life.

Then he actually smiled at her and began to talk to her about Diana.

"I never thought I could care about anyone again, but Diana has been there from that first morning in the hospital after surgery. Did you know that even before you and Joseph believed in me that she did first? She fought the police when I was first arrested. I never knew that until a few weeks ago."

Pea paused for a moment and then sat her coffee mug on a new table he had bought. She was very surprised, but it explained some of the changes in the apartment and in Thomas. She was glad that he had been able to shed some of his pain, but she wondered how he had done it.

"How have you moved forward? I feel so alone. Trey tries to make me feel better and I don't think there's a more patient man around than him," she said and attempted a small laugh.

"But I sometimes think that I just work on his house and help him with business just so I don't have to think about what happened. And I don't know if you can understand this, but I feel so much guilt, including guilt for killing someone."

Thomas had raised his eyebrows as he leaned back in his old recliner, one of the few pieces of furniture he hadn't thrown out. He raised his arms and held his hands at the back of his head. The physical therapy had given them a definition that was more muscular than before the shooting.

"Why? I mean, why should you feel any guilt? He was an evil man, Pea, and you should think about the women you saved rather than the women he killed," he said.

"I think he would have killed whether he met you or not. He might have killed Diana instead of Shawnette if circumstances had been different. You just can't carry this load by yourself."

"And I know you," he had continued.

"You won't talk to a therapist about it. I know for a fact you haven't even talked to Joseph or Mary. So, you've got a choice – move on or let it ruin your life. And, if you let it eat at you, you let him win, even if he's dead. Think about that."

He leaned forward and took her hands in his and she could feel the calluses that had formed on his palms from his working with metal again.

"You're right," she had said. "It's just hard to stop thinking about it.

She had stood, and as she did, he stood with her and hugged her against his broad chest. She wiped a tear away from her eye and had tried to smile.

"I will always be here for you, Pea. If you hadn't dragged me from this apartment, I might still be lying in that bed. You gave me the strength to move on, now let me do it for you," he said.

She hugged him back and then had headed to the door to leave. All she could manage to say was "Thank you" and that just didn't seem like enough.

That had been the last time she had mentioned any of it to any of them, but Trey knew she slept little and sometimes he woke up to hearing music from her playing the new baby grand he had bought her when she had moved in with him. Sometimes he would go sit at the landing and listen and other times he would stay in bed and drift back off to sleep. He loved her enough to have learned one truly important thing about her – she had to do it herself, no matter how much he wanted to help her.

So, while Pea thought about guilt and Thomas and Diana thought about how they had found one another, Trey wondered if Pea would ever heal or if he could wait or how long he would be willing to wait. He was 36 this year and he wanted to start a family. He just wondered if Pea would ever trust him enough to do that with him. And finally, he wondered if she couldn't do it, could he stay with her?

By the time the last of the trucks was pulling away from the house and driving down the gravel road and over the cattle gate, the four of them each rose and headed into the house.

Thomas put his arm around Diana's waist and whispered something to her that made her laugh out loud.

They said their good-nights, headed up the front staircase and left Pea and Trey standing in the wide front hall. It was almost one o'clock and neither of them felt sure for the first time in a year about what to do.

It was as if they had tried to stay so busy with the house and the business and then the wedding that they never had really talked about what had happened or about anything but getting through the next day. But here they were, for the first time in a year, faced with new and old questions about where they were going.

"Want some coffee?" Pea asked.

Trey laughed and shook his head no.

"That's the last thing I need. Anymore caffeine and I'll be up all night as it is."

Pea walked into the living room and stretched out across the red suede sofa, raising her arms upward and looking at her grandmother's ring and her hand that seemed very thin.

Trey followed her and sat in the large leather armchair adjacent to the sofa. He picked up a copy of one of Mary's weaving magazines, but didn't open it and lay it on his lap. He sighed and covered his eyes with his hand.

"What are we doing, Pea?"

"Well, I guess we'll head back to Lexington sometime Sunday. We need to finish the proposal for Fredericksburg Farms for later this week," she replied.

He sighed again and then slammed the magazine against the glass table top. Pea immediately sat up. She tried to pretend ignorance, but she knew what he was talking about.

"I'm not talking about the Fredericksburg proposal. I'm talking about us. What are we doing? Are we lovers or friends or something else? You told me once, before last year, before what happened at Goshen, that you wanted a life with me and then after everything happened, you stopped talking. Every time I bring up the subject of getting married or having children, you change the subject to something else."

He leaned back in the suede chair and held his hand to his forehead. He could feel a headache coming on. This wasn't doing any good and after a few seconds, he stood and told her he was heading up to bed.

"Wait, Trey, wait. At least let me . . ." But it was too late by then. His leaving told her that now he didn't want to talk about it.

Pea watched him as he climbed the stairs, not sure whether to follow him or let him go. As much as he was ignorant of how she felt, she was ignorant of her own feelings as well. She lay back down on the sofa and buried her face into the sofa cushions and wept.

While Joseph and Mary celebrated their wedding, while Thomas and Diana celebrated a weekend away from work, Pea and Trey spent the night apart, each of them carrying very different fears that they were afraid to speak about to anyone, including each another.

She lay on the sofa for what seemed like hours, hoping that he would come back downstairs to her. She wanted to change things, but every time she thought about what she could lose, about what she had done, she was frozen in place.

If life were perfect, she thought, she would march up those stairs and go to him, tell him she loved him and wanted to have a family with him and he would be forgiving of all the horrible things she felt she had done. But she did not feel worthy of a happy ending. She just could not understand nor accept that she was not responsible for the pain that the people she loved and it had not begun with her own blindness to the monster she had married.

She fell asleep trying not to think about what had happened a year ago or her fear that she might lose Trey. She closed her eyes and began to focus instead on anything but those things.

Chapter Six

Pea woke up to the voices of Thomas, Diana, and Trey in the kitchen. She had spent the night on the sofa where she had cried herself to sleep, no matter how hard she had tried not to. She remembered wondering as she fell asleep if tomorrow would be better, if she would ever stop punishing herself for the ghosts she lived with?

She walked into the kitchen still dressed in her clothes from the night before and Thomas greeted her a little too enthusiastically while Trey quietly said "Good morning," handed her a cup of coffee and then moved back to the stove where he was starting breakfast. Thomas either knew or at least realized something had gone wrong between her and Trey last night. Then she realized that both Thomas and Diana knew something was wrong since she was still wearing her gown from the night before. Sometimes she thought Thomas saw more in her pain or at least understood it better than Trey ever would. She looked across the room at Thomas and saw an understanding in his eyes that no one else seemed to have. Sometimes she thought that he might have forgiven her, but he would never forget that it was she who had brought Manley into their lives.

Diana and Trey were now laughing at the stove and cracking eggs into one of her mother's old Pyrex bowls, good naturedly arguing with one another about the right amount of cheese to put into scrambled eggs and whether it should be grated or sliced.

Thomas raised his cup to her silently, took a deep drink, and tilted his head toward the back staircase as if to tell her to make her escape while she could. She smiled at them, said "Good morning" and excused herself to go upstairs to shower and change.

She went up to her old bedroom where she and Trey had planned on sleeping. She noticed that the bed was made and wasn't sure whether Trey had slept there and then made the bed this morning or had simply lain on top of the covers. She pulled clean clothes from her suitcase and headed to the shower to wash off the remains of yesterday. She realized that Mary and Joseph were probably boarding the plane to Rome right now and smiled. If nothing else good had come from last year, it was Mary, Joseph, and their tiny yet-to-be-born baby.

Although she could hear Thomas, Diana, and Trey in the kitchen after she had showered and changed, she walked to the front porch and sat down in the old swing out there instead of joining them for breakfast. Her guard was up a bit and she wasn't really ready to face Trey right now. She didn't want a repeat of last night. She just wasn't ready to face him.

As she sat in the swing, she could smell the lush old-fashioned roses and she thought of her dad and how he had always picked a bouquet of them every May for her mother, bringing them in as a surprise as though he had not done the same thing for her every year for almost 25 years. The roses made her feel as if her dad were there with her and the thought of how much he had loved the three women in his life gave her great comfort and still made her tear up.

She missed her parents more today than she had in years. They were always so close and she could talk to them about anything and right now she wished she could talk to them about Trey.

Her father had been so good at seeing the truth in people. She wished now that she had had Manley spend more time around her dad before her parents had died. She wondered if her dad would have seen the ugliness that Manley disguised so well.

Once, when she had been in high school and had rushed into what she thought was "true" and "everlasting" love with a boy who would later turn out to be a wife-beater, her father had warned her away from the boy very subtly.

"Don't let your heart get in front of your feet, Pea," he had said to her. She should have kept that thought in mind when Manley had swept into her life. Her dad would have certainly reminded her of it had he lived long enough to get to know Manley.

She knew what Trey wanted and she wanted to give it to him so much, but she was terrified that she would fail again and lose her way. If she lost another child, if she lost him, what would she do? Could she survive it? Was she as strong as those who loved her thought she was? She drank the last drink of the coffee and wrinkled her nose at the cold bitterness of how it tasted since it had cooled off while she had showered.

Pea knew that Trey would stand by her and would not leave her unless she pushed him away. She just had to be brave and stop looking back. If she could bury Alicia and still fight Manley, if she could kill the man she had thought was her soul mate, she knew deep within herself that she could do anything, including risking her heart again and allowing herself to forgive herself for the crimes Manley had committed that she could never have stopped.

Good god, she thought, how could I have stopped him when I didn't even know what a monster he was? It was one thing to ignore the truth of a philandering and greedy husband, but to see that he was a murderous, evil man who took joy in the death of others, including his own daughter was beyond her comprehension.

Just as she was about to rise from the swing to join the others in the kitchen, Thomas came outside with a fresh cup of coffee for her. He sat down on the swing next to her and took a deep breath of the aroma of the roses. He wore a white t-shirt that made his beautiful chestnut skin glow. He swung one muscled arm behind her along the back of the swing and sat with her without speaking for several minutes, just breathing in the fresh May morning air and pushing the swing back and forth slightly with his bare feet.

"Forgiven yourself yet?" he asked, facing out to the sheep in the pasture and not looking at her.

Pea thought about it for a moment and took a sip of coffee to forestall her answer. Finally she looked forward and replied, unable to face him.

"Have you forgiven me?" she asked in return.

He said nothing for a few moments and then walked over to the porch banister, leaning against the old fashioned turned support posts, his dark blue jeans a contrast to the white posts.

"Nope. Never had to. You didn't do anything wrong, but you did do a lot of right things. Pea, I've told you before it wasn't your fault. I don't know what's going on with you and Trey, but I suspect it's got something to do with the load of guilt you've got strapped on your back"

He walked back to the swing and held his hand out for her to take.

"Girl, when are you going to forgive yourself? You cannot live like this. I know. I did it to myself for too long. Remember that I told you that you saved my life that morning you showed up at my apartment and refused to leave?"

"Hell, I didn't know what to make of you. You were like a woman obsessed. I still don't know why I listened to you, but I did and you saved me from my own misplaced guilt. Now you've got to do the same thing for yourself."

Thomas jerked his head in the direction of the kitchen.

"Go make things right with your man. He may be hurting more than you think. Diana's gone upstairs to change and he's cleaning the kitchen up. Maybe he needs a hand," Thomas said and pulled her to her feet.

Pea held Thomas's hand, kissed him on the cheek and smiled. She brushed her hand against his cheek after the kiss.

"You might want to shave before tearing Diana's face up with that scratchy stubble, too," she replied and they both laughed as she walked back into the house alone.

Trey was just putting the last of the dishes into the dishwasher when she walked in with the two Fiesta Ware mugs.

He smiled at her as she entered the kitchen. He was making an effort to pretend that last night hadn't happened.

"Are you hungry? I can still fix something for you," he said.

She put the cups on the counter and wrapped her arms around his neck.

"I'm sorry. Too many memories last night and suddenly I turned into Chicken Little," she said.

Trey bent his head and kissed her nose and then her lips. He wanted to tell her that she had nothing to be afraid of with him, but he had done that too many times over the past year. It would just be redundant to keep telling her. She was going to have to start trusting him with more than just living together.

She smiled and moved her pelvis against his, rubbing his jeans just enough to make him hard.

"Oh, if you do that, I'm never going to go riding with Thomas and Diana and I promised them a ride along the property," he said, groaning a bit.

"Ok, but you owe me for later. That sofa was hell last night," she said.

"I didn't tell you to sleep there. I stayed up half the night waiting for you come upstairs."

She grimaced and stepped back from him, but still held onto his arms.

"I'm a fool sometimes. Last night was one of those times. I should have come to bed."

"Well, Thomas and Diana weren't unhappy or arguing about little things. I think they enjoyed last night a great deal. Almost made me come looking for you," he said and laughed.

Pea kissed him and walked toward the backdoor, twisting her rear end a bit in his direction.

"Well, maybe you should have. I don't think I would have said 'No'," she said and headed out to the stables to help Mr. Dickson get the horses saddled.

Trey smiled and hoped that this change in her attitude meant better things for both of them.

Chapter Seven

1982

The white water enthusiasts were thick on the New River the year that Pea was two years old. Mary hadn't been born and Joseph was just entering adolescence, Trey was only a few years away from losing his mother and Thomas had just started playing Little League baseball. Not one of them realized that the two young men who were watching the white water tourists, trying to select the perfect victim for their annual hunt, might be hunting them 30 years later.

Most of the groups the two men dismissed immediately. They sat in Tim's squad car on an old dirt road several miles from where the old Thurman Hotel had once sat. From their vantage point, they could sit unquestioned by the tourists and the guides. Most of the people assumed that the squad car was there in case of an emergency since March was one of the more dangerous months on the river because of the snow melt in the upper elevations.

The car could be seen, but it was far enough from the tourists that no one could clearly identify it if any questions were later raised.

Doug had driven to his mom's house in Gladstone Gap and Tim had picked him up in the cruiser. No one thought twice of it. They were old friends and football teammates who only saw each other once or twice a year. They had been football heroes in high school and were considered by their neighbors to be good boys who were becoming good men.

No one suspected that they were anything else. They were respectful, kind, and generous. How could anyone have had a doubt about their character?

And, with the exception of old Mr. Harrison, they usually hunted strangers, people passing through or tourists who no connections with anyone in the Gap. They were careful. They knew from the moment that they had succeeded in eluding suspicion in the first murders that they could do this for years and never be caught as long as they were careful.

While Tim was beginning a slow advancement within the Gladstone County Sheriff's department, Doug was still working the floor at the print shop in Charleston. He had only had one or two raises in the few years he had worked there and no promotions, but he didn't want a promotion or the extra responsibility that one might bring with it. It was so much easier just to walk around the floor and pretend to be busy, picking out a girl to take home on any night he wanted sex.

Somehow he had managed to sleep with most of the young women who worked there or left there without any of them discovering that he had slept with the others.

He had found the story of his drunk, and now 'tragically' dead, father, a man who had beaten him and his mother, but a man he forgave, was a story the naïve girls couldn't resist.

He used the possibility of losing his job as an excuse not to be around them at work and never met any of them in the same bar within months of one another. When they started to get serious, they were treated to the next section of his seduction process – the rejection via the story of the poor mother he had to support and had to visit often to make sure she was doing ok.

He failed to tell them that he did nothing to help his mother or that his brother Sam had been sending her money for years now, nor that his father had left a generous pension to see her through her later years. It was true that she was happier and safer now that Doug's father was dead, but no one knew that Doug and Tim had killed Doug's father when Doug lost the scholarship to Morris Harvey, which was by then in the process of becoming the University of Charleston.

One of the girls had given him the clap, but he went to the county health clinic and given them a fake name and gotten the antibiotics he needed to get rid of the gonorrhea. He decided that the bitch who gave it to him was going to move to the top of his list and he just had to figure some way to get her over toward the New River area to take care of her.

Tim dated a girl they went to school with. She had been a year behind them in school and had been popular and was pretty. He figured he would marry her in a year or two and that would help his career. He even thought about joining the Rotary Club to help establish a good reputation.

He was smarter than Doug gave him credit for being, except when it came to hunting. When it came to hunting, it was an experience that overwhelmed any good sense he possessed. Had it not been for Doug, he would have been caught early on. But then again, had it not been for Doug, he might never have discovered his almost animal need to torture and kill people. Either way, without Doug, he knew he could end up in real trouble.

But this year was Tim's choice and Tim was having a hard time picking his prey because everyone seemed to be clustered in groups this year. Personally, Doug thought white water season was the worst time to hunt because they were always in groups, but Tim just couldn't wait. He had felt the need to kill growing in his chest until he thought he would burst. When he called Doug and asked him to hunt a little earlier this year, Doug didn't argue with him since Tim had helped him so much with his father's "accident."

So far their "hunting" had been mostly men. Women were rarely alone and they hadn't taken on the thought of hunting a couple. The men were easy targets, often oblivious to the danger that the two men represented. Tim, in his uniform, made them feel safe, although Doug sometimes made them nervous. Once or twice he had spooked them enough that the men picked up their own guns to leave and Doug and Tim let them walk away rather than cause any suspicions to fall toward them by killing rashly, without a plan.

But this was the year they would learn to kill two at once. For some reason, Tim chose a couple that had exited the river alone and were obviously fighting with one another. Even at this distance, they could see the man and woman gesturing at each other as they slogged through the river next to the bank.

Dave Johnston was exhausted. If Melanie opened her mouth one more time he was going to start throwing gear at her. She had whined from the moment they had left Blacksburg. Dave loved the outdoors. It was the only time he felt free of his family's expectations and Melanie had made him absolutely miserable for two whole days. Her idea of roughing it was to wear merino wool instead of cashmere.

Oh, she had tried. He had to give her that. But showing up with all the right REI equipment and Eddie Bauer clothing still did not give her the necessary patience or appreciation of the wild mountain landscape around her.

The ground was cold. The water was cold. The tent was too complicated and where were the trashcans to throw the trash in?

When he had explained the rule that you carry out what you carry in, she was peeved. When he explained that there were no bathrooms or even outhouses, she became angry. The trip went downhill from there with every word out of her mouth a complaint.

Dave had thought that they had a lot in common when this trip started. They were both pre-med. They loved Monty Python and came from similar backgrounds when it came to their families. While they weren't trust fund babies, they did have families with enough money to make their lives easier than many of the other students. They both came from the Washington area – he from Alexandria and she from Georgetown and both gone to private schools. Their families were thrilled that they had found each other and each of them were unaware that their futures had been mapped out by their families long before they ever found out that they really had no say in what their future would be.

Melanie didn't mind the plans her parents had for her or what Dave's family expected of him. She believed she loved him and that he loved her. They were exactly matched as far as she was concerned. She had the prep school shoulder length bob with perfectly applied sunlit streaks in her brown hair that accentuated her delicate features and Dave's muscular build, blond hair and handsome face made a perfect picture of their Wasp background. They could have been models for the cover of any upscale preppy catalog.

But right now, they were tired, damp, and lost. Dave's head hurt and Melanie's whining was starting to make him rethink their relationship, especially when she would not make love with him under the stars last night. It was a memory he had imagined that would have been magical. Funny how what you imagined never quite turned out to be what reality was, he thought as he dragged the boat out of the river.

Dave wondered if she really knew him or had ever listened to him when he talked about his future and his family and his fears. She would cuddle next to him in his bed and nod in agreement, stroking his chest and caressing him as if she shared his concerns about life. When they were in Blacksburg, they were the perfect couple, the ones everyone else wanted to be. One of his friends joked that

Dave and Melanie's parents had secretly betrothed them when they were born and simply sat back and let fate take its course.

But Dave had found that so much of what he thought was real in Blacksburg might have just been wishful thinking on his part. He was beginning to believe that Melanie really didn't know him. He did think that she loved him as much as she thought love was supposed to be and he now wondered if that were enough for him. He didn't want to wind up 50 years old and full of regret for the wasted life that he had never chosen. Why the hell couldn't Melanie understand that?

He shook his head and tried not to think about any of it. He just wanted to find their Jeep, stow their gear and get back on the road to Blacksburg. He decided to drop Melanie off at her place. He needed a night or two away from her to forget the hell of this weekend.

Melanie, on the other hand, was completely confused by the man with whom she had spent the past two days. Where was the kind, sweet man who took care of her, protected her, and who stood by her through any problems that arose? Where was the man who shared her idea of what their lives would be? She thought that they had both decided to go to UVA for medical school where he would specialize in cardiology and she would specialize in pediatrics.

They would finish school together and do their residencies at the same hospital or at least at hospitals in the same city. They would wait a few years and then buy the perfect home where they would have three children who would be raised as they were.

This weekend had been bad and, if she had to admit it, she had not been fully prepared for the work it required. But was it her fault when she didn't want to make love on a blanket in the woods where anyone could see them or where wild animals might come on them at a most vulnerable moment? Why did they bring the tent if not for protection? And this business of really "roughing it" was nothing like she had expected. She had thought the weekend would be a quaint camping experience in a National Park that should at least have had restroom facilities.

No, she decided, it wasn't her fault alone. Dave had not prepared her for this properly.

"Dave, you know if you had just told me what you really wanted to do, you would know that you hadn't prepared me for this mess. I mean, seriously, using the bathroom in the bushes. Girls just don't do that," she said, almost whimpering.

Dave closed his eyes for a moment to stave off what he really wanted to say to her.

"Melanie, girls do that all the time. You may not have, but many girls do. Now can we just get out of here and go home?"

And just after he finished that sentence, he looked up to see Tim get out of the car and head down the hill toward the two of them.

Great, he thought, now they were probably going to get a ticket for something from some local yokel cop.

Doug jumped from the car and followed Tim, looking to see if any other people were around. He hated the years when it was Tim's "turn". He was always afraid that Tim's Barney Fife routine was going to get them either killed or caught.

By the time he reached where Tim stood talking to the couple, he could hear them still arguing over where they had left their Jeep. Tim was smiling and offering to give them a ride down the river to find their vehicle. Both of them seemed relieved and exhausted, so much so that they didn't question why a civilian was with Tim as they climbed up the hill to where the cruiser was parked.

Tim was directing most of his attention to the woman and when they reached the cruiser. He opened the front passenger door for her and told Doug and the man to climb in the back.

All of this made Doug very nervous. If Tim had a plan, he hadn't told Doug about it and if he didn't have a plan, he could bring a world of trouble down on them. While Tim chatted with the woman about the trip, her male friend sat next to Doug in the back seat, sullenly watching the scenery pass by and not speaking.

The woman told Tim that they were taking a weekend vacation to camp out along the New River, that they were pre-med students at Virginia Tech, and that she thought West Virginia in the spring was beautiful, but that the river had scared her.

The man in the back seat grunted and Doug thought that their relationship was going to be over soon even if Tim and Doug didn't kill them.

After a few miles, the man in the back seat noticed that they were heading up into the mountains instead of following the river back down toward the main road.

Before he could say something, Doug pushed a pistol into the man's side.

"Just keep your mouth shut and you'll get out of this alive," Doug whispered. "Don't act like you know something's wrong. We just want to have some fun with her."

"Afterwards, you can both go as long as you remember that we'll find you if you tell anyone."

The man's face had drained of all color. He looked at the girl still chatting with Tim and started to open his mouth.

Doug jabbed the gun hard into the man's ribs and the man closed both his mouth and his eyes. Doug realized that the man cared more about the girl that he had thought.

Too fucking bad, Doug thought. The man should have thought about the girl before bringing her into such a desolate and dangerous area. Anyway, she wasn't important, just another stupid woman who was only good for two things – fucking or killing.

"Don't give her a second thought. Most girls are just whores anyway. You're lucky she hasn't given you the clap or something," Doug said, thinking about the woman from work. He really wanted to kill that bitch. Maybe he and Tim could do another hunt this year before deer season began Thanksgiving week.

Dave turned and just stared at Doug. He was becoming more terrified with each passing second and his mind was racing with thoughts of how he could get Melanie and himself out of this. He had no illusions about these men. He could see the dead look in Doug's eyes and that told him that these men would never let them leave this mountain alive.

Doug saw the fear in Dave's face and he laughed and then tapped on the partition between the seats with the gun.

Tim knew that meant that Doug thought that they were where they needed to be and he stopped the cruiser. While Melanie opened the car door and stood looking around for the Jeep she and Dave had lost, Tim opened the back door and Doug pushed Dave out of the car where he fell hard onto the ground.

When Melanie heard the noise, she turned to see Tim standing next to her with a gun and saw her boyfriend lying on the ground with Doug's foot on his neck.

For a moment, Tim thought she was going to run and that he'd have to chase her down, but she just stood there in shock at what was happening to them. Before she could do anything else, Tim hit her hard with the gun and she, too, fell down on the cold ground.

Doug got Dave up and took him over to a maple tree and pulled his arms behind and around the back of a hickory tree where he handcuffed him. The man's hands didn't quite reach backward enough so Doug jerked at his arms to cuff him, dislocating one of the man's arms in the process.

The man started to scream and Doug rammed the gun in his mouth, breaking one of Dave's front teeth, muffling then stopping any sounds Dave might have made almost immediately. Dave twisted his upper body in attempt to relieve the pain in his shoulder.

"If you say a word, we'll kill her and then we'll kill you. Remember what I said in the car," he said, pulled the gun from the man's mouth and walked over to Tim and the girl.

Dave spit the broken tooth and blood from his mouth. He could feel the tears on his face as he watched them go after Melanie. He tried to struggle with the cuffs, but he couldn't do anything with his messed up arm. He regretted his earlier treatment of her. He couldn't bear watching what they were doing or seeing her in such pain.

Tim grabbed the girl by the hair and dragged her over in front of her boyfriend. She looked up and was weeping.

"So, partner, what's the plan?" Doug asked. They never used each other's names just in case someone really did get away from them and Tim never wore his name badge when they were hunting. Doug always thought it strange that Tim insisted on wearing his uniform, but the uniform had come in handy a time or two.

The girl was trying to crawl backwards away from them, but Tim held firmly onto her hair and she began to wail in fear. She knew she was about to be raped. She just wanted to somehow stay alive.

"Dave, help me. Please," she begged, looking over at her boyfriend.

Dave hung his head down and began crying hard himself. He began begging Doug and Tim to let them go or at least let her go.

Doug laughed and punched Dave in the gut as Tim began rip the girl's clothing from her. She was still trying to crawl away from him and toward Dave, but Tim grabbed her now bare legs and pulled her back to him. While Tim was tearing the rest of her clothes away, Doug went to Dave and shoved the gun back into Dave's mouth.

"You watch. Everything. If you look away, you're dead and we'll just have some more fun with her before we kill her."

In front of them, Tim pushed her face in the softened March ground and raped her.

When he was through, he stood up and looked at Doug and said, "Your turn, partner," and grinned.

While he was standing and brushing his clothes off, the girl was still trying to crawl away from them, making small whimpering sounds in her throat.

"Remember. Watch," Doug said to Dave.

"Don't even think of trying to look away or my partner will blow your head off."

"Watch her face and you'll see she's a whore. She's going to like it. You'll see it on her face. I've never seen any woman not get that glazed look when she comes," Doug said.

Dave was almost crazy with fear and frustration and pain by then and for some stupid reason he kept thinking of T. S. Eliot. At that moment, he lost control of everything that was keeping him sane, keeping him from believing this was happening the them, the moment when he lost the last sliver of hope that they could make it out of this alive.

Eliot was wrong, he thought. The world did end with a bang and not a whimper and he began to giggle and howl simultaneously, his body slumping forward, his mind gone.

Both Doug and Tim paused for a moment and stared at Dave in confusion. They'd never had anyone react this way.

"Is this guy mental?" Tim asked.

Doug just shrugged and turned his attention back to Melanie.

Doug pulled her up and threw her back on the ground in front of Dave again, hoping to bring him back to reality. Instead of pushing her into ground, he rolled her over so he could make sure that he, Tim, and Dave could see her face.

He tried to rape her, but no matter how aroused he was, it just wasn't working for him.

He decided that he was having trouble achieving orgasm because she would not look at him. She just stared up into the grey sky as if he weren't there and as if he wasn't giving her the fuck of her life. He got mad and slapped her, but she didn't respond. He couldn't finish with her like this no matter how hard he tried. He stood and kicked her hip hard as he zipped his jeans.

"Get me the bat," he said to Tim. Tim raised his eyebrows, but shook his head and went to get the baseball bat out of the trunk of the cruiser. He figured he knew what Doug was probably going to do, but it was ok with him.

Dave continued his howling and Doug kicked him in the balls to shut him up. Doug nodded at Tim and Tim took the bat and broke both of Dave's legs and then went to work on his arms.

After Tim finished breaking Dave's limbs, he went around to the back of the hickory tree and removed the cuffs from Dave and threw him on the ground next to the girl.

Even bleeding and broken, Dave had finally regained some semblance of his senses again and he leaned his head against Melanie's head as if to let her know she wasn't alone. She was catatonic. There was no recognition of him or anything else in her eyes. The only thing that gave Dave any idea that she might be in there somewhere were tears that streamed from her eyes.

"Ok, do it now and we can finish 'em. I need to get back to town for my shift and I've got to call Tiff and take a shower and put on a clean uniform."

Doug walked over to the girl whom he had tried to rape and wiped the tears from her face.

"It's ok. Don't cry. It's going to be ok," he said smiling.

She still wouldn't look at him. And even then she didn't make a sound or blink. Dave was whispering something in her ear and Doug kicked his back and told him to shut up.

"She's gone," Tim said. "We might as well finish up."

Doug stood back as Tim poured gasoline over the two of them and Dave tried one last pathetic attempt to cover Melanie's body with his own, but his body was so broken and splintered by the bat that all he could manage to really do was roll around in the dirt a bit.

Doug lit a cigarette and inhaled deeply, the taste of the cigarette and blood filling his lungs. Finally tired of them, he flicked his cigarette at them and their bodies lit up the night sky from the gasoline bath Tim had given them. Dave's screams from the flames were short lived and Melanie made no sound as the flames enveloped her as her mind had long since ceased fighting to live.

"Should we do something about the bodies?" Doug asked.

Tim shook his head and said, "No, if the animals don't pick them apart first after the fire burns out, there won't be any evidence left from the fire. It should destroy anything we might have left on their bodies."

The two of them watched the couple's burning bodies for a few more minutes before the smell of the cooking flesh began to get to them.

"You know, someone might miss these two and there might be a hunt for them," Tim said.

"We should probably work down river next time. We don't want anyone to think someone's killing on the river. That could bring the Feds in and we'd have to stop. Too many disappearances could get us noticed."

Doug nodded in agreement. The last thing they wanted was for anyone to figure out that people were being killed along the river, especially in a national park.

"Let's go. But next time, I want to plan things a little better. This making it up as we go isn't a good idea," Doug said.

Tim took once last look at the bodies and then smiled at Doug. "Yeah, you're right. But that was really fun."

Doug shook his head and laughed. "You're fucking crazy."

Later that year Doug brought Sally, the girl who had given him gonorrhea to the New River Valley under the pretext of showing her where he had grown up and meeting his mother. Sally had no idea that Doug's mother was visiting his brother and that he had spent the last few months planning her last moments on this earth.

He hated her so much that every time he kissed her made him physically ill. She was a whore. He had been unaware that she had slept with several other of his co-workers. He hated the fact she had made him look like a fool in front of those men more than the fact that she had given him the clap.

Doug had not told Tim about this little excursion because he didn't really think of it as a hunt. He looked on it as ridding himself of a truly bothersome pest. He had made sure that no one had known she was with him that weekend. He had planned to bring her up to the mountain, kill her quickly, and then get back to Charleston in time for a bowling game with some of the guys from work.

It was a lot of driving and a lot of work for one day, but he figured he could do it and when the police started looking for Sally, he had an airtight alibi and six witnesses who were with him that evening. And no one thought he had dated Sally except for the one time months ago.

He decided he'd tell Tim about it after if he needed to give Tim as a character witness. Tim could vouch for his character, saying that Doug always came by when he came home and since Tim didn't know he was there Tim wouldn't appear to be lying.

After the police called Tim, Doug would tell Tim the truth and why he hadn't involved him in his little problem and he definitely was not going to tell him that the whore had given him the clap. It was humiliating to think about what she had done to him. He could never tell anyone about it.

When he drove Sally to the top of the mountain, he went around the truck to open her door for her, telling her made-up stories about how happy he had been living in Gladstone Gap and how great his family had been. The mountains glowed green that day and he showed her the gap near the top of the mountain where you could see the distant mountains for miles and miles.

As she chattered on about how beautiful the valley was and how lucky he had been to have grown up there, he walked up behind her and pushed the hunting knife deep into the base of her spine. She crumpled to the ground like a piece of tissue paper.

He rolled her over and began stabbing her chest repeatedly. She cried and screamed, her hands and arms carved to the bone as she tried to ward off the blows..

He continued stabbing her until his anger was thoroughly spent – 37 blows in all and with every stab he called her "whore".

When he finally stopped he took off his clothes and balled them up and tied them to her body. He had found another small cave to put her body into where it wouldn't be found. He had thought of burning it, but he worried that the smoke might attract attention of any campers in the Valley this time of year so he dismissed that thought.

He stuffed her body through the mouth of the cave and heard it fall down into the little cave. If he were really lucky, he hoped that maybe it was used by bobcats who would feast on her dead flesh. Either way, she was gone. He threw the knife down the hole as an afterthought and went to bury the blood pool and trail to the cave before getting dressed again and racing back to Charleston.

Doug had to admit that this stuff was easier with Tim to help, but he couldn't tell Tim the truth about this time. It was just too damn embarrassing admitting what she had done. No, he thought, better that Tim never know.

Chapter Eight

Doug and Tim were 53 when Pea saw a newspaper article in the Beckley Observer about a body found along the New River near the new Visitor's Center up the river from Hinton.

The man was unidentified, but the article noted that he had died from stab wounds inflicted by "person or persons unknown."

She was sitting on the front porch of the house in the swing, waiting for Thomas, Trey and Diana to return from their ride. She never rode anymore. She loved the horses, but she couldn't ride and she never let anyone near the palomino. Some things were just too painful and she knew in her heart that no amount of time would change that fact. The others understood and never questioned her decision.

They waved to her as they rode off and she buried her face in the newspaper, looking for the events section to see if anything was scheduled for Carnegie Hall that weekend.

It was another case of "ifs" as Doug called it. If she had gone with her friends, if she hadn't picked up Friday's paper instead of Saturday's which she thought she had, if she hadn't seen the article on the dead body or the mention of other bodies found along the river over the past 15 years. If. If. If. They would have all been safe and no one would have known. No one would have even guessed.

But the one person in the world who saw the pattern saw the article and life began to change for Doug, Tim and the survivors of Manley's rampage.

Pea had spent many outings on the river and she knew it well. In her mind, she could see the location of the body just found and then connected the other bodies on an imaginary map in her mind. The New River had been a place on which she had spent many whitewater trips before she met Manley.

She went back to the article to see if there were any details about the other deaths, but there were none except for places and the years the bodies had been found. She carried the newspaper inside and sat down in her dad's old office to do a search of bodies found on or along the New River.

Other than new computer equipment and detritus left by Joseph and Mary both, the office had changed little since their parents had died 12 years ago. She normally avoided the room and just used her laptop. When she entered the room she missed her parents so much that it seemed that her heart actually hurt in her chest. Too many memories of growing up and running into the room to talk to her dad about her day, memories of sitting on his lap in there as a small child as he kept financial records of the farm for quarterly taxes and records concerning the animals.

But today those thoughts weren't present. She sat down as obsessed as she had been when she began the research on Manley's victims. She was surprised by the number of deaths that appeared close to the river – 30. Once she removed the accidental drownings and solved murders, she still came up with a number closer to 20, far too many for coincidence especially considering the deaths listed in her search went only as far back as the online archives to the 1990s.

By the time her friends had returned, her dad's desk was littered by print outs of articles from the Beckley paper's online archives. When Trey walked in the room, her face flushed red and he saw the guilty look on her face. He picked up some of the papers and his faced turned bright red.

He threw the papers back on the desk and went outside, storming past Thomas and Diana and got in his Celica and headed out the gate and down the road.

Pea had walked out to the porch and watched him drive away. She wanted to cry. Why did she do it?

Thomas bounded up the steps followed by Diana.

"What the hell just happened?" he asked "I thought things were ok."

Pea sighed. "I screwed up. Come on in and I'll show you."

After Thomas finished reading the print outs, he waved some of them in Pea's face while Diana was beginning to read the others.

"What the hell were you thinking? Haven't we all been through enough? Jesus H. Christ, woman, do you think you're some kind of super detective? And did you really think he wouldn't be angry?" Thomas asked.

Pea sat in her dad's old leather chair.

I didn't think. I just saw the newspaper article and came in here and started looking up things on the computer. It all just snowballed. One article led to another. Before I knew it, you guys were back and I was surrounded by this," she said and held her spread hands out toward the papers around her.

Tears were falling fast from her eyes and she couldn't seem to stop.

Thomas walked around the desk took her hand and stood her up.

"He almost lost you last year. I don't think he could go through that again. I know I can't. Get rid of this now. He'll be back, but you've got to let this go. Can you imagine what this would do to Mary and Joseph if they found you doing this?"

Pea nodded. "I know. I know. I'll put it away. I won't do this again. I promise." She wiped her eyes and tried to force a smile.

"Go fix some lunch. I'll be there as soon as I get rid of this stuff. I'm sorry. Diana, I'm sorry. None of you deserves this madness. Go eat. I'll just be a few minutes. I'll burn this stuff in the fireplace. I promise," she said.

Thomas looked doubtful, but took Diana's hand and left for the kitchen without speaking.

Pea started gathering the papers together and was about to put them in the fireplace when she stopped herself. She couldn't explain to any of them later why she hadn't burned them. She just felt it was too important to ignore the lives on those papers. She opened the side drawer of her father's desk and took out an old folder of farm inventory and replaced the inventory with the print outs. She threw the inventory papers into the fireplace and lit them, making sure that they were burned before she went to join Thomas and Diana.

Thomas raised an eyebrow as he was making turkey, ham and cheese sandwiches for them while Diana was pouring glasses of iced tea.

"Should I pour a glass for Trey?" she asked.

Pea shook her head. "He may not be back any time soon. He may not be back tonight. I'm sorry. Ever since Mary and Joseph left for Washington, I just keep screwing this weekend up. I got rid of the papers."

She sat down at the table, the sandwich and tea in front of her.

"Shit. I may have to get you guys to take me up to Staunton to get my stuff and my dogs if he doesn't call or come back by tomorrow evening. I think he may be through with me. Heaven knows I probably deserve it."

She picked up the sandwich and began to eat as if her whole life hadn't just completely changed. Thomas and Diana just stared at her and then began to eat as well. She didn't say it to them, but she had been alone before and she certainly didn't have to tell Thomas that she had survived worse. What she didn't realize was that tears were sliding down her face as she continued to eat.

"We'll take you to Staunton tomorrow evening. Don't worry about it anymore," Diana said and placed her hand on Pea's shoulder. Pea was shaking a little bit, but she was still struggling to finish the sandwich and have a normal lunch.

Diana glanced at Thomas and under the table he took Diana's other hand and squeezed it. He loved her for her kindness. He only hoped that Pea really was going to let this go.

Chapter Nine

Pea woke up around midnight to find Trey sitting in the armchair next to her bed, the moonlight streaming in through the open window and illuminating his face. She sat up on the side of the bed and waited.

He pressed his fingers against the bridge of his nose, then wiped one hand across his eyes and rubbed his temples.

"I can't do this, Pea. I love you, but I won't watch you destroy yourself. I want a normal life with kids and a stable home with a wife who isn't out trying to get herself killed because she thinks she doesn't deserve those things. I can't have a child who had the empty childhood I had."

He stood and looked out the window, remembering the first night he had spent in that room with her and awakening to see the fog in the pasture and her beautiful face asleep on the pillow. He had thought at one time that he could fix her, but he realized tonight that only she could do that.

He turned back to her and rubbed his eyes again.

"I went home and got your stuff. I even managed to fit the dogs in the car, too. I put your bags in the hall downstairs and the dogs out in the barn."

"Trey," she said, "Please wait . . ."

He walked to the door and didn't give her a chance to finish.

"I'm sorry, Pea. I can't do this," he said and headed out the bedroom door.

She leapt up and grabbed his arm.

"After a year, this is how you want to leave it? You said you'd wait. You promised," she cried.

He pulled his arm from her hand.

"Pea, I can't do this. I thought I was stronger. I'm not. It's not as if you didn't know what I wanted, what I've wanted all along. You lied to me once over the business with Manley and now what to keep you from doing the same reckless things again? Am I supposed to believe that you won't do it again?"

He left the room and she fell to her knees in the floor and wept until she could barely breathe.

Thomas had heard their voices and had stood at the end of the hall and watched Trey leave. He walked to Pea's room and saw her in the floor and took off down the stairs after Trey.

Trey was almost to his car when Thomas reached him.

"You chicken shit son of a bitch. You're the most selfish man I've ever met. So she isn't perfect. So she hasn't given you what you wanted yet. Have you even thought about what she went through? You motherfucker, she killed the man who killed her child, my fiancée and 11 other women."

Thomas pushed him into the car and said, "Go! Go now, you little bastard. Go back home and have a little pity party for the little orphan whose mommy died. Pea deserves a better man than you."

Trey drew his arm back and hit Thomas on the jaw, knocking him to the ground. "Shut up!" he yelled.

"You don't know. You don't . . ." Trey stepped back and remembered that Thomas did know. He thought of what Manley had done to Shawnette and fell down to the gravel drive opposite where he had knocked Thomas down.

"Sorry. Shit. I'm sorry," Trey said.

Thomas was working his jaw back and forth with one hand.

"You've got a mean right hook for a white boy," Thomas said and laughed.

Trey looked up at the second floor of the house and then stood and kicked the rear panel of his Celica.

"I think you'd better stop that before you end up with a cast on your foot.

"Have I ruined it?" Trey asked.

"The car or something more important?" Thomas asked.

Thomas stood and looked up at where Trey's eyes were focused.

"I don't know. You'll have to find the courage to face her yourself. She's a strong woman, probably stronger than you know. She might tell you to go to hell," Thomas said and shrugged.

As the two men walked back to the house, Trey was shaking his right hand out and limping at the same time. He looked up at the light in Pea's room.

"I don't know what hurts worse, my hand or my foot. Hell, do you have a titanium jaw or something?"

Thomas laughed. "No just fast enough to only let you clip my jaw instead of hitting it directly.

"Damn, I'd hate to think of what my hand would feel like if I'd really connected," Trey said.

Thomas held the door open and looked at Trey.

"I'd worry more about how you're going to explain about being an asshole than clipping my jaw," Thomas said.

Trey nodded and walked up the steps back towards Pea's room. She wasn't in the floor anymore. Diana had followed Thomas down the hall and had stopped at Pea's room and helped her to her bed and gotten a box of Puffs which Pea had used quite a few of, judging by the white pile of tissues next to her.

"Diana, can I talk to Pea alone?" he asked.

Diana stood and gave him a dirty look, then closed the bedroom door and headed downstairs to join Thomas.

Trey sat down at the foot of the bed and leaned over to hand Pea another tissue.

"I was stupid. I let my temper get the best of me and I never even gave you a chance to talk to me. If you want me out, tell me. I deserve it."

Pea blew her nose and wiped her eyes again. She wasn't sure what to say to Trey. She loved him, but she knew that she had changed and she wasn't sure if it would be fair to expect him to be happy with the woman she was now.

When they met she was almost emotionally crippled by her daughter's death and Manley. When she sat down that February morning and discovered the other Pearl Montgomery, she began to change. Slowly she was no longer tortured by panic attacks or the doubt or the fear that had doggedly followed her everywhere for years. She was stronger now and needed Trey to allow her to be strong and not to have her depend on him for her happiness.

So, the questions of their relationship weren't just his or hers alone. If they were to survive, they had to accept one another, she thought. Love always seemed enough, but she knew in reality that it was just the start.

"I can't be the woman you want me to be," she said quietly.

"I'm not the woman you met at Baker's last year. I can't go back to that woman again even if I wanted to. I can't change anymore than you can."

She looked down at the tissue in her hands. She had wrapped it around one of her fingers liker a bandage. She sighed and looked back up at him.

"I've tried for the past year to be the woman you wanted me to be and I can't do it. So if you want out now, I understand. I'm not saying that it won't hurt, but I can't be anyone but who I am now. I think maybe I was living a childish dream of what I thought marriage was when I was with Manley and I have to admit that I'm afraid of what a real relationship might be."

Trey moved down the bed and sat on it next to her. He took another tissue and wiped the tears from her face.

"I know, Pea. I know. When I saw those papers downstairs, I could only think of the danger and fear from last year."

"I'll admit that I wanted you to come to Staunton and live a conventional life with me without having to worry about if you were safe," he said.

He tucked a stray strand of hair being her ear the way he had the day that they had met. He loved her so much, but he wondered if he could live with the fear of losing her to someone like Manley. He wasn't sure, but he knew that walking away would be just as difficult.

"Maybe we can meet this problem somewhere in the middle. I won't ask you to change, but you can't expect me not to worry or sometimes lose my temper. I do need to know that you love me and that you'll forgive yourself, that you'll talk to me before doing anything rash," he said.

She nodded her head and fell forward against him, sobbing.

"I'm sorry. I do love you. But I'm scarred, Trey. And you've got to let me heal my way. I want to be with you. One day I may want to have another child, but right now the thought of losing a child or losing you just kills me. Give me time. Just give me time."

He pulled her closer to him and said, "All the time you need, Pea. With or without children. We'll just take it a little bit at a time."

They lay back down on the bed on held onto each other until they both fell asleep, exhausted.

An hour away, another couple lay down on the muddy river bank next to one another, exhausted and taking in their last breaths. The man tried, but failed to lie close to the woman as they felt and smelled the diesel fuel poured over them. They were luckier than other couples had been. They had been tortured so much that few sounds came from them as they burned. Their bodies had mercifully let their souls escape just as the cigarette cart wheeled through the air toward them.

Doug and Tim did not know it, but they had just murdered two people who would bring the wrath of God upon their heads through a woman they had never met. Not that the woman who would stop them was a friend of the couple. She wouldn't know of their deaths for several weeks and they were strangers to her. That night she was falling asleep in the arms of the man on earth she loved. But she was tenacious and she would see something in the murders that no else saw just as she had with the murders Manley had committed.

Although she knew that she and Trey would often be at odds in the future, she also hoped that he would be there when she needed him in the future.

Chapter Ten

"You are crazy!" Mary yelled and walked out into the July sun, her face almost as red as her hair as she slammed the door behind her.

Trey raised his eyebrows and looked from Pea to Joseph, whose slack-jawed expression said as much as Mary's words and the slammed door she left in her wake. Trey had shown his own displeasure at Pea's ideas which had worked about as well as if he had slammed every door in the house the way Mary had slammed the kitchen door. In other words, it didn't do a thing to change Pea's mind. Then he tried to dissuade Pea from telling Joseph and Mary about it. Again, he failed.

He watched her frustrated body language and thought of the fragile blonde figure he had first seen in Baker's, the woman so broken that she couldn't even enter a book store without having a panic attack. But he also came to understand after Manley's death that she was not a hot house orchid who needed tender attention and care. If anything, she was more like kudzu – tenacious, overwhelming sometimes, and covering everything around her with her own notions of justice.

Joseph sat across from them and was experiencing his own form of déjà vu. Before the others, he and Thomas had seen the unstoppable force that Pea could be when she had tried to solve the murders of the women last year. He would have agreed with Trey's assessment of Pea being tenacious, but because he was angry, he would have also chosen adjectives closer to selfishness and thoughtlessness right now. His concern for Mary colored his opinions of Pea right now.

"Pea, how can you even think of pursuing this right now?" Joseph stood and walked toward the door to find Mary.

"This is damn stupid and selfish. Your sister is almost six months pregnant. You want to endanger her again? And what about Trey? How fair are you being to him? I know you. I know you better than you may know yourself. What? Did you blackmail him into not trying to stop you by threatening to walk away from him? What on earth would make you pursue this?"

He looked from Pea to Trey and realized he was right.

"I know what you went through was incredibly . . . I know it almost broke your will. But I also knew even then that you were stronger than anyone gave you credit for being. Let it go, Pea. For god's sake, don't pursue this."

Joseph paused and lowered his head as he rested his hand on the door knob, then looked into her eyes and was almost in tears.

"I can't believe you've involved Thomas in this. He's happy for the first time in almost three years. And as for me, you can forget my help. You were lucky last time. We all lived. What if this time we're not so lucky?"

He shook his head and followed Mary out to the fence where she was standing watching the lambs whose wool would be sheared in the next few weeks. He dug his hands into his pockets, forming them into fists as the thought of how Pea could just spring this on them after everything they had gone through.

When he reached the fence where Mary stood, he put his arm around her shoulder and kissed her on the cheek. She reached out to him and rubbed her hand across his back as she leaned into him for support. He had put weight on in Italy as he was unable to resist eating as she ate everything in sight, but she hadn't noticed his slight weight gain and wouldn't have cared if she had. She was so in love with him that his slight paunch meant nothing.

Mary was so angry with Pea. She wanted to slap her sister, but she knew that Pea was more stubborn than any of them. She also knew that Pea's stubbornness had brought pain and misery into their lives, including the ten years of Manley's evil at Pea's expense.

And now, she had come up with some crackpot theory that there was a serial killer in the New River Valley. How did she come up with these ideas? Mary thought. Was there some arrogance in her that made her think she could see things that people such as Joseph couldn't see or did she just not think at all when she started it?

"Joseph, I can't go through this again," Mary said.

"I just want to stay here for a while, have our child, and let the craziness out there stay out there. Please don't get involved in this.

Joseph hugged her tighter and frowned. How could he tell Mary that he believed that Pea had found something? Right now Mary and their child was the only thing that truly mattered to him and he couldn't risk the health problems himself.

Looking out into the pasture, the sheep kept the grass there better manicured than some professionals could. Who knew that grass could be so naturally and brilliantly green, he thought, allowing his mind to drift away from the problem at hand.

"Joseph, shit, you're going to help her," Mary cursed and pulled away from him.

He raised his hands as if trying to surrender, but she knew him as well as she knew Pea.

"Mary, she's onto something. Even Trey and Thomas have looked at what she's found and they agree. And if the pattern she's found follows true to form, we've got months to look into it," he said.

"Months? You mean about the time the baby's due?"

Mary almost spat the words at him.

He moved closer to her, but she was too angry to touch him. She wanted to kick him as much as she wanted to slap Pea.

"Damn you both! I am not going to raise this child without you. Get someone else to help her or just let Trey and Thomas do it. But not you, not you," she grabbed his shirt and pulled at him, before beginning to cry.

She buried her face in his chest.

"I can't lose you, Joseph. Please. I can't sit there and wonder if you're going to live or die. Please. Don't," she shook in his arms as he held her against him.

"Let's go in and rest for a while. I don't want this stress on you or our little guy," he said placing his hand on her swollen belly.

She nodded and they walked back to the house. Not a word was said until they reached the porch steps where she stopped and faced him.

"Little guy? Maybe you should be saying 'little girl. I know you want to know the sex, but I like the idea of being surprised," she said.

"Mary, I don't care as long as both of you are ok," he said and led her up the steps and into the house.

Pea and Trey were no longer in the kitchen nor were the papers Pea had previously spread across the old poplar farm table when she had presented her case for the murders to them.

When Joseph had walked out, he had left Pea in tears and Trey angry. Trey had gathered the papers together while Pea went to the kitchen window and stared. He had known that they would not be happy, not any happier than he had been, but after he had sat down with Pea and Thomas and Diana and had listened, he saw the pattern as well.

What made him angry and what Joseph and Mary did not know because they had not given Pea the chance to tell them was that they had contacted law enforcement, including the FBI, and no one would listen or even look at the evidence Pea had pulled together.

It wasn't as if Pea were trying to drag them through hell again. It was just that no one wanted to listen. They would look at her, remember her history with Manley, and turn away. None of them wanted to have such things happening in their backyard and the New River area was such a big tourist draw that no local official wanted any taint on.

They also didn't want anything to do with Pea. It didn't matter to them that she had stopped a man who had killed 12 women and his own daughter. But it did matter that she had walked away without a trial. Some of them even thought she should have been arrested. One of them in Gladstone County even said so.

They had been so shocked at that reaction that their only hope was that Joseph could use any influence he had with the Bureau to get someone interested in murders occurring over a six county area, some of which included a national park.

Trey sat the folder on the table and placed his hand on Pea's shoulder in much the same way Joseph had placed his hand on Mary's shoulder.

"She hates me," Pea said.

Trey shook his head and watched Joseph and Mary at the fence.

"No, Pea, she loves you. She's your sister. She's just scared. She's pregnant, with a husband who's had a heart attack and she probably thinks about what happened in that farm house as much as you do."

Pea turned to him, shock showing on her face.

"Yes, I know you think about it all the time. I can see it in your face sometimes. You put up a very brave face, but Joseph does not know you as well as he thinks he does. I've been there when you've cried yourself to sleep thinking that I was already asleep. I can see the fear that you hide. I may not know how you feel about it, but I do know how you torture yourself over it."

He lowered his head and kissed her on her forehead, cupping her face in his tanned hands.

"Come on. Let's drive into Lewisburg and go by The Bakery. We'll get Mary some sweets and give her and Joseph some time alone."

Pea nodded and as they headed out the front door to his Celica, he scooped up the folder and carried it out to the car, putting it in the trunk of his car. Pea got in the passenger side and leaned her head back and closed her eyes. She realized that she should have expected their reaction, especially after Trey's initial anger. She just hoped that she and Mary could cross the distance between them right now. She felt as if she had no family but Mary unless Trey proposed and so far she felt like that was a far off dream.

By the time they were on 219 South, Joseph and Mary were heading up the stairs to their bedroom. Mary didn't know where Trey and Pea had gone and at the time she didn't really care, but she felt as if she just kept holding onto Joseph, everything would be better. She wanted no more misery, just peace.

Chapter Eleven

Tim had been expecting someone in the last 30 years to notice the deaths and disappearances, but he was stunned that it was a beautiful, well dressed young woman with two men who seemed as if they were body guards, both of them checking out the office while she asked questions about any unexplained deaths, murders, or missing people in the county.

While the men made him nervous, the woman's questions terrified him. Now, here was what he had dreaded for 30 years. It only after he recognized Pea and the two men that he relaxed. He remembered how she had killed her ex-husband, supposedly because he had been killing women in Virginia. Just another rich bitch with a grudge against men, he thought, but she and her questions still frightened him.

But her actions last year were what he needed to find a cause to dismiss her and the men with her. Everyone knew she had stabbed her ex-husband to death and had gone free. He hated women like her and she was just the type of woman he liked to hunt – the type who thought she was better than him, who didn't know her place.

Tiff had been like that after they had married, but he'd taught her fast to watch her mouth and to mind him or she'd be feeling the back of his hand.

When he saw that Pea was the one asking him questions about the murders, he turned the questions on her own actions in the past year and asked her how much money she had spent keeping herself out of jail. Instead of allowing her to ask him any further questions, he attacked her verbally, showing her and what he thought of as the gutless wonders she had with her the door, telling her just how despicable he thought she was.

It was only after he left that he began to sweat. He had used every inch of his deputy's training to intimidate them, but he also knew he was lucky because everyone else was either out on a call or out to lunch. He could not sleep that night thinking about what might have happened if she had come in there when someone else might have been there. No matter how careful he and Doug had been, that could have been bad. It could have been very bad.

He and Doug had been hunting together for a long time now. Sometimes, when Doug called him up, he just wanted to say "no", but he knew deep down, somewhere inside his gut, he was afraid to tell Doug "no". He wouldn't admit it to himself, but he was afraid of Doug.

Over the past 30 years he had seen Doug do some fairly sick things, especially to the women he took when snatch the boyfriends or husbands. He thought that Doug did it not so much to hurt them, but to try to make them see that neither one would or could do anything to help the other.

Tim knew that a streak of cruel sickness lived inside Doug. He thought that it had come from his father, but Tim never mentioned Doug's dad after they had killed him. He also knew that Doug hated most women except for his mother and he believed that Doug's devotion to his mother just wasn't quite right. But he had tied his destiny to Doug over 30 years ago and he knew of no way out.

Tim thought of the look on the men's faces as they were forced to watch Doug rape and torture the women in ways that Tim had never thought of. When the last couple somehow managed to touch their hands together right before Tim doused them with gasoline and lit their bodies against the darkening sky, Doug was furious. Tim had never, in all their years together, seen Doug so out of control. The couple barely touched their hands together before they died and Doug began screaming at the burning bodies. He was almost incoherent, screaming at them that they couldn't love one another because love didn't exist, just pain and fear. It made him wonder if Doug had demons inside him that had to do with Doug's mom and dad and the way he was raised.

Doug called him back the night after the three people had come by asking questions. Tim told him what questions they'd asked and who they were, but Doug had laughed and told him he worried too much. He told Tim not to be stupid or to do something stupid. Doug had said things like that to him for years and every time it just made Tim angrier, but Tim never said anything.

"Well, I just thought you should know, Doug," Tim said.

Doug dropped the subject and began to discuss a second hunt this year, maybe this summer. Tim said for Doug to just let him know when, but as Doug talked about the new hunt, Tim could feel a tightening in his chest. He'd always trusted Doug, but now that he was over 50 and getting close to retiring, he wasn't as eager as Doug to hunt anymore. He just couldn't tell him "no".

Tim wanted to come home to a good supper that Tiff always had waiting for him, have a beer and watch a game on the box. He wasn't as excited sexually as he used to be and sometimes just rolling over on top of Tiff every now and then was so much easier than wrestling around on the cold ground near the river with one of their victims. With Tiff, he didn't have to do or say anything afterwards. He'd just roll over and fall into sleep.

While Doug had wandered from job to job, never staying anywhere too long, Tim had stayed with the sheriff's department. He and Tiff had bought an old company house and had raised three children together. It wasn't much. The old coal company houses were small, but affordable on his salary.

They had saved some money and every now and then Tiff talked about his retirement and their using the money to go see the country. Tim thought it sounded good, but he knew Doug wouldn't let him go so he just nodded while Tiff talked and he thought about all the things he and Doug had done through the years.

And that made him afraid. Not of getting caught, but of what might lie ahead of him one day. He'd never been religious, but his parents had dragged him to church until he'd been in junior high and he remembered those sermons about the abominations of hellfire and the eternal pain of damnation. Yes, that made him afraid. He didn't want to die a sinner, but if he got saved, he knew Doug would kill him or maybe even his family.

The irony was that Doug went to church in Kanawha City every Sunday and the congregation thought he was such a good man, taking care of his mother, devoting his life to Christ. Tim got angry about that. At least he wasn't a hypocrite. Doug could go to church from now until kingdom come and it wasn't going to save his sorry ass.

Tim had thought about turning himself in, too, but then he thought about his kids having to live with the shame of what he'd done. He was stuck. He knew it and he had no idea of how to stop any of it. But worst of all, he knew that deep inside himself, when he was hunting, he wanted it more than anything in the world. He was getting older, but the hunt, the hunt never did. Deep down he just wanted to do nothing but hunt. And he knew he'd never turn himself or Doug in because then the hunt would be over. Forever.

Chapter Twelve

Mary woke to the sound of muffled voices. She could hear Joseph, Pea and Trey talking quietly through the antique vent that was placed in the kitchen ceiling and the floor of her bedroom.

She sat up in bed and swung her legs over the side of the bed. She wiped angry tears from the corners of her eyes and looked out the window to see the setting sun above the pasture where the sheep quietly grazed.

Damn, she thought. Joseph was going to help them, not matter what she had to say. How could he do this? She realized that he was never going to change just as she knew that she wouldn't change her love for him or her fear for him.

And she didn't truly blame Pea for what had happened. Manley, definitely, but not Pea. None of them saw the monster that lived inside him. Mary watched as the sun set and thought about whether she should have told Pea when she first found out about his cheating. Would Pea have left him? Mary didn't think so. She often wondered what had finally pushed Pea over the edge and then she remembered that Pea hadn't left Manley. He had left her, but only after he took money from Pea.

Good god, she thought, Pea could still be married to him. He would still be torturing women and murdering them. And she suddenly recognized that she had not been there for Pea.

She had been so caught up in school and falling in love with Joseph that she had left Pea to sit here, feeling forever guilty for the death of her daughter, perhaps even still married to Manley and living in the private level of hell she had put herself into.

Would I have ever really gotten involved in everything, would Joseph have, if she had left Pea to sit here on this farm, alone and destroyed? She knew the answer and so she walked down the back stairs to the kitchen where the three of them sat of the old farm table.

Joseph jumped up immediately to offer her a chair, but she waved him away and headed toward the Bunn coffee maker that Trey had insisted on buying, unable to take Pea's cowboy coffee any longer. She poured a cup and drank in the thick, bitter liquid before she turned to face them.

No one had said a word since she had entered the kitchen and she knew they were waiting for her to speak. She frankly didn't know what to say to them. One minute she was furious and the next resigned. She saw the box of pastries next to the coffee maker. Pea's peace offering. She smiled before she took one from the box, turned and sat down in the chair next to Joseph.

"So, who the hell is the bastard murdering people this time? I'd like to see you people catch him before this baby decides to pop out because I would like to have my husband back for a while," she said and took a large bite from the fudge brownie she had on a napkin in front of her on the table.

She wasn't surprised to hear the sighs of relief from the three of them that they probably didn't even know they had uttered.

Trey was the first to speak.

"We have no idea," he said and pushed his chair back from the table and then slapped both hands against the table.

"And no one thinks anyone is murdering anyone. The local law enforcement thinks we're seeing things that aren't there and one county deputy even wanted to arrest your sister for murder as he threw us out of his office." He was frowning and Mary saw that anger was behind that frown. He had seen how close Manley had come to killing Pea and her in that farmhouse in Goshen and it obviously pissed him off that anyone would accuse Pea of murder after she had stopped a serial killer, almost dying in the process.

Mary looked to Joseph and he reached out to rub her shoulder. He shrugged his shoulders and took a drink of coffee before speaking.

"I haven't called the bureau yet. I'm just getting caught up on everything myself before I call and possibly get dismissed by agents who are really busy going after terror suspects," he said.

"I'm not saying that these deaths and disappearances aren't important. They are. And I know they matter to the families involved. I think of Pearl Montgomery's family and how after 12 years they were finally able to bury her. What we did last year was right. I don't regret working on it with Pea and Thomas. It helped a lot of people, especially Pea," he said and nodded at her, "though I know we should have told you and Trey and I'm sorry for that."

"But there is so much going on right now and all we have are hunches, newspaper clippings, and no real pattern. I doubt if the bureau or even the state police have the time to really look at this. However, we do, for whatever that's worth."

Mary looked across the table at Pea who had remained silent throughout everything Trey and Joseph had said. Pea hadn't taken her eyes off her sister. She sat waiting to see how Mary would respond.

"Pea, sometimes I want to smack you and sometimes I want to hold you and protect you from yourself," Mary said.

Pea smiled a little and hid it with the coffee cup from which she took a long drink. She was as concerned as Mary was about Mary's pregnancy, Joseph's health, about the safety of all of them and of the complete lack of cooperation from many of the counties along the New River. Many of the officers had said the same thing. The Summers County deputy had said it the best.

"People die on that river every year. Doesn't mean there's some crazy person killing them. Most of them drown and often their bodies aren't found. It's a dangerous river and people don't take it seriously and they end up dead."

"So where are the files," Mary asked.

"You guys aren't the only ones involved. Maybe I'll see something you haven't."

Joseph shook his head. He did not want Mary involved in any way.

"No, Mary, let us take care of this. We've done it before and Pea, Trey and Thomas have already started the process of trying to put the puzzle pieces together."

"Well, I'm very good with puzzles," Mary said. "And if you're doing this you're going to have to let me help. I'm not going to argue about it. So don't even try to stop me," she said.

Joseph looked at her and then reached up to touch her cheek. She could help from the house, but there was no way she was going out with any of them.

"Alright, but just from here for right now. And if you have any problems we all stop. Everyone agreed?" he said turning to Trey and Pea.

"Absolutely," Trey said and Pea nodded in agreement.

"That includes you, too, Joseph," Mary said. "If you're not here for our child's birth, I'll kill you myself."

Joseph stared at her for a few moments and then said, "I'll be here. I will. I promise."

"Well, then what are we eating for supper. This pastry has just made me hungry," Mary asked.

They all laughed at once and Joseph leaned in to kiss her forehead.

"Whatever you want, dear. Whatever you want," he said and smiled.

Across from them, Trey took Pea's hand and squeezed it under the table. She exhaled a deep breath, felt some of the weight from the last few days lift from her, and returned his hand clasp.

"There is just one problem, Ree," Pea said.

"We're all going to gain a hundred pounds if we don't stop eating every time you do. Seriously, I've gained five pounds since you've been home."

At that they all laughed again and began to pull food from the cabinets and refrigerator to prepare a light supper for themselves. When all else fails, Mary thought, cook and people will eat and listen.

Chapter Thirteen

Doug had just had a good night with one of the new girls at work and he had sent her home with the false promise to call her after church tomorrow. The stupid whores always believed him and then when he didn't call they pouted, sometimes got angry, but not one of them had ever tried to get back with him.

His eyes scared them after he was done with them. He had dead eyes after he slept with them and that was enough to make them want to stay away. He didn't really care as long as they stayed away. He wanted nothing to do with them afterward. He really believed that if they slept with him that they were whores and that the ones who wouldn't were bitches.

It wasn't always easy, but it worked out for the best. He didn't think they were worth anything but for the sex anyway and even that never came close to how some of the women he had hunted had made him feel. Those women made him actually feel something - desire, lust, anger, and rage, a rage that felt sometimes as if it would consume him.

He sat on the edge of his bed smoking a Marlboro and drinking the last of a can of Bud and thought about that idiot in Gladstone Gap. That stupid son of a bitch could get them both in a lot of trouble if he didn't calm down. In all the years that they had been hunting, no one had suspected that someone was killing on the river and as long as Tim kept it together, no one would.

Maybe he needed to take Tim on a little hunt to remind him what was at stake and if Tim still couldn't handle it, then maybe he'd have to take care of Tim cause there was no way he was going to stop and he'd be damned if he'd let Tim's stupidity got in the way.

Although August was a busy month on the river, they could probably pull someone off the trail. He would like it to be a woman, but the odds against a lone woman were low so Doug figured a man would be just as fun. No sex, but the torture would more than make up for that and he could always get a whore from over on Washington Street later on for the sex.

About five or six years ago, they had found a man who had gotten lost on the trail along the ridge. Out of nowhere the blows from the hammer had taken the man down fast. Doug knew just how hard to hit the back of a man's skull without killing him. Well, once or twice, he'd fucked it up and killed the person, but he was good at it now. They usually walked beside Tim and they never even knew what Doug had planned for them.

The man from six years ago, they'd staked to the ground and had taken a opossum they'd starved for a few days and had opened the cage door quickly against the man's leg, jamming the cage next to his leg so that the hungry animal had begun to take large bites, trying to feed his hunger and escape the kill-free trap at the same time. Even though they'd duct taped the man's mouth shut, they could still hear screaming.

But the real screaming started when Doug turned the cage up to the man's genitals and the opossum's long jaw had taken off the man's penis in one quick swallow. That had really surprised both of them. They didn't think it could eat a penis in one swallow and they had looked at one another in shock and then had laughed so hard that their sides hurt.

They moved the cage around the man's body until he passed out from the pain and then they had pissed on his face to wake him up.

He was barely holding on, barely breathing when they put the cage down on his face. His screaming stopped after just a few minutes after the opossum ate enough of his face to escape through the door.

They had watched as it waddled off into the bushes and thought that it was going to be a happy little beast for a few days.

As they removed the ropes and stakes from the man's ravaged body, they decided to just leave it there, with the man's sleeping bag covering part of the body so it would look like an animal attack. They figured that if the man's body was eventually found that there wouldn't be much left anyway for the coroner's office to come up with anything other than an animal attack.

Doug noticed that he was stroking his penis as he remembered the opossum eating into the man's body. He headed to the shower to wash the whore's smell off of his body and finish what the memory had begun. He had to get up early for church tomorrow. He was scheduled to be a greeter and he didn't want to disappoint his minister.

Chapter Fourteen

Pea snuggled up against Trey's back and he rolled over to face her and brushed his fingertips against her soft lips. They lay there together staring into one another's eyes for a few moments before their hands began to anxiously explore the small places on each of their bodies that they knew lit their desire for one another.

He kissed the side of her neck as his hands softly cupped her buttocks and pulled her legs to him where they separated and wrapped around his own hips. She rolled on top of him and he lifted himself up to match her downward thrusts.

He watched her face as it glowed with pleasure, her cheeks turning soft pink and he sat up, with her legs still wrapped around him, their bodies rocking together until their desire had grown so strong and fast that the release left their bodies throbbing like two violin strings struck in unison.

They sat holding one another like that for what seemed like an endless time, before they lay down, their bodies still entwined as they fell into a deep and dreamless sleep.

Down the hall, Joseph watched as Mary undressed and slipped under the cream down the comforter, their baby bump having grown quite larger in the last six few weeks, especially with what seemed like Mary's unending appetite. He could not tell her just how much he loved her. There were no words for the depth of what he felt for her. He still could not believe that she had wanted him.

He still felt like the short, fat guy who had somehow won the lottery. What was it that made them fit? He would never understand, but he knew it worked, whatever it was.

He had finally stopped trying to eat with her as he knew the foods she was eating were feeding their child and would kill him if he tried to keep up with her. He had gained 20 pounds since the wedding and he knew his cardiologist would read him the riot act over the weight gain.

She lay down on the bed, rolled on her side away from him and pushed her hips against his groin. He groaned and she laughed and said, "Sorry." He pulled her back close to him and buried his face in the nape of her neck, breathing in the sweet smell of her. He reached around, his hands moving from her breasts and down to their baby. Just as he was about to move his hand lower he felt a flutter against his palm and jerked his hand and the comforter away.

"What was that? Did you feel that?" he asked sitting up.

Mary laughed and pulled the comforter back up and put his hand back against her belly.

"He's been doing that for a few days. But don't stop what you were doing or I'm going to turn over to you and take things into my own hands," she said.

His eyes widened and he smiled.

"Oh yes, ma'm, gladly," he paused, "Are you sure it's ok?"

"If you stop, it won't be," she said.

"Oh, I'm all yours," he said and dove under the comforter. Their laughter would have been heard down the hall had Trey and Pea not been so involved in their own lovemaking.

In Staunton, Thomas slept alone, thinking of what had transpired the past three weeks. He lay flat on his back, his arms propped behind his head. It was one of the nights that Shawnette would not leave his thoughts and he wished that Diana had not left for the week. She kept him grounded when the world seemed too hard for him to face. She had made him learn to smile again and taught him to forgive himself for mistakes that he had never really made, helping him remove his guilt over losing Shawnette.

But tonight, he wondered if his thoughts of Shawnette were warning him of the dangers that might lie ahead with Pea's latest search. Last time he had helped Pea because of Shawnette and his need for revenge.

This time he knew that he was helping her because she had been the instrument of revenge against Shawnette's murderer. He knew very little about the area where these new murders had occurred and he frankly did not like wandering through the New River Valley. The place felt bad to him and he had always paid attention to that feeling.

Once that feeling had saved his life in Raleigh, North Carolina, when he pulled into a shopping center and every nerve in his body told him to leave and leave as soon as possible. Instead of getting out of his car, he had put it in reverse and exited the parking lot.

He had been in Raleigh for a training seminar and when he had returned to his hotel, he turned on the evening news as he prepared to pack to leave the next day, packing everything but the clothing he would need to wear in the morning.

He was stunned as he heard the blonde anchorwoman describe a shooting between two drug dealers in the very shopping plaza he had left. He sat on the edge of the bed and watched the news, learning that the shooting had occurred less than five minutes after he had driven away. Two bystanders were wounded and both dealers were dead. After that, he never ignored that feeling about some places and several of the places along the river had made him feel that way, especially the place where the deputy had thrown them out, acting as if they were crazy.

That place had felt really bad and he had literally dragged Trey and Pea to Trey's Celica in order to leave there as fast as possible. Something in his gut told him that if they had stayed that they would have somehow ended up as dead as the people they were inquiring about.

And that was when he began to think that that town held the answers to their questions. He made a mental note to ask Joseph to do one of his maps to see how many people had disappeared from that county and how many bodies had been found there or nearby.

He rubbed his eyes and rolled over to try to sleep and for a brief second Shawnette was lying there next to him, her sweet smile unmatched by the sadness in her eyes. The sight of her frightened him so much that as he jumped from the bed and knocked the bed lamp to the floor, the bulb shattered as it hit the floor and glass flew around his feet.

Reaching out for the wall switch he felt a piece of the thin glass pierce his foot. The light lit the room and Shawnette was gone, if she had ever really been there. He limped to the bathroom and washed his foot after pulling a long splinter of frosted glass from the sole of his foot. From where he sat on the edge of the bathtub, he could see the side of the bed where Shawnette had been lying. The covers were undisturbed, but the pillow, the pillow indented with the shape of a woman's head and he began to shiver.

Was Shawnette trying to warn him away from this search? He didn't know, but he went to his recliner and turned the TV on CNN. He didn't look back into the bedroom and he fell asleep with the lights and the TV on. It wasn't that he was afraid of Shawnette, but he was afraid of what he thought seeing her might mean. And that scared him to death.

Chapter Fifteen

The next morning Mary locked herself in her father's study and read carefully through everything that Pea, Trey and Thomas had accumulated while she and Joseph had been in Italy.

Pea had been very precise in her recordkeeping, including her own notes, which Mary felt revealed more about the possibility of a serial killer than Pea herself had probably seen.

When she finally exited the study, she followed the smell of tuna salad sandwiches and deviled eggs into the kitchen where she found not only Joseph, Trey and Pea eating and talking, but also Thomas standing off to the side, holding a sandwich wedge next to his mouth. His eyes were dark and troubled and the sandwich did not move as he stared out into the pasture.

"Thomas?" she said.

The rest of them stopped talking and looked up to see what she had seen on Thomas's face - a look of complete and utter fear. It was only then that he turned to them and took a large bite of the sandwich, nodding his head and pointing at the eggs on the plate on the table.

Mary did not like what she had seen on Thomas's face. In fact, it scared the hell out of her. What could possibly have frightened a man like Thomas, a man who looked to most of the world like an extremely strong, handsome and confident man?

"Where were you, Thomas?" she asked as she took a plate and filled it with two sandwiches and several eggs.

"You looked like you'd seen a ghost," she said and sat down next to Joseph, who inwardly groaned at the sight of the food on her plate. He'd had one thin sandwich and a glass of lemonade. The eggs on her plate looked so tempting, but he knew he couldn't indulge. Too dangerous because he knew his own weaknesses were for her and for food. So instead of putting his hand on the plate, he looked down and placed it instead on her swollen belly.

"Any action this morning," Joseph asked and Pea and Trey immediately began to ask about the baby and his movements.

But Mary wasn't going to let go of the question she had asked Thomas, and after smiling and briefly answering their questions, she turned her gaze back to him.

"Thomas, what is going on with you?"

Thomas sat the half-eaten sandwich wedge on the plate on the counter and just shook his head.

"Nothing really. Just some bad memories and bad dreams."

Everyone at the table seemed to accept his answer without further pressing, but Mary didn't believe him. She hadn't seen that in his face. She had seen fear. And in the year that she'd known him that was something that she'd never seen.

"No, Thomas, something else is bothering you. What is going on? If it's about this search, then it's important that you tell us all."

"We can't risk what happened last year. We need to get everything pulled together and then let the FBI take it over. No one is getting hurt this time," she said emphatically and looked at Joseph.

Thomas sat down at the end of the table and drained his glass of milk as if he had just downed a glass of whiskey. He looked at all their faces and paused for a moment, wondering if he was about to make a huge mistake,

"I saw Shawnette last night in my bedroom. Just as real as she looked the last time she lay in bed next to me. It scared the shit out of me. I didn't imagine it. It was really her. Go ahead and laugh or try to give me a rational explanation, but I saw her," he said.

No one said anything and Joseph and Trey actually looked down and away as if they couldn't even consider that Thomas might have actually seen Shawnette. Mary reached over, placed her hand on his and was about to speak when Pea spoke up first.

"I believe you. I don't know what's going on, but I think there's something not quite right about this whole thing."

She looked over to Trey, and then continued.

"Three days ago, I walked out to the barn and I saw Alicia standing at the opposite doors at the other end of the barn. She was wearing her red riding habit, her hair loose. She was crying and she was holding her arms out to me. I ran to where she was, but when I got there, there was nothing there. Nothing except the smell of the lilac shampoo she loved so much."

Pea stood up and began to clear the table as if she were too embarrassed to face them.

"Don't ask me if I just wanted her to be there. It was her. Now you can call both Thomas and me crazy, but I know what I saw and I won't believe otherwise," she said, leaning against the sink.

"It was so real that I could even see the calluses on her tiny hands where she gripped the reins learning to ride. I was so sure that it was her that for a moment I forgot that she was dead." Pea kept her back to them so that they wouldn't see the tears brimming in her eyes.

Before anyone could respond, Thomas spoke.

"The place on the bed where I saw Shawnette laying was undisturbed except for the shape of her head on the pillow where I had seen her laying."

"That pillow had been undisturbed before I saw her next to me. She was smiling, but her eyes, her eyes were sad. I gotta tell you I've never been so scared in my life."

Joseph leaned back in his chair and looked at both Pea and Thomas. He didn't quite know how to react to either one of them. He believed in science and the thought that their guilt was manifesting itself in hallucinations crossed his mind.

"Why didn't you tell me," Trey stood and went to Pea.

"Did you think I would just brush it off and try to convince you that you were seeing what you wanted to see? Do you trust me that little?"

Joseph stood up and said, "Whoa, time out here. This is already too weird without you guys getting into some kind of fight again about trusting one another. There are three other people involved here. So stop it with the trust shit."

"There are four," Thomas said. "Remember Diana? She may be out of town, but she's part of this, too."

Trey sighed and saw the anger in Pea's face and pulled her close to him.

"Sorry. Ok? Sorry," he said and she rested her head against his shoulder.

Mary took Thomas's hand and squeezed it.

"What? No hugs for Thomas?" she said and they all quietly laughed, the tension in the room immediately breaking.

Mary went to Joseph's side and kissed his cheek.

"One for the peacemaker, too," she said.

"You know, I don't know what to make of any of this," she continued. "There is no pattern that I see except that everything has happened along the New River."

She turned to Pea and took a deep breath before continuing.

"Pea, I know you think you see something here, but I just don't know how you can find out anything without putting yourself or one of us in danger. It's very frustrating because I do believe you, but this is just not as cut and dried as . . . as last year."

Mary still could barely think of Manley, much less speak his name. She had never thought of herself as naïve and she knew monsters walked among them everyday, but she had always thought of herself as savvy enough to spot one. That she had had one involved in her family made her almost physically ill.

That she had almost lost the two people she loved the most in the world in the process of stopping him, much less her own life was simply unacceptable in her idea of what the world should be. The thought of endangering her child or her husband frightened her even more than she could imagine.

She returned to the situation at hand and could see no safe avenue for them, especially considering that no one really believed them or if they did, they didn't want to help.

As she pondered these thoughts, Joseph turned to Thomas and inquired about Diana. Thomas told them that she was spending the week in Baltimore with her family.

"I can't say that I'm not glad, either. I really don't want her near any of this shit. I've got to get back to work this week so I don't know how much help I'm going to be."

"I'll let Joseph do some of his magic on all this information and then we can maybe meet next Saturday and see if we've found anything different," he said.

Trey nodded and looked to Pea.

"We really need to get to the farm and check on things there. We've been away for three weeks and I have to make sure the restoration on the barn is going well.

Pea nodded and stopped for a minute to look at Mary. She was trying to determine how Mary would handle this.

Mary wound her long red hair into a knot at the back of her head and smiled.

"Well, Joseph, you're going to be left alone with all this. I have a farm to tend to and a baby to get ready for.

Sorry," she smiled and started to head for the back door to the barn.

Before she could exit, Thomas spoke up again.

"Since we're talking about weird shit, I've got to say that I think that deputy in Gladstone Gap was hiding something. There was something wrong with his reaction to Pea's questions. I think it went beyond arrogance. It was almost fear."

Thomas paused for a moment and rubbed his roughened hands together. "The man just wasn't right and I got the feeling that if we had stayed much longer, we might have been in real danger."

He looked to Joseph. "Maybe Gladstone Gap or Gladstone County is a place to start. I don't know. I could be wrong, but . . . it didn't feel right."

They all turned to Joseph to see his reaction.

"Can you work on it this week, Joseph?" Pea asked.

He shrugged and glanced out the window and then to Mary at the kitchen door.

Everything depended on her. He could not endanger her and he could not take a chance on alienating her. He needed more than what the farm and this "case", if you could call it that, he thought, offered him.

"I'll do what I can. Depends on what Mary says. You all know that I'm not going to do anything to hurt her," he said.

"I'll see what I can find out, but she's right about one thing – there's no real pattern unless Thomas's thoughts about Gladstone have any substance. I don't know if we can find anything more than we've already found."

Thomas walked toward the backdoor and stood next to Mary to leave and then stopped before opening the screen door.

"I just have a really bad feeling about this." He looked to Pea. "Your ex was crazy and sick, but this guy is worse and if he's been doing it for 30 years without getting caught, he's smart as well. I know you might think I'm imagining seeing Shawnette or that Pea was doing the same thing when she saw Alicia, but I was taught to never take such things for granted. Why else would we see them when this comes up?"

He and Mary headed out the back door and left Pea, Trey and Joseph to stare at them as he waved goodbye to Mary and walked toward his old Ford 150. They really didn't know what to say or even to think. But Pea shivered a moment as if someone had brushed against her arm.

Thomas was right about one thing. This was dangerous and they should all tread lightly as they looked into it.

Chapter Sixteen

Trey spoke little during the trip back to Lexington, where they would spend the night before driving up to the farm the next day.

Pea hated the drive between Lewisburg and Lexington. I-64 was one long trip through the woods with only a few exits that provided relief to the unending mountains and trees that rose higher the closer they came to Lexington before the drop down into the valley.

She could feel the tension rising from Trey and could see that he was not happy with her by his white knuckled grip on the steering wheel. She wanted to talk to him about "seeing" Alicia, but she had been afraid that he would think she was finally losing her hold on reality.

"Trey, I didn't tell you because I thought you'd think I imagined it," she said, placing her long fingers against the glass window of the Celica. It still felt warm from the sunny day. She turned to him and tried to see in the falling dusk any reaction on his face.

He took a deep breath and then shifted gears as they turned away from the Lexington exit and moved up I-81 toward Staunton.

Pea looked in confusion at the passing exit to Lexington.

"I thought we were going to Lexing . . ." she started to say but he interrupted her midsentence.

"I'm not angry. I don't know what to think about your "seeing" Alicia or Thomas thinking that Shawnette was in bed with him. We all have our ghosts, I guess."

He glanced at her briefly before focusing back on the road.

"Sorry. I missed the exit. This whole New River thing has made things seem off. I just wasn't thinking about anything except for heading back to the farm."

He was silent for a few moments and then continued.

"I just don't understand why you don't talk to me about these things. I can't keep telling you how I feel in order to make you trust me. You either do or don't. And tonight, I'm thinking you don't," he said and looked out the driver's window in order to avoid Pea seeing his face.

She placed her hand over his on the gear stick.

"I do trust you, Trey. God, I trust you more than anyone. I just don't trust myself. Please. I need you to believe me. Honestly, what were your first thoughts when I said I thought I had seen Alicia in the barn?"

He didn't know how to answer that question. The truth was that he thought she imagined it. He actually still did, if he admitted it.

"Trey?" she asked.

He swallowed and looked in her eyes before returning his gaze to the interstate.

"I thought that you saw what you wanted," he said. The conversation was making him uncomfortable.

It was Pea's turn to look away and she removed her hand from his.

"Then you think I imagined it, that I saw Alicia because I still feel guilty and I need to reconcile my feelings about her death."

Trey was starting to get a little angry as he took the exit ramp off the interstate and onto Route 11 north to the farm.

"That's not fair, Pea. You're putting words in my mouth. That's not what I said."

Pea snorted and he knew without looking that her chin was tilted upward.

"Well, then, just what definition of the word "imagine" am I missing here because that is the word you used."

Trey didn't respond. The road was dark and he needed to keep his mind on it rather than fight with Pea. By the time they arrived at the farm, her great danes bounded to the passenger side of the car to greet her.

As she knelt down to pet them, she ignored Trey waiting for her. Thomas had returned the dogs back to Staunton the Monday after the wedding for her, along with most of Pea's suitcases that Trey had managed to leave half empty. Even then he knew he couldn't leave her.

Trey refused to allow this to go any further and he walked up the stone steps and entered his home. He stood in the foyer and realized how much she had changed his house. It wasn't just a lonely farm house anymore; she had made it a home. And that made him even more frustrated.

He couldn't make her feel things she didn't and he couldn't see how she didn't see the changes she had made in his life.

Almost five minutes had passed before he realized that neither she nor the dogs had come in the house. He went back outside onto the portico and found her sitting quietly on the steps, each dog sitting on each side of her with her bare arms draped around their backs.

"Are you coming in or are you spending the night out here?" he asked.

She stood and brushed the dust from her jeans and walked past him into the house. He felt like time was rewinding to when they first began and he had brought her here for the first time. He felt an ache in his chest and looked down at the dogs that were waiting for him to follow her.

Somewhere there had to be peace for them. But he wondered if she would ever allow it. Maybe that was the problem, he thought. Maybe he allowed her to make all their decisions and then he immediately dismissed that thought as ridiculous.

He knew she needed him just as much as he needed her. She was having a snit and he'd just have to let her get it out of her system.

"Come on dogs, let's go find her before she finds the ice cream," he said and held the screen door open for the dogs to enter the house.

He found her in the kitchen doing exactly what he thought she would be doing – sitting at the kitchen table with a pint of Breyer's Vanilla Bean ice cream and a spoon. He sat down across from her and she still did not speak or look at him.

"Do I get a spoon or are you going to eat it all?" he finally said.

She slammed her spoon down on the table, stood and pulled a second spoon from the drawer and sat back down across from him, placing the spoon in front of him.

He held the spoon up in the air and she finally looked at him and offered him the pint of ice cream. He took a spoonful and let the sweet creamy taste fill his mouth as his eyes never left hers.

"I love you and I trust you, but you make me so mad sometimes," she said.

He reached across the table and took another spoonful of ice cream from the cardboard container.

"Ditto," he said.

She stood and walked around the table to him.

"You have ice cream on your cheek," she said and leaned down to lightly lick it away, but before she could, he turned his face to her and kissed her deeply, wrapping his arm around her waist and pulling her onto his lap.

She leaned her forehead against his.

"Why isn't everything easier?" she asked.

"I don't know. I don't think anything's been easy except for the day I met you at Winter's. You were so beautiful," he said.

"And such a klutz," she said as she stood, his hand still wrapped around her waist. She tousled his dark curls.

"You need a hair cut," she said. He looked up and smiled.

"I know. And we both need to stop eating every time Mary gets a craving. I've never seen your jeans quite so appealing," he said.

"Are you saying I'm getting junk in my trunk?" she asked, turning quickly so he wouldn't see that she wasn't serious.

"No, no, no I just . . ."

She turned and smiled at him.

"Oh you're going to pay for that. That wasn't fair at all," he said.

She ran from the kitchen with him quickly behind her on the steps to their bedroom.

Later that night as he lay with his head on her chest, lightly sleeping after their lovemaking, she wondered how much longer she was going to be able to keep from telling him that she was pregnant, too. Their lives were about to change completely and she was so afraid that she would lose herself the way she had with Manley. Just a few more weeks, she thought. Just a few more weeks and I can tell him.

Chapter Seventeen

The next afternoon Joseph took one of the empty bedrooms upstairs and started putting his charts, clippings and maps up on the walls of the room. The bedroom was completely painted white with high gloss enamel so it was perfect for work. He had almost finished getting everything up when he heard footsteps coming down the hall. He recognized Mary's measured steps but failed to notice that they stopped at the bedroom door.

She stood outside the room and looked around it.

"You can't work in here," she said.

It was then that he noticed that all color had drained from her face.

"Is something wrong? Are you ok?" he asked and rushed to the door.

"No," she said, pushing him from her.

"This room. It was . . . it was Alicia's bedroom. Pea can't come in her. I can't. It's just . . ."

"I didn't know. It was empty and I needed some space . . . I'm sorry. Are you ok?"

She nodded and leaned against him as he led her down the staircase to the living room. They sat down together on the sofa for several minutes in silence as he watched and waited for her to speak.

"Oh God, will that man never be gone from our lives?" she sighed.

Joseph stroked her hair and placed his hand on her swollen belly.

"It's going to be ok. We need to get him out of our lives for good. This isn't good for you and it's not good for Pea. This was your house before he came here. Make it your house again."

"I don't know if Pea can exorcise his ghost from this house. I mean she's talking about seeing Alicia and, well, I think she thinks we don't see that she still feels guilty, but I can see it. Can you? I think Trey does," she said.

"Yes, I've seen it since I first met her. She carries those ghosts with her all the time, although I think you're right in saying that she thinks she's hiding it."

Mary placed her hand on his knee and stared into his eyes.

"Do you think she actually saw Alicia or that Thomas saw Shawnette?"

Joseph shook his head.

"No. They're both still struggling with guilt. I really believe they both should be in therapy. Trey does, too. We talked about it last year when Pea was so intent on restoring Trey's family home as fast as she possibly could. He said she wasn't sleeping then. I doubt little has changed."

The thought that Pea had been, was still, so distressed by the past upset Mary. She had been concentrating so much on the wedding and the baby that she didn't really notice how Pea was feeling. Now she was feeling guilty.

"Stop it," Joseph said and laughed.

"One of these days I'm going to stop you from saying that. What do I have to do to get you to stop seeing everything I'm thinking?"

"Nothing. You can't. We'll be old farts and I'll still know."

"Umph," she said. "Well, I managed to keep you from knowing about the little one. So score one at least for me."

Mary snuggled closer to him and he could feel their child between them. He kissed the top of her head and they sat there till Mary's craving pulled her from the sofa toward the kitchen.

"If I can convince you to whip up something for dinner, I'll get the stuff out of that room," she said.

"Deal," he said and smiled, heading up the stairs as she made her way to the kitchen.

How could he do this in this house? He wondered. How could they or any of them live here if the two sisters weren't ready to let go of the past?

He could hear Mary rattling around in the kitchen, pulling pots from the shelves and scrounging around the refrigerator for food.

"How about spaghetti?" she called from the kitchen.

Oh God, turkey sauce again, he thought, but responded with a hearty "Fine" from the staircase.

What he hadn't mentioned to Mary was that he had talked about Mary as well as Pea and Thomas. What had happened before the cabin had been hard enough, but only Pea and Mary really saw what happened in that cabin. Trey had been outside and Thomas was lying in the road, almost gone. Only the two women had faced Manley down alone.

Joseph rubbed the bridge of his nose as he walked down the hall. It terrified him that the women might have been tortured and murdered, but it horrified him that no one had been able to help them. Thomas wounded, Trey, unarmed, and he hospitalized. A nightmare.

The thought of Mary's description of Pea taking the shotgun and holding the barrel of it next to her chest with Mary lying in the floor behind her made him almost physically ill.

Then he thought of the room filled with the papers, the maps, the clippings about the murders and the disappearances and he knew that somehow he had to end this before one of them was hurt again. He was calling the Bureau the first thing Monday morning. This amateur detective work had to stop now.

And he knew that Trey would agree with him on this one. This time Trey would be there and he might be able to rein in Pea's relentless search for self-forgiveness, because that was what she was actually doing. She was trying to find redemption for herself by trying to find whoever had killed those people in that river valley.

But before he made it to the room to remove everything, he heard Mary curse in the kitchen and he went to see if he could help her. She shooed him off and told him to go take care of his own work, that she had her own work to take care of.

He kissed her sweet lips and headed up the back steps to the room he had set up shop in. And that was when he knew that he couldn't stop anything, that whatever was coming, was coming with the speed and force of a locomotive.

Standing in the middle of the room was a small girl with long red hair falling onto the shoulders of her riding habit, smiling as sweetly as he had ever seen Mary smile.

Chapter Eighteen

Mary had just tasted the sauce when she heard the loud bang and thump coming from the second floor.

Oh god, please, no, not now, she prayed as she ran up the steps, holding the stair rail with one hand and the other placed under her belly. Her first thought was that Joseph had had another heart attack.

From the top of the back steps, she saw Joseph at the far end of the hall slumped in the floor staring into Alicia's bedroom.

"Joseph!" she screamed and ran toward him as he turned his head to look at her.

He first raised his hands to stop her. His own fear was that she would see what he had seen. He got to his knees and waved her off.

"I'm fine. I slipped on the hall runner and banged my head against the wall," he said trying to keep her from moving to him.

She reached him and got down on her knees next to him.

"You scared me to death. If you do that again, I'll kill you myself."

She leaned back against the wall and tried to catch her breath.

"I thought . . ." She couldn't finish the sentence.

He hugged her and tried to block her view of the room.

"I know what you thought, but I'm ok. I slipped and fell. That's all. You've got to calm down. You've got someone else to worry about," he said.

She nodded and finally calmed herself down.

"Maybe we should get rid of this old runner. Neither of us needs to take a chance falling down,"

"Mary, this runner has been in your house forever. Your great-great whatever grandmother probably wove it.

The runner stays. I was a klutz. You're the one who shouldn't be running around."

He took her hand and helped her to her feet.

"Do I smell supper?" he asked. "Come on. Let's go eat and I'll take something for this headache."

As he led her away from the doorway, he took one last look into the room and saw that the child was gone, if she had ever been there. He was starting to truly dislike this house. Now it had him seeing things, but the last thing he would consider doing would be to tell Mary what had really happened. God help them all, he thought. He shivered as he thought of what he had seen.

Could Pea and Thomas have actually seen what he had seen or was he letting their imagination and fears influence his own common sense? His head was really starting to throb where he had banged it against the wall. No, he wished he could blame it on Pea and Thomas, but he knew what he had seen. The child was so real he thought that he could have reached out and touched the velvet and wool texture of her jacket. And her face, it was so much like Mary's.

As they entered the kitchen, he went to the cabinet over a small built-in desk and took down his bottles of medicine. His nightly routine - heart meds, same time every day. He was glad that Mary was involved with putting their supper on the table. He didn't want her to see just how bad his hands were shaking.

In Staunton, while Joseph was seeing Alicia standing in her old bedroom, Pea had been playing Chopin on the piano as Trey had finished fixing his homemade potato soup for their supper. He heard her switch to Coldplay's *Viva la Vida* and smiled. He never knew what she was going to play. One minute a Mozart sonata and the next minute The Who's *Behind Blue Eyes*. He laughed remembering their first discussion of her musical choices and how he had described her tastes as "schizoid."

That should have prepared him for her discovery of the old Victrola and stacks of 78s in one of the bedrooms. He had found her sitting in the floor sorting through them with an original pressing of Hank Williams's *Jambalaya* playing on the old hand cranked console.

She was thrilled with her discovery and had danced around the bedroom, leading him in an impromptu two-step around the room, the whole time talking about how important the records were and how valuable they were as well.

He had just shook his head and followed her along. When she was as happy as she had been that afternoon, she lit up the whole house with her presence. It was afternoons like this when he wondered how he had been so lucky to have been in the Winter's Books with her at the same time. Maybe she had been what he had been waiting for while grinding through his own quiet days.

He was staring out the kitchen window as the sun was beginning its descent behind the distant mountains and he thought about the old sailor's adage about "red skies at night, sailor's delight."

He hadn't noticed that the piano playing had ceased and he went into the front parlor to look for Pea, but she was nowhere to be seen.

"Pea? Supper's about ready," he called and went through the dining room and into the solarium where he found her sitting and watching the same sunset he had been watching from the kitchen window. The sky was a brilliant orange and pink now and the light began to turn yellow in the room.

"I can see why your mother loved this room so much," she said.

"I always feel so calm and peaceful in here."

He looked down at her face and saw the colors of the sunset glowing upon her face lighting her blonde hair with a gentle wash of pastel colors. He took her hand and raised it to his lips and gently kissed it.

They walked to the kitchen together and as soon as they had left the solarium, Pea began to feel anxious.

"I want to call Ree for just a second before we eat. I promise not to stay on the phone long," she said.

"Hurry up. I'm hungry and I'm not going to have vichyssoise instead of hot soup. Did I ever tell you just how much I hate cold soup?"

Pea took her cell from her pocket, held it up to his face, and hit the number for her sister. She mouthed the word 'fast' as the phone rang. She was surprised when Joseph answered instead of her sister.

"Joseph, it's Pea. I was calling Ree. Is everything ok?"

She could hear his sharp intake of breath before he lied and said, "Sure, though she's in the middle of emptying a pot of pasta, which she should have let me do."

Pea felt he wasn't quite telling her the full story, but in her own preoccupation with her own thoughts and the knowledge that her sister was probably fine made her dismiss the edge in Joseph's voice. Usually she would have picked up on something like that right away, but not this time and Trey was starting to wave at her so everything disappeared from her thoughts but what had prompted her to call.

"Joseph, pregnant women are not helpless and are quite capable of cooking," she said.

"I know that, but I don't think you can say too much about cooking" he said laughingly referring to her distaste for the culinary skills.

"Ha. Ha. Now put Ree on," she said as she heard her sister calling out something in the background.

"Sorry, couldn't help it. Just a minute, she wants to talk to you," Joseph said.

Pea could hear a rustling noise and then the heavier breathing of her sister taking the phone from Joseph.

"What he's not telling you is that he almost scared me to death," Mary said and now Pea could hear Joseph in the background.

"What happened?" Pea asked.

"The klutz slipped on the runner upstairs and fell in the hall," Mary said.

"We should have gotten rid of that runner years ago," Pea said.

"Yes, I said so myself, but my husband thinks it belongs on Antiques Roadshow or something."

"Well, as long as you guys are ok, that's all that really matters, Umm, Ree, can you meet me in Lexington on Monday for lunch? We can meet at Trey's. He's going to be here working all day. Oh, and, uh, could we make this just our own little trip?" Pea asked.

Mary frowned. It was not like Pea to ask her not to tell Joseph something, but she agreed. She knew it had to be important or Pea wouldn't have asked.

"Well, um, I guess so if I can convince my husband that I can drive. And I'd really love to go baby shopping," Mary said and Pea could hear Joseph grumbling in the background.

"Thanks, sis. Love you and see you then," Pea smiled and clicked off her phone and went back into the kitchen.

"Where's my food?" she called out to Trey as she sat down at the little Hoosier table.

"What was that about?" he asked

"I'm going baby shopping with Ree on Monday," she said.

"Ugh," Trey grunted. "That makes staying here cutting hay sound like fun."

Pea punched his shoulder and laughed.

"That's the same sound Joseph made. Do they teach men that or something?"

He put the tureen of hot soup on the table and leaned over to kiss her cheek.

"I think it's the word "shopping" that causes it," he said and pulled a seat out next to her.

Chapter Nineteen

Doug dreamed of the ghosts of his victims standing before him, their rotting and burned and cut corpses forming a circle around him. He was wearing his old high school letter jacket and jeans. He felt 17 again, but he didn't like the feeling of being surrounded by these dead people. Once he was through hunting, he liked to forget it and move on, not think much about the bodies or what happened to them as long as they just 'disappeared'.

The ghosts were moving closer and ever closer. Some of them had rotting strips of flesh hanging from their bones and some of them had blackened skin that was peeling back from their bodies, revealing the meat of their body that looked like rare, blackened steak. And they all smelled foul.

He'd never smelled anything so bad in his life, like sewer gas and burnt pork barbeque together.

He had no weapon in the nightmare and saw only one small spot to escape from their silent cursing stares. He ran to it and found himself standing above the small cave where they had thrown the old man from their first hunt. He looked down and saw the skeletal hand of the old man clutching a hard Lucite key ring in the shape of a faded rainbow. Part of it was broken off and the keys were spilling onto the ground.

Suddenly the old man's hand grabbed his ankle and he could hear a voice from the hole saying, "Why son, why?"

Just as the other hands were reaching out to touch him, he woke to find himself in his bed screaming like a little girl. He was alone and he flailed about trying to find the bed lamp. He turned it on and sat up on the side of the bed and realized that his body was dripping with sweat. He looked for the glasses that he had had to start using a few years ago and put them on in order to bring the bedroom into full focus.

Nothing. No corpses. Just a nightmare and he hadn't had a nightmare in decades. He thought about Tim and the phone call about the people who had been asking about the missing people and the bodies that had been found. It was Tim's fucking fault he had had the nightmare. The idiot was going to get them either caught or killed.

Doug reached for a t-shirt to pull on and noticed for the first time that his chest hair was starting to turn grey. He stopped for a moment and stared down, running his hand across his chest. The skin was looser than it used to be. He had a sudden though and pulled his boxers open to see if the same thing was happening down below. Sure enough. Fuck. When his hair on his head had started thinning and turning grey, he'd shaved it off and now kept it neat and smooth. The chest hair he could probably do something with, but what the hell was he supposed to do about his nuts?

He didn't feel as if he were older. He still felt the way he had when he had been wearing that letter jacket in the dream – buff and strong. It angered him that his body was aging. He thought of how he had swaggered across the football field and how the crowd had cheered. He still felt that way. Why was his body doing this?

He knew. Worrying. Tim was making him worry too much. He needed to put a stop to it and a hunt would make him feel much better. And if those snoops came around again, then he and Tim would have to take care of them, too. He'd have to think about a good plan – one that wouldn't point to either him or Tim, something that looked accidental.

Yeah, he'd have to think about it for awhile.

He got up to take a piss and as he waited for the stream to start, he thought about those corpses again. Something bothered him about it. Something wasn't right. He couldn't figure it out. What was it?

He flushed the toilet and thought it needed cleaning. He thought he'd bring his mom up for the weekend. She'd clean everything up just to spend some time with him. She was a big believer in cleanliness being next to Godliness. That made him think about the beer in his fridge and he knew he'd probably have to drink it all before he brought her down. He walked to the kitchenette in the small studio apartment and got a Schlitz out of the fridge. The red lettering on the can caught his eye and he felt a chill going up his back.

Red. A red coat.

A red coat on a little girl with red hair. What the fuck? They hadn't killed any kids. Why was there a little girl standing in the middle of his kills in the dream?

He sat down on the old sleeper sofa that he'd had since he moved in there 20 years ago and looked at the red words on the can. There was something else wrong, too. Something about the little girl.

Doug closed his eyes and tried to see the corpses in his dream. Some of them made him smile for a moment. While he truly didn't like to think about them much, he did enjoy the memories of some of the hunts. Some of people he had forgotten about till now. Some of them meant nothing to him but being able to enjoy the hunt, especially the men. The men always bored him. After so many years, they really weren't any fun. The couples were best and sometimes the women . . . that was it! He realized there was a woman standing next to the little girl. She was one of the most beautiful women he'd ever seen, with coffee colored skin, tall and with a face like a model. She had one hand on the girl's shoulder, but the other arm was raised and pointing at him and her eyes looked like they were on fire.

What the fuck? He'd never seen either of them before, but he was sure as he was sure that his father was dead that the two of them were dead in real life as well as in the dream.

He tilted the beer back and chugged it down fast. He could feel his heart pounding and cold sweat forming on his body. Fucking Tim! This was his fault. This had to stop. He hadn't killed either of them and Tim's fear was tainting his own enjoyment of the hunts and he couldn't let that happen. He threw the empty can across the room and hit the trash can dead center.

Fuck this shit. He was going to hunt. And he wasn't going to dream.

He stood and went back to bed thinking of where the next hunt was going to go down.

Tim was having his own bad dreams that night as well, but he couldn't remember clearly what had been chasing him. He just knew it was bad and it was going to get him.

He rolled over and spooned up next to Tiff, who was snoring lightly. He cupped her breast and lifted her night shirt to reach around and start to grasp her closer to him.

She brushed his hands away and scooted away from him.

"Don't Tim, I'm trying to sleep," she mumbled.

He got angry and rolled her whole body to his.

"Don't tell me no," he said and started pulling at his briefs.

"Oh, Tim, please. I'm really tired. I want to sleep," she said and rolled away from him again.

This time he didn't pull her back to him. He wanted something and he knew he wanted to hunt. He rolled in the other direction on the king size bed and was as close to the edge of it as he could get. He thought about the last woman he and Doug had taken and began to stroke his penis. He thought about what they had done and was just about to get off when he thought about the nightmare he'd had.

His penis went limp in his hand and he tried to get it hard again, but the fear was still hanging on in his head and nothing he could do would help.

He had planned on jerking off and then rolling back over to Tiff and let her deal with the mess in the morning. But that wasn't going to happen now.

All he could think about was the color red. He couldn't understand why. He crawled closer to his wife. He was going to call Doug tomorrow and tell him that he wasn't going to hunt anymore. He was too tired and old for this shit anymore. He was 54 and he just wanted to stop before they started hunting someone who might just take them both down.

This was enough. He was done. And when he closed his eyes to go back to sleep, he didn't see red anymore, just darkness and that was ok with him.

Chapter Twenty

Pea reached the Lexington house early and prepared a light lunch of a basic garden salad for herself and added pasta to Mary's, along with embellishments such as a chopped hard-boiled egg that did not sit well with her morning sickness. She wasn't really very hungry and she was still ambivalent about whether to tell her sister that she was pregnant as well. She did know one thing – both her husband and her sister would be thrilled with her decision to forget about the New River stuff.

What had she been thinking? And now, the pregnancy had sealed the deal, so to speak. She could take chances with her own life, but she would not, could not risk the life of another child.

She thought of lying next to Alicia in bed in the early morning, listening to Alicia tell her mommy that she had read in one of her storybooks that once horses had wings and Alicia had asked her mother if her mommy thought horses could fly again.

Pea remembered her sweet smell and how Alicia's hair glowed in the morning sunlight, curls flowing across the pillows. Pea squeezed her eyes shut tight to keep from crying and tried to think of all the joy that Alicia had brought into her life.

And that was what had changed her mind about the New River murders, if there ever were really murders. She was with a man who loved her, who wanted children with her, and who, even when he disagreed with her, never made her feel stupid or foolish. She had the chance to have the family with him that she thought she might have had with Manley. But, with Manley, she had closed her eyes to so much. With Trey, her eyes were wide open and she needed him so much and she wanted this child so much.

She had been so deep in thought that she hadn't heard Mary enter the house. She jumped a little when her sister's voice suddenly broke her from her thoughts of Alicia and her pregnancy. Mary came in and sat down at the kitchen table, put her feet up on an empty chair and slung her leather bag onto the table with such force that the place settings shook slightly.

"Ok, what's so important that you make your preggers sister drive an hour for lunch and not tell her husband why," Mary asked.

Pea sighed and put Mary's salad down in front of her. The sight of the pasta salad made Mary's mood change immediately and she sat up and breathed in the aromas of the salad and smiled.

"Well, maybe I can forgive you since you made this."

Pea put her own meager salad at her place at the other end of the table. She had intentionally placed a low floral arrangement between them so that she could see Mary's face, but not her food.

She seemed to have morning sickness most of the day and nothing seemed to help. It had been this way with Alicia as well. The last thing she needed was to look at the eggs on Mary's plate.

Mary finally took a look around and realized that her sister was sitting as far away from her as she could get. Trey's kitchen table was almost as long as the one at the Greenbrier farm. She sat her fork down and sighed herself.

"Pea, if this is about that New River stuff, I really don't want to talk about it. And sitting five miles away from me is not going to change my mind."

Mary picked up her fork and began to eat again. Now it was Pea's turn to smile.

"Don't you even say 'Hello Pea' and 'Gee what a great lunch you've made before you start fussing at me?" Pea asked.

Mary stopped eating and said 'Hello Pea. Great lunch' and took a long drink of her lemonade.

Pea leaned forward, looked down and shook her head.

"Ok, ok, Ree, you win. Good heavens, why do always have to be the bossy sister?"

Mary laughed and said, "Cause I am."

She looked down the table at Pea and finally noticed Pea had not picked up her fork and that her skin was devoid of color.

"Are you ok, Pea? You look like hell. What's going on? I know you wouldn't have called this secret sister meeting without a good reason."

Mary moved from seat down to the chair next to Pea and leaned in to take a good look at Pea. Pea looked like she was going to faint.

Oh great, fainting woman and pregnant woman stuck in kitchen. She could just imagine that 911 call.

She helped Pea to her feet and led her into the front room of the house and sat her down on Trey's saddleback leather sofa.

Once out of the kitchen and away from the smell of the food, Pea's nausea began to subside. She took a deep breath and held her sister's hand tightly.

"I'm sorry, Ree. I didn't expect to get so nauseous. I thought fixing lunch here would be better than going to a restaurant."

"What, do you have a bug or something? Let me get you some water. I thought you were going to pass out on me for a moment," Mary said.

Pea laughed and shook her head 'no'.

"It's 'or something'," she said.

Mary was puzzled for a second and then saw all the pieces fall into place – the nausea, the pallor, the lunch.

"You're pregnant!" she exclaimed.

Pea started laughing and leaned against her sister and nodded yes. She was laughing and crying at the same time.

"Oh, now I know why you wanted the secret sister lunch! You haven't told Trey yet, have you?"

Pea wiped her eyes with the back of her hand and nodded again.

"I'm afraid to tell him. He wants a family so much and I'm so scared. If I fail him . . . if I fail him the way I failed Alicia, I don't know if I could go through it again. I'm so scared to try this again."

Mary hugged her sister to her and then held her at arm's length.

"You have absolutely nothing to be afraid of with Trey, Pea. You know that. He's not Manley. And how could you possibly fail him by giving him the one thing that he has wanted for years?"

"I know, Ree. I miss Alicia so much. All I've done is think of her the past few days. Do you think . . . no, God, I don't know how to do this. I need you to help, to help me be strong and not afraid."

Mary smiled and looked down at her own widening belly.

"Don't you think I'm afraid? I'm afraid of so much. Childbirth. Being a bad mother. Having my husband have another heart attack or, or, or something worse. Giving up a law career because I got knocked up first. But I don't think about any of that. I just concentrate on bringing this child into our lives, to having this child and Joseph at my side," she said.

"I don't know how you bore the pain of losing Alicia and I know you'll always have her with you, but this is a blessing, Pea. Be happy. Go home to your husband and tell him. Make him happy, too."

Pea pulled a tissue from a box on the side table and blew her nose and tried to compose herself.

"You're right, Ree. I know."

She smiled at Mary and leaned back against the sofa.

"Are you feeling better? Your color looks better," Mary asked.

"Yes, yes, the morning sickness is really bad. I don't remember being this sick with Alicia." Pea asked.

Mary laughed.

"Oh, that was easy. You guys were always eating breakfast and I'd get up early, get sick and then go for a long walk. By the time I came back, you were always through and everyone was so busy with the wedding that no one noticed . . . well, except for Joseph's Nana, who must be the best detective in the world."

"And you were dreadfully sick the first months with Alicia. I remember calling from school and you were always in the bathroom and when I did come in you never wanted to go anywhere that served food. But it passed quickly. It did," she continued.

Mary leaned back against the sofa next to her sister and looked around the room.

"This is the most boring room. Do you think Trey hired someone to do this? I can't imagine he picked this stuff out."

Pea laughed.

"Believe it or not, he did pick this stuff out. It's all quality stuff. Great antiques and beautifully hand made furniture and not one hint of his personality."

Mary patted her hand.

"He was waiting for you to fix it. Listen, that gives me an idea, though not about the room. Would you want to go do some real baby shopping or do you still feel too yucky," Mary asked.

Pea smiled and stood up.

"Let me go straighten up my face and we'll go shopping. Oh, goodness, I've forgotten all the stuff you need for a new baby."

She and Mary were out the door within ten minutes and spent the rest of the afternoon hitting every boutique and baby store in town. The warm July sun and their happiness shone the whole day and people who passed them smiled without knowing why.

Chapter Twenty-One

Pea didn't arrive home until the sun was beginning to fade in the horizon and she took the bags from the trunk of the Audi and put them on the foyer settee so she could go in search of her husband.

Trey walked in the foyer just as she was turning towards the kitchen. He had already showered and changed from his day in the field.

"Haymaking over?" she asked and kissed him hello.

He took her in his arms and said, "Very funny. Haymaking while the sun still shines is not fun. I think I got a little too much sun. I should have cut the day short, but the morning sun wasn't so bad."

Pea stroked his arms and could feel the heat rising off of them.

"Didn't you wear sunblock?"

"Yes, and a hat, but it only works for so long. I wanted to get the west field cut and it took longer than I expected. Did you have fun shopping?"

She was about to open one of the bags when the smell from the kitchen hit her along with her new friend nausea.

"Hey," Trey said. "Sit down. You don't look so good all of sudden. Lean over and put your head down. It will help."

As he helped her onto the settee, he knelt on the black and white marble tile floor in front of her. One of the shopping bags fell open and tiny, white silk baby shoes in little clear boxes slid out. He picked up one of the boxes and held it up.

"Shouldn't Mary have taken these home?"

Pea raised her head and her white skin began to flush.

"What? Are these a surprise for her?" he asked.

Pea smiled, shook her head and raised her hand to his cheek.

"They're not for Ree's baby."

Trey looked down at the tiny shoes and was confused.

"Is another one of your friends pregnant?"

Pea leaned forward and kissed his forehead.

"No, dear, we are."

Trey stared into her eyes and then lowered his head onto her lap. He stayed that way for so long without speaking that she began to be afraid he was upset. Oh God, she had not even given thought to the idea that he might not want a child right now. She lifted his face to hers and saw the joy in his eyes.

"Are we really?" he asked.

She nodded and he hugged her and kissed her face and neck.

"How? When?" he asked, a grin spreading across his face.

She draped her arms across his shoulders.

"Why do men always say 'how' and 'when' first? You were there, dear. We women don't usually do it alone."

They both laughed and he sat down in the floor and pulled the bags over. They were full of tiny shirts and socks and shoes and little blankets.

"Everything is so tiny. Are babies really this tiny? I don't think I could get more than two fingers in this sock?"

She nodded and laughed again.

He leaned back against the settee where she sat and looked upwards at the ceiling, his face suddenly looking very serious.

"God, I've got to get a lot of work done on the house. We've got to get the nursery updated. And don't we need new furniture? Isn't the old stuff unsafe? And car seats? Maybe we should stay in Lexington to be closer to the hospital?"

Pea stood and held her hand out to Trey.

"Slow down, cowboy. We've got time."

She kissed him and the world felt so, so right.

"I love you so much," she said. "And no, we're fine staying here until it gets close to late winter. Then we can think about Lexington."

Trey stood and took her hands and kissed them.

"We're going to be a family," he said smiling.

She almost cried then, realizing how long he had lived without one. She now understood Mary's anger over her 'fixation' with the New River stuff. This – life – was so much more important.

In Greenbrier County, Mary was telling Joseph the news at almost the same time that Pea was telling Trey. He had fixed dinner for them, making sure that his food was not quite as heavy on the calories as Mary's. He was really getting tired of turkey.

"How's she dealing with this?" he asked Mary as he pulled the baked chicken from the oven and placed it on the table.

"Seriously, Mary, I don't want to concern you, but I've been worried about Pea for the past year. She really, really doesn't deal with the past well. I saw things in her that you've probably never seen."

"When, well, when we were looking at the Manley situation, for example. She dove in head first and didn't think about the repercussions," he said.

"Well, Joseph, right now I think she's mostly just trying not to be afraid of losing another child or telling Trey."

"No, Mary, you're not listening to me. She might tell us all that she's given up on the New River murders, but I'm telling you that she won't." he interrupted her and sat down at the table across from her.

"Shit, Joseph. You stop it. Stop interrupting me and listen to me for a change. If you had talked to me last year, you might not have ended up in the hospital with a heart attack and I might have been prepared when Manley showed up at our apartment," she said and slammed the serving spoon on the table.

She stood and glared down at him.

"I am so sick of this "murder" shit. All of this just makes me miserable. We're supposed to be happy right now and all you want to do is tell me that things are going to get worse. Well, fuck you. Go back to New York. Just take all this serial killer stuff with you," and she stormed from the room.

Joseph closed his eyes and took a deep breath. How could he tell her that he had spent the entire day working on the 'New River stuff' and that the Bureau was already aware of what was going on, but didn't have enough to go on to make an arrest yet. What they did have were suspicions about a deputy in one county and one of his old friends, but no real proof.

And unfortunately, that deputy was the one who had thrown Pea, Trey and Thomas from his office, which meant that the deputy knew that someone might be on to him and that they were in danger. The deputy had access to information on all of them, including Thomas. Who knew how far he might go to protect himself if he were killing in the New River Valley?

As Joseph got up from the table to go find his distraught wife and try to calm her down, he thought about going into town tomorrow and buying a new gun and ammunition for Mary's dad's hunting rifle. They were not safe here and somehow he had to protect her without upsetting her. What happened a year ago could not happen again.

Joseph found Mary upstairs in one of the guest rooms they were turning into a nursery. She was unpacking the shopping bags onto the dark cherry changing table, taking each item out and examining it carefully to make sure that each piece was perfectly made. He knew it was an attempt on her part to keep from turning to face him.

He ran his hand over his head and slumped against the door. She was going to have to hear what he had to say no matter how painful the words might be.

"Mary."

Nothing.

"Mary, look at me. Now," his voice was a little more strident than he had intended and she whirled around to face him, surprise showing on her face for she had rarely heard him raise his voice.

She laid a soft minky blanket on the table.

"We're supposed to be happy now, Joseph. Happy."

He shrugged his shoulders. "Man plans. God laughs."

"What the hell does that mean, is that some Italian saying?" she said angrily.

He held out both his hands, palms upward in surrender. At least he had her attention, now.

"No, I think it's an old Yiddish proverb I heard somewhere. I think it means that we should be happy with each moment, love and laugh and live and not tear ourselves up with what we want to happen when it does or doesn't go the way we thought it would," he said.

Mary turned back to the red and gold minky blanket with Winnie the Pooh dancing in the center of it. She stroked the soft velvety texture of it. She waited for Joseph to continue. She could not speak.

"These things were put into motion before you were born. Even if we wanted them to stop, we couldn't make them stop. I called the Bureau today to see if this was even on their radar and it is and has been. For a while," he stressed.

"Unfortunately, your sister's uncanny ability to see patterns in things as simple as a few newspaper articles took her to the one place she should never gone – straight onto the radar of the one suspect the Bureau has."

Mary fell into the rocking chair that had been in the family for decades.

"God, no. Please tell me no, not again" she said in shock, unknowingly cupping her belly protectively.

Joseph crossed the room and brought her close to him.

"I'm so sorry, Mary. I'm so sorry," he said as she leaned against his side and wept.

Chapter Twenty-Two

"No." Pea was adamant.

She looked at Trey sitting next to her on the living room sofa. She refused to look at Joseph or her sister.

"Pea, don't be stupid. We can't go without you and we're not safe now. The FBI will be moving in on this man in the next few months and we can come home," Mary said.

The men sat next to their wives waiting for them to come to terms with Joseph's discoveries.

Trey took Pea's hand in his and she pulled it away. She felt ambushed, as if she were the target of some intervention, which she supposed this probably was.

"And how long are we supposed to be gone while we wait for the FBI to act? Joseph, you said that they'd known about this for awhile. How long? Months? Years? Just when are they going to go after him?" she asked.

"And, is everyone forgetting about Thomas and Diana? That deputy knows who we are. When he recognized me, he certainly has the ability to find out all of our names. Thomas doesn't have the resources to just leave his business, which is just starting to take off, and Diana has her dissertation to finish."

Pea stood and strode across the room, stopping at the hand carved door facing. She studied it for a moment, running her hand against it, and thinking of the work she had put into restoring the house. She had had the painters match much of woodwork to the original colors of the house's interior.

"No. I will not run. I will not give up living my life because of that . . . man," she said.

Joseph stood and walked over to her. He placed his hand on her shoulder. He had to get her to see reason.

"Men, Pea, men. We're looking at two men according to what I've been able to find out. They work and kill in pairs. They torture their victims and no one knows how many victims there have been."

"And what about Mary? What about the fact that you and your sister are pregnant? We can get Thomas and Diana out of here, too. Money is not the problem, so why are you being selfish, Pea? There are a lot of other lives at stake here, now. This isn't a puzzle you need to solve anymore," he said.

She turned to him and saw the fear in his eyes, the fear for his wife and unborn child, for all of them. Whatever the people at the FBI had told him had been enough to convince him that they were all in danger.

She shook her head. No. She refused to be afraid again.

"Joseph, I can't. I hid from a man for almost ten years. I let him take from me the person I loved most in my life. I won't run again. I wouldn't run from Manley if he rose from the grave and haunted me and I won't run from this man. I'm sorry. I'm not leaving," she started to walk away and then continued.

"Well, not unless Trey throws me out and then I guess I'll just go back to the farm. But . . . I am not leaving," she slammed the front screen door behind her as she headed down the path to the barn.

The three of them just watched the door for a few moments. Joseph could say no more. It was up to Trey and Mary now. He rammed his fist against the plaster and oak lathing wall hard enough to actually crack it and then went toward the kitchen to find ice to put on his knuckles, the whole time cursing under his breath.

Mary sank into the love seat and wiped the quiet tears that were falling down her cheeks. Trey moved across the room to her without her realizing he was there next to her on the love seat, offering her a handkerchief. She cried for another few minutes before finally taking a deep breath to calm herself down. She could feel the baby kicking and moving around and she knew she shouldn't let herself get upset for the baby's sake. She held out Trey's handkerchief and looked at the pressed white cotton.

"I didn't even know that men carried these anymore," she said to him, studying the straight stitching in overlapping lines.

Trey smiled as she started to hand it back to him. He waved his hand for her to keep it.

"Old habit. Our housekeeper seems to always keep putting them in my dresser drawer. I just grab one when I grab my socks and stick it in my pants' pocket."

"Joseph and I should start thinking of finding a housekeeper. Mr. Dickson's there to help with the farm, but I think the house might get busy in a few months," she said and returned his smile.

"Trey, Pea won't go. And I sort of understand why. I don't really want to go either. Joseph just seems so determined to get us out of there."

She sighed and sat up, turning to look at him.

"What do you want? I mean, do you think leaving our homes will mean that they can catch these bastards? What if Pea's right and they don't? How long are we supposed to run? And, I don't think Thomas will go anywhere. He might try to convince Diana to go, but he won't."

"Pea and Thomas have been through some things that I'm not sure anyone will ever understand," she added.

She took a deep breath and started to say more, but decided against it.

"I'm going to go find my husband and make sure he hasn't broken his hand," she said, using Trey's shoulder as leverage to raise herself from the deep love seat.

She stopped and stared down at the love seat and smiled.

"Pea's going to regret buying that sofa and love seat in a few months," she said as she walked to the kitchen.

Trey was left alone in the living room that looked nothing like it did when he had first brought Pea there. He sank back into the love seat and rubbed his temples. He didn't know anything for sure except that he wasn't going to let Pea go.

He hurt so much right now that he wanted to hit that wall as much as Joseph had, but he smiled a little then because he did know better than to do that. Two hundred year old walls didn't yield the way dry wall did to a satisfying punch. Joseph would be lucky if he hadn't broken his hand, but Trey decided to let Mary tend to him. He needed to go find his own wife right now and talk to her.

He walked out to the front steps and didn't see her in any direction. He headed toward the barn and then saw her over at his family plot standing there, staring off into the distant fields.

He took his time making his way to her. She was safe and he knew she was thinking about all the aspects of the situation, including her sister and both their babies and everyone else involved in this mess. He also knew she was probably blaming herself for getting them involved and that she was in more pain than any of them could imagine.

So, when he reached her, he just stood next to her and put his arm around her shoulder and let her silently stand there. In the distance, the unmown east field of hay was bowing beneath a breeze that travelled across it.

"I think I'm going to mow the east field next week, after we get the west field hay rolled into round bales," he said squinting in the sunlight that dappled the ground where they stood.

Pea's blond hair had grown below her shoulders and the breeze that had blown across the pasture finally reached them and whipped her loose hair across her face. She pushed it away and Trey could see that she had not been crying. She was hardening herself for whatever was coming. She squinted in the sunlight as well, her lips firmly set. She was not going anywhere. He knew that then and decided not to say a word to try and change her mind. He felt she deserved that. For so long, everyone had treated her as precious bone china, but she was far from that and he would respect her for her strength even if the others didn't see it.

"I'm getting thirsty. Let's go get some iced tea," he said and she nodded in agreement as they headed back to the house.

Chapter Twenty-Three

Tim was furious. He slammed the phone down on the receiver so loudly that Karen, their office manager, almost jumped out of her seat. She turned around to face Tim at his desk behind her and what she saw scared her to death. She had worked with the man for 15 years and had never seen him ever lose his temper, even with the most rowdy drunk or belligerent suspect. But right now, he looked ready to kill someone.

"Tim, Jesus Christ, are you okay?" she asked.

Tim didn't even bother to look at her or answer her question. He just pushed himself up from his desk and stomped down the hall to the men's room. He paced back and forth several times before stopping to look in the mirror and he saw the murder in his eyes that had probably scared Karen half to death.

He shook his head like a dog trying to shake off a leash and leaned forward into the sink to rinse his face with cold water. When he looked up again at his image in the mirror he saw that his eyes now were filled with fear and he could feel his arms shaking as they held onto the sides of the white porcelain sink.

What the hell was he going to do? In over 30 years he had never felt so helpless or lost. The phone call had been from Doug who wanted to go hunting again. Soon. And what was worse was who he wanted to hunt. No, Tim thought. Oh, hell no. He liked his life and Doug was a complete asshole if one ever walked the earth.

Doug had informed him that he wanted to hunt the people who had come here asking questions. Doug said they were too dangerous to be allowed to keep asking questions. They just might find someone who would listen to their nonsense. And worst of all, Doug informed him, the bitch's sister was married to an ex-FBI agent.

"How do you know that?" he had asked Doug.

"Read the fucking news accounts of what happened in Virginia last year, you moron. Read the society pages of the

Beckley newspaper for June. They got married then. How can you be so stupid?"

"We gotta do something and we gotta do it fast before this gets out of control," Doug had said.

Tim had sat at his desk with the phone gripped too tightly against his ear and had simply nodded and said "Yes" and "I see" and finally had ended the call with a terse, "Well, we'll have to get back to you about that, sir."

Tim couldn't take it anymore. He and Doug had killed more people than he could remember since they were 17 and drunk on that ridge above the New River Valley. Now the only person he wanted to kill was Doug.

He looked over to the frosted restroom window and then back to his own face. He didn't look too bad for 54. He was tanned and his face a little more wrinkled around the eyes than most other people from the sun, but he still had a full head of hair that was just starting to get a little grey. He hadn't let his body go. His job had kept him fit enough and he'd given up cigarettes years ago. If he had a real vice, he thought, it was having a beer after supper. He didn't think to include his hunting as a vice.

He sighed and headed back out into the squad room. It had been empty except for him and Karen. He was going to have to come up with some kind of excuse for losing his temper or he knew Karen would gossip.

He walked over to Karen's desk and sat on the corner of it and bowed his head.

"I'm really sorry, Karen. I wouldn't want to upset you over my family stuff, but that was my uncle on the phone. He lives in Cincinnati and his grandson has gotten into trouble over drugs."

"Oh, Tim, how awful," Karen said with real concern. She had always liked Tim because he had always treated her like a real person and not just someone to throw files at the way some of the other deputies did. She was ten years younger than Tim, not as pretty as some women but not unattractive. At one time she had had hopes of something developing between them, but found those hopes quashed when he talked about his "Tiff" and his boys.

"He wants me to try to help them out somehow, but I don't think there's anything I can do. It's way out of any jurisdiction I might even have a contacts in and it just breaks my heart that I can't. My uncle's good people. He doesn't deserve this, not at his age," Tim continued now almost believing the yarn he was weaving for Karen's benefit.

"Well, Tim, these drugs are just tearing everyone up. I don't know any county or state that isn't being affected by them. I know this has just got to be horrible for you," she replied.

"Karen, could you do me a really big favor? I'd like to keep this in the family. You know how that is and if any of the others here were to find out, well . . ." his voice trailed off.

"Tim, don't you think twice about it. Nobody here has to know. I won't say a word about it. Just don't let it eat at you. You're a good man and you don't deserve this trouble. Why don't you take the afternoon off and go home to talk to Tiff and your family about it? I'll tell the others you came down with some kind of stomach flu. They won't ask twice about that," she said.

He stood and grabbed his hat off the rack on the wall.

"Karen, you're truly an angel. I owe you a big favor for this," he said and headed towards the front doors.

"No problem, Tim, and I'll say a prayer for your uncle and your family at prayer meeting tonight," she called out as he exited the sheriff's offices.

Prayers weren't going to help anyone, Tim thought. But he stopped as he opened his cruiser's door and looked up at the mountaintops around him. Actually, he thought, a prayer might be the only thing that could save him.

When he arrived home early, the house was empty. Most likely Tiff had driven over to the IGA for groceries, he thought. He headed straight to the fridge and grabbed the last beer in there and began to drink it down in an attempt to make the whole nightmare phone call just disappear from his brain.

He went to his recliner and when he turned the TV on, there were a group of women sitting around a table talking about how President Obama was always being disrespected by Fox News, only they called it Faux news. He almost threw the remote at the TV, but switched the channel over to the History channel. The last thing he needed to hear about was what some group of cackling hens thought about politics.

Tiff never talked about politics except to nod in agreement whenever he made some comment about the state of the country and the world.

"If they were out there everyday seeing what I see, they'd be thinking different," he'd said on more than one occasion. Although he was what his grandfather had used to call a "yellow dog" democrat - a democrat who'd vote for a yellow dog if it was on the democratic ballot, he was also very conservative. He'd been raised in a union household and democrat was the only way they voted.

As he watched Hitler's storm troopers marching in a parade while an English guy's voice narrated, he finished his beer and hoped that Tiff had remembered to pick up a case of beer while she was out.

On the whole, he believed that he had been a good husband and father to his family. He had provided a decent income for them. He had been a faithful husband and had coached his sons' sports teams when they were younger. He'd never missed their ballgames and he'd never hit them or Tiff the way he and Doug had been beaten by their dads. He'd really tried to be a better man than the man his father had been.

Tiff certainly had nothing to complain about. He'd never asked her to get a job and she'd been able to spend her life raising their sons and keeping the house clean and cooking good food for them. He never complained when she'd asked for a new sewing machine or said anything about her quilting club or women's club meetings. As long as he had a meal waiting and clean clothes, he decided she was keeping up her end of the marriage bargain.

There had been a few rough spots at the beginning when they were young and she fussed about his going hunting and drinking with Doug whenever Doug showed up in town, but he'd put a stop to that fast. He told her to be grateful for what she had and that he was going to see his best friend and have a few drinks whether she liked it or not.

Of course, she'd pouted as he left, but he always felt so good after hunting that he'd stop and buy her some flowers or candy and come home and let her know in more ways than one just how much he appreciated her.

She forgave him and hugged him as if the argument had never happened. He always told her he loved her, but he didn't think he'd ever meant it. And as the years passed, it just became easier and easier to say without even thinking about it.

Maybe this was what love was, he'd come to think, just having a good woman and a good home to come to every night.

When he was home and not hunting with Doug, he never thought about what he did to the women they hunted or how he felt about what they did, even to the men. As the years passed, he didn't feel those urges to go out and look for prey as much. It was just so much easier staying home with Tiff and the boys.

As he heard Tiff come in the back door, he looked up at the TV and realized that Hitler was gone and now some guy was talking about the pyramids in Egypt.

Where had he been? Yeah, now he remembered. Trying to forget about that fucking phone call from Doug.

"Tim, are you ok?" Tiff said as she came into the living room, while putting her purse in the closet.

"Yeah, I think I may be getting one of those summer colds. We had an inmate last week who was coughing all over the office."

She placed her hand on his cheek and smiled at him.

"Well, you do feel a little warm. Let me get you some Advil so you can try to get ahead of it and not get any worse."

He took her hand in his and kissed it.

"Thank you, babe. That's real sweet," he said.

"Oh, would you get me another beer, too. I'm mighty thirsty for some reason," he added as she went into the kitchen.

As she handed him two Advil and a new can of beer, she said, "You really should be drinking some juice or something besides beer. Why don't you go lie down till supper?"

"Oh hon, I think I'm just going to doze here in front of the box. Thanks again for the beer," he said and turned his face back to the TV.

By the time he'd finished the second beer, he had dozed off in the chair and didn't wake up until he heard Jake and Riley in the kitchen with their mom.

They were talking rapidly and excitedly about getting picked for starting positions on the football team. Tim had forgotten that football try-outs were this week.

Tim got up and stretched before walking into the kitchen where the boys pounced on him with their news. The football coach had picked them both as starters, even though Riley was still a junior.

He laughed with them as they told him about some of the seniors getting really upset that Coach Varney had chosen Riley over them.

Coach had said Riley could run faster than any of them and so Jake, who was going to be quarterback, would be passing to his brother. Nobody was going to beat them this year, Jake said, and that the state championship was going to come back to Gladstone Gap again, even if Gladstone

County had consolidated its two high schools into one now.

"Dad, we've got the best team since you played. We might even get scholarships if we can get to the state finals," Jake said.

Tim grinned. Scholarships for his boys. He'd make sure they didn't screw it up the way Doug had. He had never even been offered one, but Doug had and Doug had thrown it all away.

Tim walked back to his recliner and sat down. Fucking Doug had screwed up his life for the last time. He'd be damned if he'd let Doug screw up his boys' chances at having a better life. He decided he'd help Doug with this one last thing and then he was done, even if he had to kill Doug himself. His family's future was at stake.

He never gave another thought about the lost futures of the people he and Doug had killed or were going to kill.

Chapter Twenty-Four

Joseph had not broken his hand, but it hurt like hell. Mary grabbed a bag of frozen peas from the freezer and wrapped it around his hand.

"That may have been the dumbest thing I've ever seen a smart man do," she said and sat down at the Hoosier table.

He grimaced and sat down next to her.

"Your sister . . ."

Mary pushed the frozen peas down on his hand and tilted her head slightly.

"Oww," he said.

"My sister has every right to do what she wants and I'm not going to argue with her about it, Joseph. In fact, I agree with her. We just can't run away and stay away until the FBI decides to arrest this guy," she said.

"Guys," he corrected her. "You people keep conveniently forgetting that they believe that the deputy has a partner in crime. Listen dealing with one serial killer is hard enough. Two is really, really hard."

He took her hand with his hand free from the bag of peas and squeezed it.

"Mary, serial killers are smart. They usually get better the longer they kill and these guys have been killing a long time. This is very serious. Protective custody may be our only choice."

She pulled her hand away from him and looked out the kitchen window at the afternoon sun.

"No, it's not our only choice. We can go on with our lives and not live in fear. Besides, Thomas will never do it and Pea won't either. So just you and I and Trey go into hiding? I don't think so. I'm not leaving them. Thomas almost died trying to save us. So, no, I'm not going."

Joseph looked up at his wife's face. He saw that there was no convincing her.

"Don't you think that Trey can convince Pea?" he asked.

She shook her head.

"No, and he's already told me he's not going to try. Joseph, you didn't see how broken she was for so long. I'm scared to death for all of us, but I honestly believe that if she runs from this that she'll never trust herself or anyone else again. I simply don't think she can survive it."

"Well, what if Thomas agrees? Do you think that might change her mind?"

Mary reached out and stroked the blond hair on his arm, thinking of those arms holding her at night.

"No, Joseph. He won't agree and she won't change her mind," she said softly.

"And I won't go without her. I'm sorry."

She left him at the table and walked into the solarium her sister had spent the most time restoring. It was warmer in there than the rest of the house, but the heat helped stop the shiver that ran down her arms.

Oh God, she prayed, please don't let me lose anyone else. Please watch over them. Let them be safe and healthy and happy.

It was at that point her baby decided to give her a healthy kick in the rib and she laughed, laying her hand upon the top of her ever growing belly.

"Don't worry, little one. It's going to be ok. I know it's going to be."

As if in response to her words, the baby kicked again and then she could feel him roll around and settle down.

She sat out there for almost an hour watching the birds and butterflies flitting around her sister's garden. August was almost over and back at the farm the leaves would be starting to change. The higher elevation of Greenbrier County always brought an earlier autumn than the Shenandoah Valley. By the time her baby would be born, November would be there.

She was still at the end of her second trimester and hoped that her third wouldn't be as rough as Pea's had been with Alicia. Alicia had kept Pea off her feet and had stopped her from driving because of the way Alicia had positioned herself in Pea's belly. Manley had taken Pea's keys away from her and with them, her freedom. He had also left Pea alone for days on end and had it not been for Mr. Dickson, Pea would have had no way of even getting groceries.

Mary had known none of this until several years after Alicia had been born. She and Pea had been setting in a pair of old metal tulip chairs in their mother's garden watching

Alicia trundle about the yard with her baby doll in a toy stroller. Manley was in Louisiana and this time Mary knew that he had told Pea the truth as Pea had had to endure a conversation with Laura that was just a repeat of the same one they'd been having since before the wedding – why didn't they move down there?

When Mary had asked Pea why she hadn't told her about Pea's virtual imprisonment, Mary had felt anger flowing through her body. Pea had just shrugged and ignored the question, rising to walk with Alicia along the stone path that led to the back porch.

Now when Mary thought about that time, she became so sad for failing to see the pain her sister had been going through. She was already off to college and had been lost in her own world at Washington and Lee. College had overwhelmed her life then.

If Trey or Joseph knew every detail of the pain and torture that Pea had suffered at Manley's hands, they might understand why she refused to run now. Even Mary sometimes forgot just how many awful things Manley had done, some in front of Mary and friends of their family.

When she hadn't lost the baby weight quickly enough, she was forced to diet by him. He had called her "chubby" in front of others and pretended it as a joke, but Mary could see the pain in Pea's eyes. Mary realized now that when Pea began to flinch when Manley approached her later on, she was hiding even darker secrets which Mary could only imagine now. She knew Pea would never talk about Manley again.

And this made Mary tear up, realizing how lucky she was to have found Joseph. As she held her belly with her hands feeling the baby rolling around, she didn't hear or see Joseph enter the room until he sat down on the wicker sofa next to her. He had taken a dish towel and wrapped the bag of peas in it and tied it around his hand.

Mary smiled and took his left hand and placed it on their baby. He grinned as he felt the baby moving around.

"He's certainly active this afternoon. Maybe he'll let you get a good night's sleep tonight," Joseph said.

Mary sighed and then punched Joseph's shoulder.

"You keep saying 'he'. Haven't we had this discussion a hundred times? What are you going to do if 'he' is a 'she'?" she asked.

Joseph moved closer to her and laid his right arm with the peas and towel attached behind her on the top of the sofa.

"Well, if you weren't so stubborn about letting the doctor tell us the sex, I wouldn't have to keep saying that," he replied.

"I don't want to know and I know that you won't be able to keep it a secret if you find out, so, no, we're just going to have to be surprised."

He removed his arm from behind her, unwrapped the towel from his hand and took the peas away. His hand was still swollen, but he could flex his fingers, although the movements made him wince.

"I think the peas are done."

Mary laughed and stood up, taking the peas with her as she headed towards the kitchen. As she took some steaks from the refrigerator and began to fix supper if only for herself and Joseph, she looked out the kitchen window to see if her sister or Trey were within sight. She saw neither of them outside.

She hadn't realized how much 'bump' had grown until she had tried to maneuver around Trey's tiny kitchen. Every time she turned she had to move sideways in order to get around between the table and the counters. She could understand why Pea didn't like this kitchen and she was fairly certain that her sister would hate it as her pregnant belly grew larger. Who the hell designed this room, she thought as she heard the back screen door open and close.

She turned to see Trey without Pea.

"No luck?"

He shook his head.

"No, I found her sitting under one of the old oaks out along the west pasture. She's still angry, but she'll come in when she starts to get hungry, which should be soon," he said and sat down at the table on the opposite side of the room from where she was struggling to cook.

"Want some help?" he asked.

"No. I can do this. Just some thawed out peas to cook. I've already put the potatoes in the microwave and I just need to wait a few minutes before putting the steaks on the stove."

She bumped into a drawer she had left open and groaned.

"Trey, for the love of god, who designed this damned kitchen? I do not know how the women in your family cooked in here."

Trey laughed and said, "They didn't."

"We always had a housekeeper who did the cooking. Probably always did. The kitchen was added to the house in the 1920s. Most of these old antebellum houses had a kitchen that was separate from the main house with a little dog trot between them," he continued.

Mary rolled her eyes and slammed the iron skillet onto the gas stove.

"I know what a dog trot is. Remember where I grew up? Our house was just updated much better than yours was."

"Is one of the dogs trotting through the house," Joseph asked as he entered the kitchen. "And are my peas ready? I smell food."

Trey and Mary looked at one another and began to laugh. Mary held her belly as she bent slightly and continued to laugh at her husband's question. Neither one of them could stop laughing so they didn't notice Pea's entrance through the screen door.

"Joseph, they're having a little fun at your expense. I apologize for their rudeness," she said.

The two of them laughed even harder when they saw Pea, although they were trying hard to compose themselves.

"I thought the dogs were outside with you. I was just asking if one of them was in the house," he said, still puzzled.

Mary finally managed to straighten up and wipe the tears of laughter off her face.

"I'm sorry, dear. We were talking about a 'dog trot', not a trotting dog."

"A dog trot?" he asked.

Trey started to laugh again and Pea jabbed his shoulder and he tried to stop.

"When a lot of the old houses were built before the Civil War, the kitchens were separated from the main house by a short, covered walkway that was called a dog trot. Don't ask me why they were called that. I've just always heard them called that. Sorry," Trey said.

Joseph's face turned red.

"Oh, so it's a southern thing?"

Trey shrugged.

"I don't know. As I said, it's just what we always called them here."

"I see. Well, in New York, the kitchens are in the houses," Joseph said a little too tersely.

Mary turned round to face him.

"Why Joseph Jordan Hallett, I do believe you're being a little snooty. Yeah, we were slow putting kitchens in, but we had our own shoes," she said and began to giggle.

This time Pea couldn't help but laugh as Trey and Mary began to laugh loudly again.

Joseph didn't say another word and just turned and left the kitchen quickly.

"Joseph, come back. I'm sorry," Mary tried to say through her laughter.

Pea jabbed at Trey again and made her way around the table.

"I'll go talk to him, Ree. I don't think this has been an easy day for him," she said and patted Mary's belly as she passed.

"Bump's getting bigger," she said and giggled as she squeezed past her sister.

Mary sobered up immediately.

"Oh you just wait, Miss Pearl! Just wait till you try to cook in this kitchen. I can barely turn around in here," she said.

"You forget that I don't cook," Pea laughed from the front hall and tried to figure out which way Joseph had gone so she could try and make things right with him.

She found him on the front steps with the dogs and sat down next to him as she shooed the dogs away.

"Are you mad at me?"

He shook his head no and took a deep breath before speaking.

"Pea, I'm just so frustrated that I can't get you guys to see how deadly serious this situation is. What if they come to the farm looking for you and find Mary alone, almost six months pregnant and very vulnerable? Can you live with yourself if they kill her or Trey or Thomas?" he asked, gesturing with his hands as he spoke.

She put her hand on his shoulder.

"Your Giordano blood is showing," she said.

"For god's sake, will you take this seriously? No one is going to do anything unless you agree. This is all on you this time. You can't blame this on your ex."

Pea stood up quickly and moved down the steps away from him. She stared at him and then walked away from the house to her Audi. She was crying as she dug the keys from her pocket and got in it to drive away.

Shit, what the hell did I just do, he thought and even as she was walking to the car, he was calling out to her, trying to apologize for his stupidity.

She ignored him and drove away.

"You son of a bitch."

He turned to see Mary standing there and as he started towards the front door she slammed it firmly in his face.

He went back to the steps where both dogs just sat and stared at him.

He looked at them and shook his head.

"I think I just royally screwed up," he said to them as much as to himself.

How was he going to fix this? How was Trey going to react when he found out what Joseph had said to Pea?

He already knew how Mary had reacted. He'd be lucky if she ever spoke to him again. He began to pace back and forth on the portico and wondered where Pea had gone and what he could possibly say to Trey and Mary, much less Pea, to fix this. He rubbed his forehead as he walked and mumbled different epithets under his breath as the dogs watched in silence.

He was still pacing when Trey stormed out of the house.

"Trey, I'm sorry. I didn't mean it to sound like it did. I, well, I shouldn't have said anything. Jesus, I'm sorry. I spoke without thinking."

Trey stood in front of the door with his hands firmly placed at his waist.

"Trey, seriously, I'm really sorry. I wasn't thinking. It just spilled out of my mouth and I regretted it the moment it came out."

Mary had told Trey what had happened, including Pea leaving in tears in the Audi.

He clamped his teeth together to keep from yelling at Joseph and then took a moment to control his anger.

"I'd like to call you a few choice names right now, but I think Mary's going to do that for me. Do you know where she might have gone?" Trey asked as he pushed past Joseph and headed down the drive to his Celica.

Joseph shook his head and kept saying how sorry he was.

As Trey unlocked the car, he turned to Joseph.

"You know you're lucky those two dogs didn't see her crying. They get very upset when she gets upset," he said as he entered the car and sped out of the driveway after Pea.

Joseph sat back down on the steps and wanted to cry himself. How in the world could he ever make this right?

Chapter Twenty-Five

Trey drove down Route 11 past the old Augusta Military School toward Staunton. He was hoping that she was heading to Thomas and Diana's. He hated the thought of her driving around blaming herself for the very things he had been trying to convince her weren't his fault.

He wanted to scream at Joseph. He even wanted to hit the man, but part of him, deep inside, understood why Joseph had been so desperately stupid. He was just trying to hold onto Mary and keep her safe.

Trey pounded the steering wheel. Just why did Joseph have to hurt Pea in the process, he asked himself and gritted his teeth as he headed down the street to Thomas's apartment.

When Thomas answered the door, he was surprised to see Trey standing there. He and Diana had just finished their dinner and were cleaning up when Trey had pounded on his door.

"Is she here," Trey said and rushed into the apartment.

"Who?" Thomas asked as Diana came into the room from the kitchen.

"Do you mean Pea?"

Trey paced the small living room much as Joseph had paced the portico of Trey's house. Finally, he sat down and began to really worry about where Pea might have gone.

It took more than a few tries for Thomas to get out of Trey what had happened. He was stunned when Trey told him about the deputy being a suspect, Pea's refusal of protection and Joseph's angry and astoundingly stupid remarks.

"Oh shit," was all he could think to say at first.

He was the only one with whom Pea had spoken about her guilt about the murders. Diana sat down on the sofa next to Trey and placed her small hand on his shoulder. Thomas was immediately struck by the juxtaposition of this scene with the one that had occurred last year when he had been sitting where Trey sat now, blaming himself for Shawnette's death and Pea trying to comfort him.

"Can you think of anyplace else she might have gone?" Diana asked.

Trey said no, and that with everything else going on, including the pregnancy, that he was very, very worried.

"Wait, did you say she was pregnant?" Thomas asked.

Trey nodded his head.

"We just found out a few weeks ago."

Thomas struggled to take all this information in.

"I can think of three places she might be," Thomas said. "I'll check one, Diana can check one, and you can check the third. We can call on our cells if we find her."

Trey stood and said, "Okay, then let's go. Where to?"

"I'd say she's either in Greenbrier County or at your place in Lexington or maybe the Horse Center in Lexington. Two of those places connect her to Alicia who she's probably thinking the most about right now," Thomas said.

"I'll check the Horse Center and Diana can check your Lexington house, but I'd say she's probably on her way to Greenbrier because that's where Alicia is so I'll let you make that drive. If I'm wrong and she's at the Horse Center or at your place, we'll call you immediately."

Trey took a key from his key ring, handed it to Diana and headed to the door. Just he was about to leave Thomas grabbed his arm and stopped him.

"Trey, she's talked to me about feeling guilty about what Manley did. I think she talked to me because she knew what I put myself through over losing Shawnette, except that she thought she had to apologize to me for some reason," he said.

"She hasn't said a word to me," Trey said and started towards the door again and then stopped, but didn't turn to look at either Thomas or Diana. "But I knew. I've known for a long time. I knew how she was feeling and I should have tried to get her to talk to me."

"I should have tried," he said and headed down the stairs back to his car before Thomas could respond.

Thomas had been right about Pea going to the Greenbrier County farm. It was just getting dark as Trey pulled his Celica onto the farm road and drove around to the rear of the house. Her Audi was sitting there and Trey put his hand on the hood of the car as he looked up at the dark house. The hood was cool to the touch and he looked around to see if she might be outside somewhere. He thought about walking over to the little cemetery first and then decided that she probably had already been there, which left the barn or the house.

He decided to try the house first and got out his spare key she had given him last year before everything had gone sour. He bounded up the steps and was about to insert the key when he saw that the back door was ajar.

Oh, god, he prayed, please let her be ok. Please don't let them have gotten to her.

He pushed the door open and walked into the dark kitchen.

"Pea," he called out, but heard no response.

He flipped the light switch for the kitchen and headed toward the front of the house.

He called her name again and still heard no response. He turned on more lights and saw that everything looked in place. Where the hell was she? He headed up the dark staircase to the second floor.

The entire second floor looked dark as well. He started down the hall opening doors and without thinking opened the first door at the top of the stairs. He had only been in there one time. Alicia's empty bedroom. A room that neither Pea nor Mary ever entered. In his desperation, he flipped the light switch on thinking that maybe Pea had gone there.

The little girl standing in the center of the room looked amazingly like Mary. She had a sad look on her face and was dressed in a red riding habit. She had her arm extended, pointing away at angle that seemed to be aimed at Pea's parents' old room. He froze for a moment and blinked. When he opened his eyes again, the child was gone.

Oh, god, I'm losing my mind, he thought, but instead of going down the hall to Pea's room, he went across the hall to her parents' room. He paused at the door, almost terrified at what he might find in there. He slowly reached for the door knob and started to turn it, praying that she was in there and ok.

He hadn't been in this room more than a few times either and it took a minute for his eyes to adjust to the darkness and the unfamiliarity of the furnishings inside it. When he finally could see somewhat more clearly, he made out the shape of a body lying on its side on the bed.

He walked to the edge of the bed and paused above Pea and sighed. She lay there asleep, holding some sort of doll to her chest.

He knelt at the bed side and reached out to touch her cheek. It was warm and still damp from probably hours of weeping. As he pushed her hair away from her face she opened her eyes and reached out one arm to pull him close to her. He got on the bed next to her and held her as she began to cry again.

"Hush, now, it's ok. I won't let go. It's ok. Everything's going to be fine," he said as he kissed her forehead and stroked her hair.

She finally calmed down and looked up at him.

"I'm so sorry. I should have called you. I shouldn't have run away. I'm so sorry," she said.

He continued to stroke her hair and pulled her body close to his.

"Stop now. You have nothing to apologize for. It's okay. It's all okay. Just hold on to me. And promise me one more thing – please don't ever take off like that again and make me worry."

Minutes passed and each of them could feel their bodies breathing together, each breath like a whisper in the dark room.

"Joseph . . . he's so worried about Mary, but what he said cut deep," she finally said.

Trey waited for her to continue. He knew at this point that just letting her pour out everything would be the best thing.

"I think of those moments in Goshen all the time. I think about how I blinded myself to his, his evil that I couldn't even see that he destroyed everything in his way, including his own child. And I think of all those women and their families and their children."

"How could I have been so stupid, so blind?"

"And then, because I thought that I had to prove I wasn't weak or stupid because I had finally opened my eyes to what was already in front of me that I had to go chasing after some other murderer. I thought that if I could do that then I wouldn't feel so, so guilty and that maybe Alicia could rest then, too."

She sat up and held the small doll out.

"This was Alicia's baby. It's the only thing I kept. I put it in my mother's dresser. The pain of losing her was more than I could bear, but I thought if I kept just this one thing hidden away then maybe one day I could pick it up and just remember her smile and not her dead body on that field."

She placed the doll to the side and looked down at Trey.

"I know you don't believe me about seeing Alicia. Maybe it was just my guilty conscience, but Trey, seeing her made me feel stronger, as if everything was going to be okay."

Trey sat up and put his hands on her shoulders. How was he going to explain this one to her without her breaking down again, he thought. He contemplated not telling her for a few seconds and then decided that in order for her to trust him, he had to give her a reason to trust him by telling her the truth.

"I do believe you when you said you saw Alicia," he said.

"I think, I don't know what I saw, but when I came up the stairs in the dark, I opened the door to her room first. I forgot it was empty. I was just desperate to find you."

He looked out the window at the stars shining in the blackest sky and then turned back to face her.

"When I turned the light on, there was a child there. She looked like Mary and she was pointing towards this room. I closed my eyes and when I opened them the room was empty," he said.

As he finished speaking, Pea scrambled across the bed, grabbing the doll and running to Alicia's old room. She threw on the light switch, but the room was empty - bare wood floor and white walls.

"I'm sorry baby. I'm sorry I didn't save you," she whispered and switched off the light.

When she turned back toward her parent's room, she saw Trey standing in the doorway. She started to walk toward him and then went back to the room, opened the door and sat the doll on the floor at the baseboard and closed the door.

She and Trey walked down the hall to her own bedroom, undressed silently and climbed into the iron bed.

Trey sat up in the bed remembering he had promised to make phone calls.

"I've got to call Thomas and Diana and Mary and let them know you're okay," he said.

"Give me just a few minutes. Everyone is looking for you and I'd say that Joseph is still pacing the portico, maybe even locked out by your sister."

As he dialed his own phone number at Staunton, Pea touched his arm and said, "Tell Mary I said not to be hard on Joseph. He's just scared for her. Tell her I'll find a way to fix this. Joseph was right. This is my mess. I've got to find a way to fix it."

He looked down at her as he listened to the phone ringing and said, "Funny, when I left, Joseph was pacing the portico and saying the exact same thing."

Mary answered after a few rings and he assured her that Pea was safe and relayed Pea's message. Pea could hear her sister's muffled and still angry voice.

"Okay, I'll tell her. Okay, good night," he said and hit the end call button on his iPhone.

He dialed Thomas's number next and Thomas answered on the first ring. "Yeah, she was where you thought. She's okay. We're going to stay here tonight and then drive up to my farm. Can you and Diana meet us there tomorrow afternoon? Good. Great. See you both then."

He put the phone on the nightstand and lay down next to Pea, holding her close.

"I am so tired. I feel like I could just sink into this bed," he said and looked at Pea who had slipped away into sleep as soon as he had laid down with her.

He wished there was something, anything, he could do to fix this for all of them, but was asleep before his mind could think of anything else.

At Trey's farm, Joseph was still sitting on the front steps of the house with the dogs next to him. He had been sitting there for hours now hoping to see headlights coming up the drive to house so he could figure out a way to take back his awful words.

In the Shenandoah Valley a cool breeze was blowing clouds in from the west and they began to obscure the stars shining above him.

Joseph heard the door open and jumped up and saw his wife standing on the other side of the screen door. He stood there silently waiting to see if she was going to throw his suitcase at him or cuss at him again.

Instead, she walked out on the portico and came to the steps next to where he stood. She was barefoot and dressed in oversized sleeveless nightgown. She rubbed her bare arms as she looked up at the sky.

"A storm's moving in," she said.

Joseph still didn't say anything. He just bowed his head and shoved both his hands in the pockets of his khaki pants so she couldn't see how bad his hands were shaking.

She touched the sleeve of his polo shirt and said, "Trey found her at home. She's ok. Come on in. I'm tired and I want to go to bed."

Joseph followed her in the house, closed and locked the door, then trailed her as she made her way up the steps to the guest suite Pea had spent time renovating for her sister and Joseph.

He slowly stood at the dresser and took off his watch and emptied the pockets of his pants onto a tray on the dresser. In the mirror he saw Mary go into the bath room and then return. He turned off the light as she climbed into bed and he finished undressing and got in bed with her.

She had turned her back to him after getting in bed. He was still afraid she was going to push him away, but when he was lying next to her, he reached out and placed his hand on her belly. He expected her to push it away, but was surprised when she pulled him closer and twined her fingers in his.

"I love you," he said, finally breaking his silence.

"I know. Go to sleep, Joseph. I'm too tired to talk," she said quietly, but she moved closer to him and tried to put the evening out of her mind.

Chapter Twenty-Six

Thomas and Diana arrived at Trey's farm long before Trey and Pea came down the drive in their cars. When Thomas and Diana walked in the door, they could feel the tension like a wall between Mary and Joseph. Outside, the storm front that had settled in the night before had barely moved and the grey rainy landscape made everything feel chilled. Every now and then a gust of wind would blow the rain against the window and streak the glass with rivulets of water that obscured the vista.

Joseph said very little and sat in a side chair watching out the window as if a miracle might appear at any moment to get him out of this room and this house. Pea's great danes lay at his feet, their great heads watching everyone in the room carefully.

Mary, on the other hand, looked tired and yet tried to maintain some sort of conversation with them about the most inane subjects, from the rain that seemed relentless to the size of Trey's kitchen and how hard it was to cook in there.

After almost a half hour, Trey and Pea had still not arrived and Mary asked Diana if she had ever seen the rest of the house and the renovations and restoration Pea had been doing to the house. The two women headed through the dining room to the solarium and left Thomas and Joseph sitting there in silence.

Joseph covered his eyes and wouldn't or couldn't look at Thomas, who was getting tired of just waiting here.

Thomas got up and walked over to the piano and flipped through the music Pea had on the top of the Steinway baby grand. He reached down and hit a chord and heard the deep resonating tone that only a Steinway could produce.

He looked over at Joseph who had not moved or changed his view from the chair since they had arrived.

"Well, are we going to have a guilt fest, a pity party, or a knock down, drag out fight when they arrive?" Thomas asked.

For the first time that afternoon, Joseph looked up at Thomas and his face became bright red. He put his hands on the ends of the armrests as if he were ready to bolt from the room, but then released them and sank further back into the chair if it were possible.

"I said something very stupid and very cruel last night. I regret it deeply and I have no idea how to fix it," he said.

Thomas walked over to the love seat near the armchair and sat down next to Joseph.

"Well, you're speaking now. That's a start," Thomas said.

"I know a lot more about some of this than you or Mary or, for that matter, Trey, at least until last night know. Pea came to me a month or so after I got out of the hospital. She was and, I think still is, filled with guilt. She kept trying to apologize to me for Shawnette's death. I tried to talk to her and I tried to listen, but she just has so much tearing at her that I don't think anyone but a therapist can help her. She certainly didn't listen to me.

Thomas leaned back and placed one elbow on the back of the love seat, his hand at the side of his head.

"You know, Thomas, I knew, too. We all did. She didn't have to say anything. Maybe it was because she wasn't saying anything that we all knew. But last night, I lost my temper and I said the most hurtful thing I could to try to get her attention. It was fucking stupid. I would never want to hurt her, but I did," Joseph said.

He shook his head and looked out the window again. The limbs of the two live oaks on the other side of the drive were bending down with the wind. The fields beyond the trees were still green, but were dotted with dark gold round bales in preparation for feeding the cattle this winter.

"I just hope they both get here safely. This is a bad storm," he said.

Thomas glanced out the window and then back at Joseph.

"Joseph, I'm not going to make you feel any worse than you're making yourself feel. And Mary has probably put in her fair share, too."

Joseph smiled wryly. "Other than calling me a 'son of a bitch', she's barely spoken to me, which is almost worse than cursing me or slapping me, which I deserved."

He pinched the bridge of his nose in an effort not to tear up.

"Oh, so we're going with the guilt fest. Okay, well, then, here's something for the four of you to feel guilty about – why the hell didn't you or the others call me? Didn't you think Diana and I had some say in any of this? Remember, I was at that sheriff's office with Pea and Trey," Thomas said.

Joseph looked at Thomas in surprise and his face reddened again.

"We just got here yesterday morning to try to talk to Pea and Trey. You're right. We should have called you guys as well. I'm sorry."

Thomas looked down and brushed lint from his pants and laughed.

"It's okay, Joseph. We're here now and we'll work something out. Don't be so hard on yourself. You aren't responsible for taking care of all of us. You're more like Pea than you realize."

Joseph shook his head.

"How the hell did we get into this mess? All I wanted to do was love Mary and have a normal life with our family, safe from all the craziness out there. It seemed that things were going okay and then everything just fell apart," he said.

Now it was Thomas's turn to shake his head.

"Things have not been okay. Things have just been, they've been the way life goes. Life is never fair. It just is. You know that. You've probably seen far worse things that the rest of us ever will. You know the toll it takes."

"And when it involves families and people we love, we don't always do what we should. We say and do things we regret because we let that fear and guilt get in there and eat at us."

Joseph nodded and now looked out into the house and was silent for a moment, trying to hear his wife's voice.

"You're right. All I could think of was Mary."

He hesitated for a moment and looked at Thomas.

"Do you think Pea and Trey will forgive me?"

Thomas nodded and smiled.

"I think they already have. I think they wanted us all here to talk about how we should handle the situation with the New River people and we do have to come up with a plan. You were right about that when you spoke to Pea last night. She just runs head first into situations and doesn't think, maybe because *he* never allowed her to think for herself. I don't know. But I think they've forgiven you and Mary probably has, too. She just may not know how to tell you yet."

Joseph leaned forward in the chair, looked down at the Berber rug and then up at Thomas.

"I have to tell you something and I don't want Mary to hear this. She doesn't need anymore stress than she already has," he whispered.

Thomas leaned forward to hear what Joseph had to say. He was almost afraid to her it himself. He was no better than Pea or Joseph when trying to hide his fear or guilt. Here he was trying to help Joseph and all he wanted to do was leave and forget his own role in this little drama.

"You remember telling us that you saw Shawnette one night?"

Thomas nodded again, but remained silent.

"Did you tell Diana about it? Have you seen her again?"

"Yeah, I told Diana, but no, I haven't seen her again. When Diana is there, I don't know, I think she, maybe she doesn't need to be there. Sometimes I wonder if it even happened. It was a bad night. I don't know . . ." he said quietly, his voice trailing off.

Joseph looked up at the foyer and then toward the dining room to see if Mary was in either direction.

"I believe you. And I believe Pea saw Alicia as well. Last week I was walking into one of the upstairs bedrooms at their farm when I saw, well, I guess I saw Alicia. She was standing in the middle of the room smiling. It startled me so much that I stumbled backward and fell on the runner in the hallway," he whispered.

Thomas simply looked stunned. He could not believe what was coming out of Joseph's mouth. Joseph was the most rational man he had ever known, a man who had seen death and people at their worst, a man who believed in evidence and proof.

"I know what it sounds like. I probably looked the same way you do now when you and Pea told us your stories. But I can only say what I saw. She looked like a miniature version of Mary. I had decided to use one of the empty bedrooms to put all this New River stuff up and Mary found me and stopped me, telling me it was Alicia's old bedroom. She had made supper, but told me I had to take it all down after we ate."

"And that's when I saw her, when I went back upstairs to take the stuff down. There she was, smiling like an angel.

I swear. Maybe this is all unhinging me. I have no logical explanation for what I saw. Hell, I have no explanation for how I've been acting since then, including last night."

As he had continued his narration to Thomas, he had failed to see Mary and Diana enter the room from the dining room.

"So that's why you fell?" Mary asked.

Oh, damn, Joseph thought, as he looked up to see the two women standing in the doorway, their faces as stunned as Thomas's had been.

How did she keep sneaking up on him like that, he thought.

Joseph stood and walked quickly over to his wife.

"I didn't think this day could get much worse, but I guess I was wrong again. I'm sorry. I should have told you. It's just been so hard and I've been so worried," he said.

Mary reached out for his arm and said, "Help me sit down. I don't feel so good all of a sudden."

Her face was so white that the brush of freckles on her nose and cheeks had almost disappeared. Joseph led her to the sofa and helped her to sit back.

"Do you need something, Mary," Diana said, standing behind Joseph.

"No, I'm okay. I'm just . . . shocked. I don't understand any of this," she said.

Joseph turned to Diana and asked her to get a glass of water from the kitchen. Thomas moved over to the sofa and sat next to Mary, feeling somewhat useless as Joseph sat on the other side of her, still holding her hand in his.

Diana came back with a glass of water and handed it to Mary.

"Are you okay, Mary?" Joseph said as she drank the water. Her color began to return and she nodded yes. She placed his hand on her belly and he could feel the baby rolling about. He exhaled, not realizing that he had been practically holding his breath the whole time.

"I'm okay. We're both okay," she said looking at each of them.

Thomas stood up and moved back to the love seat where Diana joined him. He put his arm around her tiny shoulders and pulled her close to his side.

"You guys are scaring me to death with all this ghost talk," Mary said and tried to laugh in a attempt to ease their fears, but even she didn't believe it herself. They had scared her half to death. But instead of showing it, she did exactly what Pea and Thomas and Joseph did. She tried to get angry and rationalize it, to move the fear as far away from herself as possible.

"And why the hell am I just now hearing this from you? Damn it, Joseph, you're treating me the way we all used to treat Pea, as if she would break if we said or did the wrong thing. I'm not an egg. I won't crack. So stop it, all of you. Stop hiding things from me."

Joseph held her hand and looked down and smiled.

"Well, technically, you are a little like an egg right now. You've just got a few months to go before you hatch," he said and glanced up and leaned away from her before she could punch his shoulder.

"I wish you'd stop play 'Punch Buggy' with my shoulder," he said, rubbing his shoulder.

"Well, I wish you'd stop making fun of me and start telling me what's going on. Stop laughing, Joseph. It's not funny."

The two great danes had moved across the room with him as he had gone to Mary earlier and now they sat at the end of the sofa next to him.

"And what the hell is it with Pea's dogs? When did they become your best friends?" she said and tried to punch his shoulder again, but missed.

Joseph looked at the dogs. He hadn't even noticed them sitting there until now. They had spent last night on the porch with him and they had spent a good part of the day going wherever he went. He had to admit that it was strange.

He shrugged and said, "What? Now I'm responsible for what those dogs do? Listen, I've got enough things I've messed up on my plate already. The dogs are on their own."

Just as he finished speaking, both dogs ran to the front door and started to whine. A chill went down his spine and then he realized that they had probably heard Pea's Audi coming down the drive. And that made him more anxious again. He breathed in and thought, here it comes - either angry people or the silent treatment. He tried to steel himself for either eventuality.

Suddenly the dogs scooted backwards as the door quickly swung open and Pea and Trey entered the house, the wind blowing them forward into the foyer. Pea petted both the dogs as their tails wagged wildly and Trey closed the front door against the wind and rain. Pea looked up and saw everyone sitting in the living room, waiting for her and Trey to appear. She glanced around the room, her eyes settling on Joseph who looked down at floor once more. And strangely enough to both Pea and Joseph, the dogs ran over to his side and then turned to face her.

Chapter Twenty-Seven

"It looks like they've become attached to you rather quickly," she said shaking the water off her clothes and trying to brush it from her hair with her hands.

Trey joined her, mimicking her movements, trying to dry himself off as well.

"Sorry, we're so late. The storm was horrible to drive through. And trees are down in a few places on Route 11 which slowed us down even more," he said.

"Why hasn't anyone started a fire?" Trey asked tilting his head toward the huge open fireplace. "It's really chilly and damp in here."

He went over to the fireplace and started building a fire, his back purposefully to everyone in the room. He knew he had to let Pea and Joseph work this out and that he had to surrender to their wills this time and not try and insert his own feelings into the situation. His feelings were mixed as it was.

Joseph stood, but didn't move forward. He shoved his hands into his pockets as he had last night.

"Pea, there are not enough words for me to say just how sorry I am and how wrong I was to speak to you the way I did last night. I am truly, truly sorry. I wouldn't want to hurt you that way for all the world," he said.

Pea stood silent, looking down at the dogs while he spoke.

"It's okay, Joseph. Well, it wasn't okay. Not at first, but after a lot of tears and time to think about what you were really trying to say and why you said what you said, I understood."

She looked up at him and stared into his blue eyes.

"It still doesn't change how I feel about the situation, but . . . I think I understand why you said it. So let's just let it go, okay?" she said, turning her face to Mary's and not to Joseph.

Joseph looked over at his wife and sat back down on the sofa next to her.

"Sure, sure," he said.

Trey had gotten the fire lit by that time and the dogs trotted across the room to him and lay down on the hearth on each side of him.

"Fickle things, aren't they," Pea said and plopped herself down into one of the armchairs next to the sofa.

"When they first met Trey, they almost ate him alive. They placed themselves between us and growled at him.

I remember that he was not happy with the way they seemed to dislike him, but by the next morning they were his best friends, following him everywhere."

"They'll probably pick Thomas and Diana for the new best friends next," she said and laughed.

"Oh we had that conversation with them the night of the wedding," Thomas said and grinned at Diana, who had snuggled close to him on the love seat as the room had grown even cooler when Pea and Trey had entered.

"They would not leave the bedroom that night until I bribed them with a slice of wedding cake. I had to have some alone time, you know," he said and this time Diana laughed, the light, tinkling sound of her laughter seemed to lighten the mood in the room.

Trey stood and turned to face the room, having finally gotten the fire going and having let the tension remove itself somewhat from the room.

"So, we've got to come up with a plan. Something that we can all live with and live through," he said.

Everyone in the room looked to him as if he had the answers they needed and he realized that they wanted him to have the answers. It was not a burden he wanted to take on. He had just wanted to get them talking. He suddenly saw that this was going to be harder than he ever thought it would be.

"Okay, Pea, you've read the most about these guys, if they are the ones. And Thomas and I have done some traveling around with you asking questions, but we probably can't contribute much more than that. But, Joseph, you've spoken to your friends at the FBI and you said that they were aware of the New River problem, had at least one suspect, maybe two, but couldn't move in because they had no real evidence," he said.

Pea, Thomas and Joseph nodded almost in unison. Diana and Mary offered nothing. Diana looked out the window behind the love seat and Mary stared at the fire with an unhappy look on her face. No, Trey thought, this is not going to be easy.

"Listen you guys, there are six people in this room. I am not the leader. You need to talk, and that means everyone, including both of you, Mary and Diana."

The two women looked to Trey. Mary now looked more angry than unhappy. Diana laid her head on Thomas's shoulder, then sat forward. Surprisingly, she was the first one to speak.

"Okay. I'll go first. I'm angry about this whole mess. I'm pissed that you guys didn't even bother to tell us what Joseph had found out until last night. I'm pissed at Pea for getting Thomas involved in yet another mess."

"And I'm pissed at all of you for thinking of me as a secondary person in this little drama. That includes you, too, Thomas. Did anyone here think to consult me about this New River mess? No, you just look at me as if I were outside your little troupe. That really pisses me off," she said.

They were all stunned by the vehemence in her voice and words. Everything she had said was true and they had nothing to explain their own selfish self-interest in what she had called their "little drama."

"Diana, I, we, god, you're right. We should have talked to you. You're in this as much as we are. It's just that we went through so much last year and . . ." Mary said.

"And you didn't think I was involved in any of that? I sat by this man's bed for over a month. I was there every day helping him through rehab. You guys would come by and talk to him and just wave hi to me as an afterthought. But I've been in this longer that at least two of you – I was there when Pea's husband killed my best friend and Thomas's fiancée. I was there fighting the police to get him out of jail a year before Pea started acting like she was Nancy Drew," she said angrily interrupting Mary and pulling away from Thomas and glaring at all of them.

"Wait just a god damn minute! You weren't there for the ten years of hell my sister went through. You didn't lose your only child to a monster who was beating you, cheating on you and killing women. Don't tell me we weren't there. If Pea hadn't had the fortitude to go all "Nancy Drew" as you said, Thomas might still be the prime suspect in Shawnette's death and possibly some of the other women. Don't . . ." Mary said as she struggled to move forward to the edge of the sofa, her face almost as red as her hair.

"Whoa, wait, stop," Thomas said holding his arm out in front of Diana who was on the verge of standing. He looked at her and realized how much he underestimated her strength. He never could see what was in front of him sometimes, he thought.

"Mary, sit back and take a deep breath. This isn't good for you," Joseph said.

"Oh, you sit back, Joseph. I have a right to be angry about someone attacking my sister," she said, but leaned back against the sofa again.

The entire time the exchange had taken place, Trey had never taken his eyes off Pea. At one point, she had turned away and wiped at her eyes, but then she had turned back to him and held his gaze. He had not known any details of her marriage to Manley, but he was starting to get a clearer picture of what it had been like.

Once the others had calmed down, they, too, had noticed that neither Trey nor Pea had spoken. The two women were a bit ashamed of their outbursts, but obviously to everyone else their feelings had been building for quite a while.

"I'm sorry, Diana. I shouldn't have lost my temper," Mary said and then turned to Pea. "Pea, I'm so sorry. I shouldn't have let those details spill out. I know I promised never to mention them. I'm sorry."

Across the room, Diana looked at Thomas and then at Mary and Pea.

"I'm sorry as well. Losing our tempers with each other isn't going to do any good. I . . . just couldn't stop. It was as if everything just came spilling out," she said.

"Tell me about it," Joseph mumbled under his breath and Pea, who was the only one to hear it punched his shoulder and began laughing.

His head popped up and he looked around the room.

"What is it with these Taliaferro women and their shoulder punching? Could we have a moratorium on it for awhile," he said and rubbed the shoulder that Pea had just punched.

Trey threw another log on the fire and sat down in the arm chair next to it where Joseph had spent most of the day.

"No more hitting Joseph, ladies," he said and smiled a little.

"We've still got to get through this. Joseph, can you go over everything your friends at the FBI told you? That would be a start"

Joseph exhaled and then thought for a few moments about everything he had been told.

"First, I'm fairly sure they didn't give me the full story. Not only would it not be prudent for them, but because it's an ongoing investigation they simply couldn't. So, what I know, what they told me, was to probably warn us away more than anything else," he said.

"You guys should have waited for me to come back before traveling the valley and asking questions, though the Bureau did get a few leads from information you gleaned, including the body dump in Bluestone and a few other deaths that were a little too random, including the death of the father of one of the men."

"From what I gather, they've been doing this a long time. They're probably in their early fifties and they only meet once or twice a year. There could be," he sighed and paused, looking at Pea, "There could be anywhere from 30 to 50 victims. Maybe more. If they killed the length of the valley for at least 30 years and only killed once a year that would be 30 people. But, I think the guys in D.C. think the number is higher."

"Most of the victims were either alone or were couples alone. They were most likely strangers. Since one of them is in law enforcement, he probably lulled them into a false sense of safety. The problem is that he is highly respected by the people in his county. He leads a very normal life, has a wife, a mortgage and two sons who are star athletes for Gladstone County. My contact said that he was expected to run for sheriff next year. That's a hard wall to break through."

Joseph took a drink of water from the glass that Diana had brought to Mary earlier before continuing.

"They think his partner is the weak link. His partner left the area and has lived in Charleston, West Virginia since he dropped out of the University of Charleston almost 30 years ago, which happens to coincide with when the deaths seemed to have started."

"Here's the thing," Joseph added. "After talking with my friend, and after reading through what Pea had gathered, I think the one in Charleston is the alpha. I think he makes the decisions about everything they do, which . . ." he paused again and looked down before addressing the rest of them. "Which is hunting, torturing, and murdering whatever unlucky person or persons happen to come along their way."

"No matter how you look at it, the two of them may be two of the most cunning and dangerous serial killers this country has seen in decades."

The entire room was quiet except for the soft sound of six people breathing.

"Jesus Christ," Thomas said. "Jesus Christ help us. What the hell have we gotten into?" He fell back against the back of the love seat and wiped his forehead with his hand.

They were all stunned by what Joseph had revealed except for Pea, who looked down at the dogs and made no attempt to speak.

Before anyone else could say anything, Trey spoke in an attempt to protect Pea from any more of their collective anger.

"Thanks, Joseph. At least we know what kind of, of, god, I can't call them men. Monsters. At least we know what monsters we're dealing with," he said.

"Before anyone starts round two of the blame game, let's leave the guilt in the past. We all have our fair share of that and it's nonproductive to what we decide to do or how we solve this problem."

"Yes, a problem that I once again seemed to have brought down on our heads. I'm sorry, Diana. I apologize to all of you. Joseph was right last night. This really is my fault. If I hadn't dove into the deep end of the pool without looking to see if there was water there, I might not have put you guys in such danger. You would be living peaceful, calm lives. It is my fault and I am so, so sorry," Pea said and bent her head.

Thomas looked on as Diana and stood and walked over to where Pea was and sat down on the arm of her chair.

"Stop it, Pea. You can't carry this guilt your whole life. Remember when I told you that it wasn't you who was responsible for Shawnette's death or the other women or your daughter? It's the same with these two men. They've been killing maybe longer than you've been alive. If you hadn't seen it, you might have gone on with your life, but they would still be killing innocent people. Hunting them down like wildlife in the forest . . ."

Joseph interrupted Thomas and said, "Wait, a minute, the forest. That's it. That's what we've missed. Serial killers mark their territory much like any other predator and they almost always hunt and kill in the same area, but they dispose of the remains in other places, usually not two far from where they kill."

"They're both originally from Gladstone Gap, right?"

Pea wiped her eyes and nodded yes.

"I think their first kill was somewhere near there. The forest around the Gap is so thick and there are so many old mining roads there that they could had a favorite place that they just continued using. I need a map of the area," he said.

"No, no, Joseph, we're not going after them the way we went after Manley. Pea and Mary are both pregnant. You've had a heart attack. Mary was right about that part. We can't go through that again," Trey said.

Joseph whipped his head around and said to Trey, "So we just let them go on killing? No. I can't do that. I can't have another death on my conscience. But I can go to D.C. and work on this with the task force assigned to it and give them the information we have. We can let them act on it."

Suddenly Mary spoke up, "And what do we do if they don't get here in time or don't act? What if these men are planning on hunting us right now, thinking we might be able to give the FBI the information they need? Didn't you write in your book that predators became most dangerous when they thought they were about to be caught? I'd say that makes these men about as dangerous as they come."

Again, the room was silent as they all thought of Mary's words.

"Trey's right about one thing. We can't hunt them - two pregnant women, a botanist, a welder, a farmer and a man with a bad heart, sorry Joseph. That would be the ultimate in stupidity," Diana said from the love seat as Trey nodded his agreement with her assessment of the situation.

Joseph slammed the glass down on the table in front of him.

"Well, then what the hell do we do? Because of the deputy, they probably have all the information they need about all of us - where we live, phone numbers, cars. Anything you can think of, I'd bet they already know, including Mary's pregnancy, although they might not know about Pea."

"Do we just go on with our lives as if we know none of this, because I think that would be the worst thing we could do – nothing," he said.

"So what do you suggest, Joseph?" Thomas asked as he crossed the room back to sit next to Diana.

"Jesus, I could use a drink right now," he said as he sat down.

Trey jumped up and headed for the kitchen.

"I can fix that," he called out as he went through the foyer.

As he went to kitchen, the dogs' ears perked up and they began to move toward the foyer. No one paid them much attention. Each of them was lost in thought until they heard low growls coming from the door. The growls turned into deep barks and the dogs began to frantically scratch at the front door just as Trey came back from the kitchen to see what the fracas was all about.

Thomas looked out the window and saw flashing patrol lights in the drive. His first thought was, oh shit, they're found us. Then he saw the Augusta County logo on the car and sighed.

"Trey, it's the local sheriff's people out there," he called out just as the knock on the door came. The dogs went wild, barking and almost knocking through the door.

"Pea," Trey said.

Pea stood and whistled sharply at the dogs. They immediately stopped and followed her through the dining room and into the solarium where she told them to stay. They sat at attention together just past the door and watched through the French door as she closed it and snapped the latch at the top of the door.

"It's okay. They're in the solarium. They won't move. You can open the door now," she said returning to the foyer. She failed to mention that she had tucked a .45 in the back of her jeans and loosened her shirt to cover it. As Trey opened the door, she put her right hand at her hip near the gun. She wasn't going to be taken by surprise as she had been by Manley. Trey didn't know she owned the .45 and she hoped he never did.

When he opened the door, a young deputy stood there and Pea thought of the day a deputy had come to tell her and Mary about their parents' deaths. Suddenly she knew that something bad had happened and her knees went a bit weak.

"Come on in and get out of the rain, Dan," Trey said.

Pea could hear sighs of relief from everyone in the room. That Trey knew the deputy by name made them all feel better, all but Pea.

As he led the deputy into the living room, Pea quickly went back to the dining room and hid the .45 back under the tablecloths in the linen press. As she reentered the living room the first words, she heard were, "When?"

"What's going on?" she asked.

The deputy turned to face her.

"Ma'am, you're Ms. Taliaferro?

"Yes, what wrong?"

"You own a house in Greenbrier County?"

"Yes." She was becoming impatient. Get on with it, she thought. I know it's bad. Just get it out, she wanted to say.

"Yes, my sister and I do. Has something happened?"

"You have a man by the name of Dickson who works for you?"

"Yes, yes, for god's sake, what's wrong? Is he okay?" Pea was suddenly very afraid for her old friend's life. None of them had given a thought to his safety.

"Yes, ma'am. The storm took out both the cell tower there and trees fell on the land line. He's been trying to get in touch with you. This afternoon he noticed smoke coming from your house. He went over and saw flames in the window and when he couldn't get the phone to work, he got in his car and drove to Renick and got the boys at the volunteer fire department. But by the time they got back, the whole place was ablaze. I think you and your sister may have lost the whole place."

Pea fell into the arm chair and looked over at Mary. Joseph held Mary as she stared at the deputy. Pea was too shocked to take it in. She had expected anything but this. Their home, their 200 year old home was gone. She looked up at the deputy.

"Please tell me the fire didn't get to the barn. The horses. Please, not the horses."

"No, ma'am, Mr. Dickson said it was just the house. He said he saw your car there this morning, is that right?"

"Dan, we were both there this morning, but we left a little after 10 a.m. We didn't even have coffee or cook. We grabbed food on the road because we wanted to get back here. Any idea of what happened?" Trey asked.

Dan the deputy shook his head.

"No, old houses, maybe old wiring."

"No," Pea said. "My parents completely renovated the house from the attic down in the 90s. New wiring and plumbing. They had an architect from Charlottesville do the plans for modernizing it, putting in new kitchens and baths. There's no way it was old wiring."

"Then the other possibility is arson," the deputy said.

"What about the storm?" Pea asked.

He shook his head again.

"No, according to Mr. Dickson, the storm had long since passed when he saw the smoke. If it had been a lightning hit, it would have been seen earlier. The thing is, was there anyone else out at the farm when you were there besides Mr. Dickson?"

Pea shivered as a finger of chill went up her spine.

"No, no one."

"And you trust Mr. Dickson?" he said, more than asked.

"Yes. He's been there since my grandfather was there. He has a small place in the barn and lives there. He would never do anything. He knows we've been . . ." she almost said 'what we've been through' but she stopped herself in time.

"Yes, ma'am, I know what you ladies have been through last year, but I had to ask. Mr. Dickson said that about a half hour before he saw the smoke he saw a dark blue Ford truck pulling out of your drive. At the time, he said he thought it was just someone who'd turned down the wrong road. But with what you've said, it sounds like it might have been arson."

He moved the brim of his hat around in a circle and headed to the front door to leave.

"The West Virginia state people are investigating it and they'll probably have more questions for you. I'm really sorry. Trey, sorry to have see you with bad news," he said and left for his patrol car.

Pea had followed Trey and the deputy to the door and as Trey closed it, Pea noticed the long scratches the dogs had left on the newly painted door.

"Oh Trey, the dogs have ruined the door."

Trey stared at her for a minute and realized she was in shock. Now they all knew just how much danger they were in. And now they knew what they were going to have to face and it scared the hell out of him.

Chapter 28

Joseph went to the kitchen and finished the task Trey had started when the knock had come at the door. He carried a tray with a pitcher of orange juice, bottles of scotch and wine and glasses. He poured juice for Mary and Pea first and then poured either whiskey or wine for the others. He poured himself a double of whiskey and downed it in one gulp. The others sat in shocked silence, holding their glasses and staring into them as if reading tea leaves.

Joseph poured another double for himself and Mary laid her hand upon his arm, silently asking him to stop in that way that couples often have of communicating without speaking.

He sat the glass down and the others seem to awaken from their reveries and drink whatever Trey had given them.

Pea put her glass back on the tray and went to the solarium to release the dogs. As she looked out the glass windows, she became worried about the vulnerability the room provided. The security provided by the French doors separating the solarium from the dining room was minimal. The one thing she and Trey had not thought about was a security system. There had never been one in the house and there were so many other things they had slated to complete that a security system was never something they had discussed.

Sadly, she realized, her home in Greenbrier County had no such system either. Her family had never considered one. And Pea couldn't begin to count the number of times that they had left the doors unlocked unless the house was empty of the family.

She went back to the living room where the dogs had run to the hearth next to Trey. God, she thought, what if we hadn't had the dogs here? They could have died. It was only then that she thought of all they had lost in the house. Not just furniture and the everyday items of life. They had lost their family's history. Paintings, photographs, family antiques, books. Everything possibly gone.

She poured herself another glass of juice and drank it quickly in an effort to forestall crying. What if she and Trey hadn't left this morning? What if it would have happened last night or when Mary and Joseph were there? She leaned forward feeling a little nauseous and faint which did not go unnoticed by Trey.

Between the trip and the afternoon and the shock of the deputy's visit, he realized that they needed to be eating, instead of sitting here morosely throwing back drinks. Pea and Mary especially needed to eat.

"I'm going out to the garage to get some steaks from the freezer and fix something for us all to eat. Anyone want to lend a hand?"

Pea stood and said, "I'll help. I can at least toss a salad."

Mary groaned from the couch.

"Not really. Sorry, Pea, but you are worse in the kitchen than anyone. Trey, let me help. Pea can set the table or something," Mary said trying to lift herself off the sofa.

Joseph put his hand in front her and stopped her from standing.

"Actually, you're not in any better shape than Pea is right now. Why don't you ladies let the men fix everything? The only thing someone has to do is throw another log on the fire at some point," he said and stood.

Thomas agreed and went with Trey out to the freezer to rummage for some steaks and Joseph headed back into the kitchen.

Pea got up and went over to the sofa to sit next to her sister, who leaned against her and was not holding back the tears now.

Diana sat across the room from them, looking out the window, watching as Trey and Thomas ran from the portico to the detached garage where Trey had put in a new, full size freezer and had filled it with food.

She turned back to look at the sisters and shuddered from the knowledge that they really were all in danger. She felt sorry for the women and she wondered just how much they had lost in the fire.

"Are you cold, Diana? I saw you shiver. Do you want a throw or I can put another log or two on the fire," Pea said.

"No, no, I'm okay, but I'll put the logs on so you guys don't have to get up. I'm probably in better shape to be lifting things and I'm closer to it anyway."

Pea sighed and put her arm around her sister who seemed inconsolable.

"I just keep thinking about all of the baby's stuff. And then I think of our stuff and Mom and Dad's things. It's all gone. Jesus, Pea. We don't have a home anymore and all our family pictures. We don't even have any other family out there who might have had any pictures," Mary said.

Pea hugged her tighter and said, "It okay. Things can be found. Houses can be rebuilt, but no one was hurt and that's what makes it alright. We're okay. That's what's important."

Diana moved from the love seat to the chair Pea had previously occupied. She poured herself another glass of wine and asked the sisters if they wanted anything. They both shook their heads.

"I think we should come up with a temporary solution before we get three more opinions thrown in. Not one of those men will admit that they're as frightened as we are," she said.

Mary laughed softly.

"Joseph frightened? He'd never admit it in a million years. He'd say something like 'I'm worried' or that he's 'concerned', but afraid? Never."

"So what do you suggest Diana?" Mary asked.

Diana looked up at the cove ceiling and shrugged her shoulders.

"I honestly don't know. Maybe we should go into some kind of protective custody. I can tell you that I'm scared as hell to go back to the apartment right now. If these guys are bold enough to just burn your house down, they're not afraid of us or of getting caught."

"I think you're wrong about that, Diana. I think they're running scared, or they wouldn't have dared to come near the house. I mean we're obviously threats to them, but they could have burned the house as a warning for us to back off. They had to know that no one was there. They wouldn't have seen any cars, including the farm truck which Mr. Dickson keeps behind the barn," Pea said and began to muse on how they could use this to their advantage.

"Anyway," she said. "In the meantime, we can all stay here. Trey has more rooms than anyone could possibly use and it's better than letting the Feds move us around while they try to gather more evidence."

She frowned.

"Seriously, how long have they known about this? We could be away from home for months or years."

"Well, that's easy for you to say, Pea, you still have a place to live," Mary said.

"Ree, that's not fair. That house meant as much to me as it did to you. And I don't think Diana wants to just get involved in some government chess game where we're all the pawns," Pea said.

"No, you're right, Pea," Diana said. "Besides, Thomas won't leave anyway. You guys know how he is. He gets shot and still thinks he has to protect us all as if his only weakness is kryptonite."

The three women smiled at that.

"I'd bet he would look good in those red and blue tights," Mary said.

"Mary!" Pea exclaimed and then the three of them began to laugh loudly.

"Oh, you ladies have no idea," Diana said, sipped the wine slyly while smiling. The three of them began to laugh more.

They heard voices in the kitchen and then saw Thomas come into the foyer and the laughter grew louder.

"What's wrong," he said.

Diana bit her lip and then said, "Oh we were just talking about tights," and began laughing again.

Thomas looked at them as if they were from another world and just shook his head.

"Well, I've been designated the table setter, so could someone tell me where the linens and plates and stuff are?"

"Yeah, they're in the linen . . ." Pea almost said press and then remembered the .45 she had tucked away in there and ran after Thomas to try to get to it before he did.

She was just a few seconds too late. He had found the gun under the top table cloth. Damn, damn, damn, Pea thought. How do I explain this?

She was amazed when she didn't have to say anything about the gun. Thomas handed it to her.

"You need to put this somewhere else. Somewhere you can get to it easily, but not where Trey's going to see it since I assume by your running in here that he doesn't know you have it."

"No," she said quietly. "He has guns in the house, but they're all locked up in the north wing in a gun safe and I think most of them probably date to the Civil War."

"I bought this myself. After . . . after Manley, I swore that I'd never be at anyone's mercy again. I grew up with guns, but a .45 is a different matter from a shotgun or a rifle."

"Trey's farm manager helped me learn how to use it and promised to be quiet about it. He said 'Women need to know how to use a gun.' He also said I was a fast learner. I guess I had to be. Not much choice."

She took the gun from him and put it in one of the lower drawers of the side board.

"It should be okay there. I don't think that sideboard's been opened in 20 years."

"Pea, I'm not going to tell him, but you should. Secrets have proven to be a bad thing for the two of you in the past and I don't think you want your relationship in a bad place. You're going to have to trust him or you'll never have what you need and want."

"I know. I'll leave you to your table setting. Sorry," she said and went back to the living room with Diana and Mary.

Before she could sit back down on the couch, her sister began to speak.

"Pea, Diana and I have been talking about your offer to stay here and we'd rather do that than take our chances with the Feds. We just need to convince the men, since two of them want to leave and one just wants to go home."

"You agree, Diana?" Pea asked.

"Yeah, though convincing Thomas is going to be damn near impossible," she replied.

"And you're all going to have to drive to Greenbrier County tomorrow to see about your house. Oh, and clothing. Thomas and I are ok on that. We can pick up our things at the apartment. But, Mary and Joseph have nothing but the few things they brought with them."

She stopped, thinking about all the things that they would need to do.

"God, I hope you had good insurance," she said.

Now it was Mary's turn to smile sadly.

"Yes, but money isn't what we have to worry about. Our folks left us pretty well off. We could build whatever we wanted with the insurance our Dad had on just the house and furnishings. But, as my sister said so well, those were just things."

"I dread tomorrow. I don't want to see our house gone. It's too depressing to think about it."

Pea stood up and took her sister's hand and smiled.

"Well, Ree, let's think about that tomorrow. I'm hungry and tired and want to go to bed. While the men finish getting supper ready, let's go get one of the bedroom suites ready for Diana and Thomas."

Pea headed toward the foyer and said, "Come on, both of you. Ree, you're not incapacitated. You can help, too."

"If we're going to share this place for a while we might as well make it as comfortable as possible and get used to where everything is. We can worry about clothes and everything else tomorrow. Tomorrow, after all, is another day."

Diana joined Pea and followed her. Mary pushed herself up from the sofa and followed them upstairs.

When they were sitting in the dining room finishing the supper the men had prepared, the women looked to one another and Diana nodded to Pea.

"You know, I've been thinking. Since Trey has lots of room here and we don't want to be shuffled about at the whim of the Feds, why don't we stay here? Would you mind the company, Trey?" Pea asked.

Trey shook his head.

"No, the company would be fine, there's plenty of room here, and we're probably safer here if for no other reason than distance from Gladstone. I was thinking in the kitchen that we should have a security system installed, including cameras along the drive as well as the outside of the house."

Thomas threw his napkin on the table and frowned.

"As generous as your offer is, I have a business and Diana has school. We can't just uproot our lives and I'm through running from anyone," he said.

Pea started to speak, but Diana interrupted her before she could start.

"Thomas, you can still go into work. Since you have several men working with you, I doubt anyone would try anything with you as long as you aren't there alone. And I can wait this semester out. I think we're safer together and as Pea said, I don't want to go into any kind of protective custody. I'm so close to finishing my work on my dissertation. All I need is a place to work."

"I don't know. I don't want to give in to these bastards," he said.

Mary looked to Joseph sitting next to her. He was still nursing that glass of whiskey and he looked miserable.

"What makes you guys think that we're safer here?" he asked.

"Has anyone listened to a fucking thing I've said? Didn't the Greenbrier house burning prove what kind of trouble we're in? Jesus, why not just drive over to Gladstone and stand in front of the sheriff's office?"

Everyone was surprised by his profanity. He had always been so calm and they thought that the whiskey was not helping him control his emotions.

"If I can stay here, you're going to," Thomas said.

"I know you think leaving is the best thing, but not all of us have the luxury of a wealthy family to run home to."

"Fuck you, Thomas," Joseph said and threw his glass across the table, barely missing Thomas's head.

"Joseph!" Mary exclaimed and slapped him.

The table became silent as everyone held their breath waiting for Joseph's reaction.

"Oh, now we've moved from shoulder punching to slapping," he said.

"Fuck this," he said and stood to leave when the room began to tilt a bit. He leaned forward and grabbed at the edge of the table to steady himself.

As Mary reached up to steady him, Trey and Thomas rose and came round the table, each taking one of his arms.

"I think you've about had your fill of whiskey for the night. Come on," Trey said and he and Thomas led Joseph upstairs to the guest suite he and Mary were sharing.

"I'm not drunk" the women heard Joseph say as he stumbled on the steps with Thomas and Trey.

"I'd better go check on him. Whether he knows it or not, he's staying here with me. I'll be damned if I'm going to Long Island and sit there with his family. I'd rather take my chances here than spend any length of time in that nest of vipers," Mary said.

Pea hugged her sister as she left the room and turned back to begin clearing the table of the remains of their supper. Diana joined her in silence, helping carry the plates and glasses to the kitchen where Pea began rinsing them before putting them in the dishwasher.

By the time Thomas and Trey rejoined them, they had managed to clear most of the dishes and Trey took over the dish detail from Pea, asking her to throw the linens into the washer in the small side room off the kitchen. Diana brought in the tray of bottles and glasses from the living room and held up the half empty bottle of whiskey.

"I'd say that Joseph is going to have one hell of a headache tomorrow," she said.

They had been so self-absorbed that no one had noticed that he had kept drinking throughout the evening. Pea frowned and looked over at Trey, who just shook his head.

"Will Mary be able to convince him to stay?" he asked.

Thomas, who had sat down at the enameled Hoosier table, said, "He won't go anywhere without her and I don't think there's a chance in hell that she's going anywhere."

Diana agreed. "She told us that she was not going to his family's house on Long Island. Not that I blame her on that, though."

Pea walked over to Trey and kissed him on the cheek.

"I'm going to bed. I'm so tired I can't think straight anymore and we still have to go to the farm tomorrow," she said.

"Diana, do you guys have everything you need upstairs?" she asked.

"Yeah, we're all set for the night. Go get some sleep."

Pea walked from the kitchen, waving back with her hand and saying "Good Night" as she left.

"Well, I'm going to check all the doors and windows and head upstairs myself. Good night," Trey said and started his rounds of the house.

Diana walked over to Thomas and sat down on his lap and wrapped her arms around his neck, kissing his forehead.

"I'm sorry you're in the middle of all this," Thomas said. "If something happened . . ."

She leaned in and kissed him to stop him mid sentence.

"As long as I'm with you, Thomas, I'm not afraid. I know I'm safe with you."

"But . . ."

"Don't say it," she said. "That was another life, Thomas. Live with me in the here and now, not the past."

Upstairs, Pea was already in bed once Trey had made his rounds of the house.

"I left the dogs to roam the house just in case," he said as he began to undress and get in bed with her.

"Good. Those guys might be louder than an alarm system if they get riled up," she said.

He pulled the comforter up and snuggled close to her.

"It is going to be okay. I promise you."

She smiled at him, closed her eyes and drifted off to sleep as soon as he turned the light off.

Chapter Twenty-Nine

Pea, Trey, Mary and Joseph drove to Greenbrier County the next morning while Thomas and Diana went to their apartment to pack their things. The Monday morning was quiet and the sun had returned, but the air was cooler that morning as they reached the farm. As Trey pulled the Celica into the drive, Mary let out a small involuntary gasp.

One entire side of the house was gone. Nothing was left but the wooden frame of where the walls and floors had once been. The farther side, away from the kitchen, was less damaged, but black strokes from where the flames had licked the outside of the house surrounded some of the remaining window frames. It was both as bad as she had expected and worse than she had hoped.

From the back seat, Mary groaned.

"Oh god, it's almost all gone. I don't know if we can salvage anything," she said.

They all exited the car and stood looking up at the devastation the fire had left of their home. Mr. Dickson, who had heard their car drive up, exited from the barn and joined them outside the house.

"The arson people were here earlier this morning and the police told me to tell you that the one side was fairly safe, but not to try and walk around the bad side," he said.

He shook his head and spit tobacco over to the side.

"Damn shame. Your folks would be so upset, but they'd be glad you're both alright.

Joseph walked closer to the house and tried to look back into it to try to remember where certain rooms had been and what might remain in some parts of the house.

"I don't think the fire reached your dad's study," he said. "We might be able to salvage anything that was in there. It looks like the far end of the upstairs might not be as damaged either."

As they stood there staring at the few remaining unbroken windows, Mary saw a small shape dressed in red at one of the windows.

"Look, do you see what I see? Upstairs? Look!"

Mr. Dickson nodded his head and turned to Pea.

"I'm sorry Miss Pearl. I was hoping that she was just my imagination playing tricks on me," he said. "I've been seeing her a lot lately, but I'm an old man and my eyes sometimes mistake things."

Pea inhaled and said in almost a whisper, "I knew I had seen her. I knew I hadn't imagined it."

She turned away from the house and walked away from them and back around the barn. They watched her as she left, all of them knowing where she was headed.

"Well, that's twice for me," Joseph said.

"Yeah, I thought I saw her the night I stayed here with Pea. I blinked and she was gone. Scared the hell out of me, though she did look just like Mary," Trey said.

Mary walked around the three men and stared at them in disbelief.

"You mean you've all seen her? Did anyone bother to tell Pea? I can't believe you didn't tell her," she said and then turned to follow her sister.

The child in the window had disappeared as quickly as she had appeared and the three men continued to stare at the window as if she might come back.

"Was that her room?" Joseph said.

"Yeah, I think, which means that their parents' room across the hall might still have something salvageable in it. That might make both Pea and Mary feel better knowing that at least some of the things that belonged to their parents may have survived," Trey said.

Mr. Dickson shook his head and headed back to the barn.

"I'll talk to the two Misses before you leave, but don't let them go into the house. The police may have said that part of the place was safe, but I don't know," he said.

"Mr. Dickson, did they say if they wanted us to come in to see them?" Joseph asked.

"They said today or tomorrow if you could. Said they could give you more information once they'd gone over everything. You might be able to get in the west part of the house I suppose," he said.

Joseph nodded and then walked around the entirety of the house, trying to assess just how much damage had been done. Trey leaned against the door of the Celica and was still shocked by the amount of destruction the fire had caused. If he and Pea had still been there, they would have died. Pea's bedroom was just an empty frame of where it used to be. Mary's bedroom had been across the hall at the front of the house and it was in the same shape – just burnt beams and nothing else. Even the back staircase was completely gone. Trey supposed that the front staircase might still be usable.

He called Joseph and waved at him.

"I'm going to try and see if I can get into the west side of the house. If you want to stay out here and watch for Pea and Mary, you could keep them from following me. Neither of them needs to go in there.

Joseph agreed with Trey's assessment and stood next to the car as Trey climbed the stone steps and then carefully made his way to one of the broken downstairs windows and climbed through it.

He had been inside the house for about 10 minutes when Pea and Mary has come back around the barn. Pea immediately noticed that Trey was not there.

"Where is he, Joseph? Did he go in there?" she said and started towards the house.

Joseph grabbed her arm and pulled her back.

"He's fine. He's trying to see what's left inside. And you do not need to be climbing around in there with him."

Pea frowned and pulled her arm away from Joseph.

"I am just as able to go in there as he is."

"Pea, for god's sake, just stay here. I'm too exhausted to worry about both of you," Mary said, opening the rear passenger door and sitting on the edge of the seat.

"I'm sorry, Ree. Are you okay? I'll stay out here with you two."

"Yes, I'm fine," Mary said sharply. "I wish people would stop asking me that. I'm pregnant and I didn't sleep and someone did a fairly good job of burning my home to the ground. I think that gives me an excuse for being tired and grouchy."

Joseph walked over to her and wanted to take her hand, but he knew that when she was this moody that she usually didn't want anyone to touch her.

Pea stared at the house and decided that if Trey didn't come out in the next ten minutes, she was going in no matter what either of them said.

Just as she was thinking that, she saw Trey climb out of the window carrying a small box and once more treading lightly on the remainder of the back porch. Once down the steps he hurriedly walked to them and handed the box to Pea. Inside was her parent's wedding photograph which had sat on their dresser since she was a child, a few other lose photos, and the small doll she had clung to the last night she had been in the house.

"Alicia's doll. I can't believe it. How does that part of the house look? Can we go in? There's got to be more in there that we could save," she said quickly.

"Slow down," Trey said. "We need to hire a crew to come out and get everything that's even remotely salvageable. Then, you two can go through everything and see what you want to keep."

"We can have it taken to the barn at my place which is bigger and mostly empty. And you'll be safer there making any decisions than here."

Joseph shook his head and went around the car to get in the back with Mary.

"Let's go. We've got too much to do to stand here staring at this," he said.

By the time they got to Staunton, they had decided to let the women out at the mall to buy clothing for Mary and Joseph while the men went to see Trey's friend who ran a security business in town. They agreed to meet back at the food court in the mall in two hours.

For Pea, the two hours were interminable. Mary was listless and indecisive, unable to even decide what basics she and Joseph needed. At one point, Pea had been talking to her about buying Joseph shirts and trousers and she realized that Mary had wandered over into the baby department, standing there just staring at everything in confusion.

Pea left her there and just started gathering clothes, shoes, and anything else she could think of that her sister and Joseph might need. She wasn't happy having to be the practical one. She wanted to just go home as much as Mary did, but she knew that no matter what had happened, they had to have clothing. After she paid for the purchases, she made arrangements with the sales associate to have the packages held for pick-up until Trey and Joseph returned.

She then went back into the baby department and took her sister by the arm and said that she had to eat. Mary nodded that she was hungry as well. Mary had barely noticed how much time had passed, but when Pea placed a large plate of Chow Mein in front of her, Mary had devoured the food. It was only then that she began to shake off the depression that had taken her over.

"Good heavens, I just realized I haven't bought a thing," she said.

Pea laughed.

"Yeah, you did. About $1,200 worth of everything from underwear to shoes."

"No, seriously, I don't remember buying anything. I remember wandering off into the baby department and then coming down here," Mary said.

"I took the size lists and bought the stuff. If you hate it, well, too bad. You can return it and buy something else. But you still owe me $1,200," Pea said.

"Wow, I can't believe I just tuned out the last few hours. What in the world did you buy?"

Pea took a bite of a egg roll and smiled.

"Well, I thought neon colors for Joseph and all chartreuse and aubergine for you."

"Okay, I get it. I owe you. But please tell me you didn't buy aubergine for me. Please?"

They talked about the clothing for another half hour before Trey and Joseph found them. The table was littered with empty Chinese food containers.

"Oh, this was a smart move, leaving two pregnant women in a food court," Trey said as they sat down.

Pea wrinkled her nose at him and finished off the last crab puff.

"Was the security guy in?" Mary asked.

"Yes," Joseph said. "He's coming out to Trey's house first thing tomorrow to start getting everything installed. He said he thought he could get it all done by Wednesday morning. He's bringing a crew with him so the work will get done a lot faster."

"I told him I'd throw in a bonus if they could get it done by Wednesday," Trey said. "That should cover any delays. Or at least we can hope."

Trey started looking in the white and red cartons for any bits of leftovers, but found none.

"Well, I'm going to get food. Joseph, want something?" he said.

"Yeah, Chow Mein and an egg roll are fine."

As Trey headed over to the Chinese buffet, Pea called out for him to get her a few more crab puffs. He feigned shock, then smiled and continued on.

"Trey also hired a couple of armed guards. I thought that they might be a little much, but . . ." Joseph said.

"I don't know how we're going to feel about strangers around the place," Pea said.

"Well, I say the more, the better," Mary said. "I don't like the idea of you walking around with a .45 in the back of your pants."

Now both Pea and Joseph looked shocked.

"You've been walking around the house with a loaded gun? Do you know how dangerous that is?" Joseph said tersely.

Pea looked at her sister and frowned.

"Thanks, Ree. Thanks so much. Can you keep it down so Trey doesn't hear it along with everyone else here?" Pea said.

"How did you know about the gun? Did Thomas tell you?"

Joseph rolled his eyes, placed his hands flat on the table and looked up at the ceiling tiles as if pleading for some help in handling Pea.

"No, I didn't know Thomas knew. I saw the damn thing in your pants last night," Mary replied.

"You know, we've got to stop this shit about not telling each other stuff. All of us," Joseph said harshly to both of them. "You need to tell Trey about the gun. We've all got to agree that there will be no more secrets until this is over. These secrets could end up getting one of us killed."

He turned to Pea and repeated his warning to tell Trey about the gun.

"I'm serious, Pea. Tonight. And it wouldn't hurt to show the rest of us where it is. I don't think it's a good idea to have guns in the house, anyway."

Mary smiled a little sadly at her husband.

"Joseph, we grew up with guns. When you grow up in the country, well, it never hurts to know how to use one. Snakes, raccoons. Although, the only thing I ever shot were old cans behind the barn. But Pea, she's a natural. I always let her take care of the snakes."

"Oh, good god, yes, I understand that guns are legal where you grew up, but you're both pregnant. What happens if someone manages to wrestle the gun away from you?"

Mary looked to Pea and shrugged her shoulders.

"Joseph," Pea said, "Our father taught us the one most important lesson about guns – if you aim it at someone, you shoot. You don't wait to be overpowered. You don't have a gun out unless you're cleaning it or you're going to use it. I would think that the FBI had taught you the same thing."

Joseph's face reddened. He looked around for Trey before continuing to try to explain to Pea why having a gun in the house was a very bad idea.

"Yes, they did, but it's a different situation right now," he said in almost a whisper.

"We're just going to have to agree to disagree. I'll tell Trey, but I don't think he'll be too surprised since I've been practicing shooting out in the pasture. I'm not going to argue with you about the Second Amendment. I'll show you where the gun is and where Trey keeps his gun cabinet. Will that at least bring an end to this discussion?" Pea asked.

"Gun cabinet? Jesus Christ. Really? A gun cabinet?" he said and rolled his eyes again.

Pea sighed and then brightened up as Trey came back to the table carrying two trays of Chinese food.

"Ooo, crab puffs!" Pea said and dug into the carton. Trey smiled at her enthusiasm and brushed her hair from her eyes.

"I guess we know what you're going to be craving for the next few months," he said.

Joseph said nothing, but looked up at Mary from beneath his eyelids. Why did he think that Pea wasn't listening to a thing he said to her? Mary pursed her lips and reached out to place her hand on his shoulder. What can I say, she wanted to say, but she agreed with her sister on the gun issue. She just didn't want her sister carrying one around the house.

By the time that Thomas and Diana had made their way back to Trey's, another storm seemed to be forming to the west. Thomas had unloaded their suitcases and boxes onto the portico and then had driven his old Taurus around to the side of garage where it was both out of the way and couldn't be seen.

The others arrived shortly after and while the women carried in groceries, the men moved the bags of new clothing as well as Thomas and Diana's things upstairs to the bedroom suites they would be occupying.

When Thomas lugged the last of Diana's suitcases up the steep staircase and placed it at the end of the bed, he collapsed into a chair next to the dresser.

"What the hell do women carry in those things," he said to no one in particular, but both Joseph and Trey began laughing.

Joseph came to the bedroom door and grinned.

"When Mary and I went on our honeymoon, she had three bags as well as a large carry-on, all this compared to my one small carry-on. She paid several hundred dollars to check those extra bags, but it was our honeymoon and I didn't want to argue over it. So we get to Rome, get our bags and drag them to look for a taxi. Luckily, from that point on either the driver or the bellhop took care of them," he said.

"The big surprise came when Mary opened the suitcases. One entire suitcase was full of nothing but shoes! And we were in one of the best places on Earth to find beautiful, handcrafted shoes! When I asked her why she had to bring so many, she said she needed them for all of her clothes. I tell you, if you can solve the mystery of women and their shoes, you might just solve the mystery of the universe."

Trey had joined Joseph at the doorway during his recitation of the honeymoon story and the three men shook their heads and just laughed.

Downstairs, Pea called for them that supper was ready and to come and eat.

Joseph and Trey sighed together.

"What?" Thomas asked.

"Just plan on lots of food if you and Diana ever decide to have a baby. Not that these women were ever delicate birds about food, but it seems to be the main focus of their attention now. We just ate two hours ago," Trey said.

"Well, I didn't and I'm hungry so I guess I'll just take your share," Thomas said.

Joseph smirked and looked away.

"You haven't asked what supper is," Trey said.

"What?" Thomas inquired apprehensively.

"Well, let's just say that you can have my whole share," Joseph said and headed down the stairs.

"How bad could it be? It's food," Thomas said as he followed them down the staircase and they headed into the dining room.

.

Chapter Thirty

Doug was unhappy that the house had not burned completely. Leave it to Tim to do a half-ass job of getting the amount of gasoline they needed. By the time they had soaked the kitchen and living room, the containers were empty. He was so pissed at Tim right now that he wanted to drive to Tim's house and put a bullet in the head of Tim and his whole damn family of idiots, especially that bitch Tim had married who always whined whenever Doug showed up. It was so much easier when they were younger and were just fucking around with any girl they could find.

But no, Tim had to get married and try to look respectable. The fact that he was a deputy was such a joke. Doug wondered how many people would be stupid enough to think that they could hide being a serial killer by being a policeman. Probably only that asshole Tim, he thought.

Neither man realized that they were nearing the end of their friendship. They had little, if any respect for one another and if not for the hunts, they would have parted ways years ago. The hunts were the only thing that kept them attached and Tim was getting damned tired of that.

He thought burning the Taliaferro home was a colossal blunder on their part. Since they didn't know that Mr. Dickson was living in the barn and that he had seen Doug's blue Ford, they still didn't know that they were even closer to being caught. But Tim felt something in his gut that he had never really felt before - real fear. He knew they were in trouble and that Doug was spiraling out of control. He also saw the murderous looks that Doug had thrown at him and he was almost as afraid of Doug as he was of getting caught. Either way, he thought, it had to stop.

Doug called him from Charleston to find out what the police were saying about the Taliaferro house fire. Tim told him that they'd heard next to nothing about it up there. They were just too far from Lewisburg to have heard much about a house fire, even if arson were suspected, he said.

"We've got to figure out our next step," Doug said. "They may know more than we think. We're got to find out where they're staying. Maybe if we took one of them, we could lure the others over to the mountain. Or, we could pick them off one at a time, but I think that might throw up some flags. What do you think?"

Tim held the phone next to his ear, his expression emotionless. He wanted to scream into the phone at Doug that he was the idiot, but the office was between shift changes and was full of people. All he could do was nod his head and pretend to write on the yellow legal pad in front of him.

"Sir, I'm not sure if there's anything we can do about that," he said to Doug.

"What the fuck, can't you talk right now? Listen asshole, we've got to take care of these people before things get worse!" Doug yelled on the other end of the telephone.

"Sir, I'll check out the situation and get back to you. Give me a day or so and I'll get back to you," Tim said and hung up the phone.

In Charleston, Doug sat staring at the cheap cell phone. What the fuck? Did that asshole just hang up on him? Oh no, that was not going to happen. He was the one who decided, not Barney Fife.

He dialed Tim's cell phone rather than his office number and waited for Tim to answer, but instead all he heard was a recorded message instructing him to leave a message at the beep and if it were an emergency, the caller should dial 911.

"Dial 911?" Doug said to the empty apartment. Outside, the sky was turning grey as a storm moved in. The light in the apartment dimmed and he turned on the table light next to his sofa.

Oh, this bastard was going to pay when this was all over. He couldn't do anything until they took care of the Taliaferro problem. He needed Tim to help him. He couldn't dispose of the bodies alone. But oh, when they were done. Then he'd get rid of Tim somehow, too. He just had to be smart about it. Tim would require the most careful planning than anyone else. But he would do it. In fact, he was beginning to enjoy thinking of the different ways he could get rid of Tim.

Maybe one of those Taliaferro women would be the key. He could save one of them for last. Tim couldn't stay away from pussy like that, he thought. Yeah, that might be one way to get rid of him and one of the bitches at the same time.

At the office, Tim got up from his desk and told the dispatcher that he had gotten called out on a neighbor dispute.

"Yeah, two senile old bastards throwing garbage in one another's yard. The one who called sounded like he was on the edge of doing something stupid. I'd better go over and try to make peace between them," he told the dispatcher.

"Oh, and if I can get them straightened out, then I'll probably head on home since my shift is almost over. Damn nuisance calls always come in at the end of the shift."

The dispatcher laughed and said, "Ain't that the truth. See you tomorrow, Tim. Oh, wait, are your boys ready for their first game with Beckley Friday night? I've got a little something riding on it."

Tim smiled. "They are 100% ready. Looks like it's a sure thing,"

"All I needed to know," the dispatcher said and waved Tim on his way.

Of course, there was no neighbor dispute and the last place Tim wanted to go was home right now. He decided to drive up to Thurman and park the cruiser up on the hill where he could smoke and think about the problem he had with Doug.

The last of the day's whitewater groups were still downstream a bit and Amtrak didn't come through until later that evening. Labor Day weekend was coming up and Doug never liked to hunt then. Too many people, he'd said and Tim had to agree with him on that. After Bridge Day in mid-October there were few people on the river except the hard-core people. They always had a small window to hunt before the weather changed. Still enough foliage to disguise their activities, but at least some people left to hunt.

Since they had always taken their victims high in the mountains to the ridgeline in the last decade, few people came up there, even in hunting season. And there were plenty of caves and sinkholes to dispose of bodies.

Tim marveled that that only a small number of bodies had been found, and those were from the days when they were younger and less experienced.

He was surprised when the one man's body had washed up on the river bank near the Park center below Hinton. They thought they had thrown that body down a deep hole halfway up the mountain. He wondered if the heavy June rains had had anything to do with it. Bad luck, he thought.

He almost felt sorry for those Taliaferro women. Why didn't they just leave well enough alone? He was about to quit anyway. His body had too many aches to be rolling around on the ground now. Oh, the hunt was always fun, but this didn't feel like hunting. It just didn't feel right.

Tim drove over to Lewisburg in Greenbrier County the next day to find out what he could. It wasn't his brightest idea, but he didn't know what else to do to appease Doug's crazy obsession with the Taliaferro women. As he took the exit to Lewisburg, he noticed how much building was going on there. If I-64 had only taken a route further north, he thought. Of course, it still was smaller compared to the explosive growth in Beckley. In ten years, Beckley had grown so fast that every exit had fast food restaurants and new motels and shops. Of course, that growth had been disastrous to downtown Beckley, just as it had been in many small towns across the country. One big box store and the downtowns started their slow and eventual decline.

Gladstone Gap was no different. Being so close to Beckley, people just drove there to shop. The only surviving businesses were the IGA, a dollar store and a couple of convenience stores. Tim remembered when they were called service stations and his dad had called them filling stations. Tim used to catch the school bus in front of the old Esso station. Gas had been 35 cents a gallon when he was in junior high. Who would have thought that it would get to be almost four dollars a gallon and you would have to pay first and then pump it yourself?

The Gap hadn't been a bad place to live then, with a small downtown street that had a real restaurant, a bakery, a dime store, an old theater built in the 1920s, and the ever present building that overwhelmed every coal town – the company store.

He had loved the company store. Three floors that sold everything from groceries and hardware to shoes and furniture. It had had a real soda fountain where he used to buy comic books when he was little.

But, Lewisburg had a downtown that had somehow survived, even with the big box stores near the exit. He supposed it was their creative use of the history of the town to lure tourists that saved it. It was pretty, he thought. Clean, like one of those made-up places that you see on TV.

His first stop was at the sheriff's office next to the courthouse. He had made up a story about some meth labs up on the border of Greenbrier, Nicholas, and Gladstone counties. He gossiped a bit with the dispatcher and glad-handed it with a few of the older deputies he'd known for a long time, but got no information.

His second stop was the one he regretted. He drove up to the Taliaferro farm, not expecting anyone to be there. He was genuinely surprised when Mr. Dickson appeared from behind the barn after he had parked and was looking around the house.

"Can I help you son?" Dickson had said and had scared him so badly that he had actually jumped.

"Sorry, bout that. Didn't mean to startle you."

Tim shook it off and introduced himself and once again trotted out a story about meth labs and arson for the old man as he had for the local deputies.

"Gladstone. Now that's a might small county for this state, wedged up between Nicholas and Greenbrier, with only the river and some old coal camps left there. Though I do hear you have a might fine football team this year. Could go all the way to the state championship," Dickson said.

Tim grinned as he always did when he had the pleasure to mention that his sons were stars on that team.

"Well, if that don't beat nothing. I'd bet you're a pretty proud father," Dickson replied and smiled.

Tim bobbed his head happily and then looked over at the house and sobered up seeing what he and Doug had done.

"So, no meth involved in this?" he asked.

"Lord, no. The misses would never be involved in something like that. And with both of them pregnant, I just thank God they weren't home when it happened. When I saw that blue Ford drive away, I knew something wasn't right, so I checked the house and saw the fire. Guess it could have been worse," Dickson said.

Two things sent chills down Tim's spine. The first was hearing that the women were pregnant. That was out of his league. He would not hurt a pregnant woman. He remembered Tiff's struggles and helplessness. No, he would refuse to help Doug hurt a pregnant woman. Absolutely not.

But the second item was what scared him the most. The old man had seen them drive away in Doug's truck. Ah, shit.

"Did you tell the deputies here about it? Could you tell who might have been in it?

Dickson nodded yes, but then said that between the falling darkness and the storm, that he couldn't see much more than the fact that it was a blue Ford.

"Ford always paints their name big on their tailgates or at least they used to. This was an older one. That's how I knew it was a Ford and not another make," he laughed.

Tim stood with his hands hooked on his belt and looked around the farm. He did not want this on his hands.

"Anyone else here besides you who might have seen something?"

Dickson shook his head. "No, I've been here since the two misses' grandfather had the place. You know they lost their parents over 10 years ago. Just been them since then, well, except for that man Miss Pea married after her parents died. But that's a story that's . . ."

"That's what?" Tim asked.

"Too sad to talk about. Deputy, if you don't mind, I've got some chores to take care of before I head up the road. Hope you don't mind."

"No, no, I need to get back home myself. Sorry to bother you."

He got in the car and started it and Mr. Dickson headed into the barn. He wanted to call his cousin to see if he could join him for prayer meeting tonight. He never heard Tim follow him through the barn, never saw Tim pick up the board, and wouldn't have turned around had not Alicia's Palomino started up a ruckus in her stall. That was when Tim saw a very angry red haired child standing in the middle of the stable pointing at him and he lost his nerve, dropped the board, and ran.

Dickson never saw Tim. Tim had run away before he'd had time to come back into the main part of the barn. It was the only thing that saved Dickson's life. Dickson had headed to the horse stall, but by then the horse had calmed down.

As Tim drove away, he thought that killing the old man probably wouldn't have done any good, except for the fear in his gut that was urging him to remove the old man from the situation. Where the hell had the little girl come from? Dickson had said that no one else was there. She had scared the shit out of him and he wondered if she would tell Dickson. He had no idea that Dickson did not see the child or hear him drive away.

And Mr. Dickson had no idea how close he had been to death.

Chapter Thirty-One

The next morning, Thomas woke to voices outside the bedroom door and listened carefully before moving. It was then that he untangled himself from Diana and got up and dressed for work. It was just after 7 a.m. and it sounded like workmen were doing something out in the hall.

He opened and shut the door quietly and saw three men at the far end of the other wing of the house measuring the length and width of the window. When they saw him, they waved and he waved back and headed downstairs to the kitchen to get some coffee before leaving for Staunton.

Trey was sitting at the kitchen table with the *Staunton Dispatch* and drinking a cup of coffee himself. Thomas nodded good morning to him and poured himself a cup and stood at the sink as he watched a group of men outside working as well.

"I know. They're really here early, but I wanted everything done by tomorrow morning and so they're all eager to get the bonus I promised them. Sorry if they woke you," Trey said.

Thomas shook his head and said that he had to get up to go to work anyway.

"Are you sure it's safe?" Trey asked.

"If it's not safe for me to be in a room full of welders, then it's not safe anywhere," Thomas said and laughed. "Besides, I get there when they do and I leave when they do. It'll be okay."

Trey smiled and rubbed his eyes.

"Long night?" Thomas asked.

"Yeah, Pea hardly slept last night. I'm surprised her piano playing didn't keep you up. I can't sleep when she's like this, so I just wait for her to tire herself out and come to bed. Some nights, like last night, are longer than others."

"I didn't hear a thing. Both Diana and I fell asleep as soon as our heads hit the pillows. Does Pea do this a lot?"

Trey folded the paper up and sat it down on the table next to his cup.

"Yeah, yeah. I don't know what to do. She's been doing it ever since last year. I know it's a coping mechanism for her, but . . . Did you know she won't play in front of other people, including me?"

Thomas raised his eyebrows in surprise.

"No, I didn't, but come to think of it, I've never heard her play.

"She's really good. Sometimes I listen from the landing when she thinks I'm asleep. Someone told her she couldn't play well and was an embarrassment when she did play so she just stopped."

"I think I know who that 'someone' probably was. Trey, I don't know what to tell you. She's buried some things real deep. I don't know what anyone can do to take that pain away."

Thomas looked at his watch and drained his cup of coffee.

"I've got to head out or I'll be late. See you guys this evening," he said and headed out the back door.

It was about an hour later that the rest of the household made their way to the kitchen. Each looking hungry and tired except for Diana who had enjoyed their health food feast from the previous night. She was also the only one to steer away from the coffee pot except for Mary. Pea poured herself a cup and ignored Trey.

"Trey, I hope this won't be even more of an inconvenience, but I need somewhere to work on my dissertation. Somewhere that I could spread out and work alone," Diana said.

Trey leaned back in the chair and thought for a few moments.

"Sure, hmm, the old nursery would probably be the best place."

"Lots of tables, including a good sized turn of the century oak desk. I don't think we'll be using that room, though the security people might be in and out of there today," he replied.

Diana jumped up and bounded up the stairs to start moving her boxes of papers and books into the room. When she saw the amount of room she would have she almost whooped with excitement.

Pea kissed Trey. "That was sweet."

Trey frowned at her and pointed at the coffee as Mary made toast and started making breakfast.

"Okay, okay," Pea said and went to pour the coffee into the sink.

"Happy now?" she said sarcastically.

Mary quizzically looked over at her from the stove.

The minute Pea saw the egg in the pan, she ran from the room to the downstairs restroom.

"Oops," Mary said to Trey. "I forgot they made her sick when she was pregnant."

Trey frowned again.

"At least you knew. I swear, Mary, she's driving me crazy. She won't talk about the pregnancy, about how she feels, about Alicia, about this mess. About anything," he said.

"I know this is probably a stupid question, but have you asked her?"

"Yes, of course. I've been trying to get her to talk to me or anyone since last year. She just changes the subject or leaves the room."

Mary finished her egg and put it on the slice of toast and joined Trey at the table. She looked thoughtful as she ate.

"I wouldn't ask you," Trey said, "But I'm at a loss as how to help her. And you know as well as I do that she needs help with this."

Mary nodded and wiped her mouth.

"Yeah, I heard the piano last night. Always a bad sign."

"A bad sign?" Trey asked.

"Yes, it started when our parents died. Then, when Alicia died and Manley left her, I'd hear her playing at the farm when I came in sometimes from school. She never slept. She took all that guilt inside and it was if playing the piano was the only outlet she had for all that pain she had. It was a really bad time."

"I sneaked downstairs one time then and watched her as she played. It was unnerving. I wanted to go to her, but I didn't. I once even mentioned hearing the piano and told me I must have been dreaming and then, as you said, she changed the subject," Mary continued.

Trey leaned back in the chair again and held the coffee mug next to his mouth.

"I've never gone downstairs when she's playing," he said.

Mary shrugged and wiped up the last of the egg yolk with the toast.

"Maybe you should," she said. "Besides she has to sleep. She's pregnant and this could be too much strain on her. I don't know. I just would try to stop it and I don't think she'll listen to anyone but you. Though, you may have to be hard about it. She's slippery about the nightly piano playing."

"Did she play much before Manley," he asked.

"God, did she play. She played for hours. At least until he embarrassed her at a dinner party one night by telling her that she was boring their guests. Actually, he was the bore. We all felt very sad for her, but she just smiled and never played for anyone again."

"After everything fell apart, the piano became her refuge, her safe place. If you hadn't had a piano, I doubt that she'd ever left the farm."

"Maybe if we could get her to play for us," he said, thinking about what it might accomplish.

"What if we all came downstairs one night and just sat down? If she gets that involved in the music when she plays, she might not notice us since her back would be to the rest of the room," he mused.

"I don't know, Trey. Her guard is really up right now. What if it backfires? Or what if she just leaves and doesn't even speak? What you're describing almost sounds like an intervention and interventions have been known to sometimes go spectacularly bad, if you remember."

He touched her hand.

"Would you just try one night? Tonight, if she plays? Please? You could ask Joseph and I'll speak with Thomas and Diana," he asked.

She patted his hand and stood to put her dishes in the sink and empty the dishwasher from the night before.

"I'll try. I can't guarantee anything, but I'll try," she said and continued putting away the clean dishes.

Trey left her there and went in search of Pea. He had one other problem that was weighing heavily on him about Pea. He wanted to marry her, but he was really afraid to bring that topic up yet. Maybe in a month or so, he thought. Maybe when this New River mess was over.

He went to the solarium first, but she wasn't there. He then went upstairs to see if she was helping Diana, but she wasn't there either. He took the time to talk to Diana about later that night before going outside to look for her. Diana agreed and said she'd mention it to Thomas, though she, too, voiced her doubts about it as Mary had. He thanked her and went back downstairs to continue his search.

By then, Mary was finished in the kitchen and was carrying a load of towels from the laundry room. She looked as if she were having trouble maneuvering it and herself through the door.

He took it from her and walked back upstairs again to show her where the upstairs linen pantry was. She thanked him and began to put the towels away.

"You know, you don't have to do that. Mrs. Franklin always does it," he said.

"Mrs. Franklin doesn't usually have a house full of people either. You'll either have to let me help or pay her more or even worse, watch me make Joseph crazy from my boredom," she replied.

"Oh, well, okay, if you want. I'll talk to Mrs. Franklin to avoid any domestic disputes."

Mary laughed at him as she carefully placed the folded towels on the shelves.

"Did you find Pea?"

"No, I keep getting sidetracked. I'd better get back to finding her."

"That would probably be a good idea. Now, if you don't mind, I'm going to get my and Joseph's dirty clothes and wash them. Everyone else can deal with theirs," she said and picked up the basket, heading for her bedroom.

Joseph was lying on the bed his arm thrown over his forehead and the curtains closed when she entered the room. He was so absolutely motionless that it frightened her until he quietly spoke.

"Migraine. Probably from drinking. Sorry," he said in a whisper.

Mary gently sat down on the bed next to him. He had been having the migraines since the heart attack. The doctors had told him that they might be a side effect of the nitro tablets he always carried in his pocket.

"Were you having chest pains?" she whispered back to him.

"No. I haven't taken any nitro in a few months. This just came on fast."

He moved his arm from across his eyes and pulled her down next to him, with the baby nestled between their bodies.

"Do you want something? Something for the pain?"

"No, it's starting to ease up. The dark and the quiet have helped."

He kissed the top of her head.

"Your being here helps, too."

"Well, since we're going to be up later tonight, maybe I'll take a nap with you," she said.

"Why would we be up late tonight?"

She explained Trey's plan to him and he groaned.

"Now that makes my head start to hurt again."

"I'm sorry," she said. "Don't think about anything right now. Just sleep for a while. I'll stay here with you and sleep, too.

She lifted her face to his and lightly kissed his lips.

"I love you, too," she said.

Trey finally gave up on searching the house and went out the front door only to find Pea sitting on the steps with the dogs on each side of her. When the dogs heard the door open, they ran around him and scrambled into the house. Pea didn't move or turn to face him. He walked over to her and sat down beside her. She was watching the security people put in the last of the cameras.

"I don't like the cameras," she said. "I feel like I'm in one of those cheap horror movies where everything is hard to see and all the cameras do is record people screaming and falling down."

"Those cameras are hooked into a central monitoring station. There are also guards on duty 24/7 in a van behind the garage," he said.

She whipped her head around to face him.

"What guards?"

"The ones you'll never see or know are here," he said.

"Trey, I don't like this. This is awful. I feel trapped here. What about shopping or leaving the farm? Can I do that?"

"Yeah, of course. But can't we be careful? You wouldn't have known about the guards if I hadn't said something."

She stood up in front of him.

"Trey, I made myself a prisoner for two years. I don't want to be a prisoner again. Can you understand that?"

He took her hand in his and held it close to his heart.

"I love you and just want you to be safe. I don't want to trap you and make you do things you don't want to do. It's not a prison. Besides, we should have put the security system in six months ago. I've just never had any problems out here or I would have done it sooner."

"I guess you're right. But I'll still be glad when we have the place to ourselves again," she said.

Trey laughed at that and patted her small protruding belly.

"That's not likely to happen again for a long, long time. This little guy is going to probably change everything. And if we're lucky, maybe in another few years, he'll have someone else to help drive us crazy.

Now she laughed and sat down on his lap.

"Another one? Seriously? Hmm. Well. It could happen, but we'd better get legal before this one comes along."

Trey was stunned. Had she just mentioned marriage?

"Of course, I'd rather we just went down to the courthouse than go through the whole wedding thing," she said, draping her arms around his neck.

"Are you serious, Pea? Is that what you want?"

"Well, I thought that with the baby . . . Don't you want to?" she asked.

"God yes," he said and hugged her close to him.

"You've just never given any indication that you wanted to and I, I didn't want you to feel forced into it."

She kissed him and then realized that the security men were watching them.

"Can we go inside? Maybe go upstairs into a room where there isn't a camera. Maybe celebrate?"

"Not a problem," he said as he stood, grabbed her hand and led her into the house.

Neither of them noticed the men putting up the camera laughing as they entered the house.

Chapter Thirty-Two

Tim called Doug from the road as he drove back to Gladstone County. He conveniently left out the part about the little girl. In hindsight, he would regret that decision, but for now he couldn't imagine that it made any difference.

"Why didn't you 'fix' the problem with the man," Doug shouted into the phone, spittle flying from his mouth. He wished Tim were standing there so he could spit on him.

"Doug, the old man's almost blind and deaf. He didn't see enough the give the sheriff's department any information. They think it was a bunch of kids breaking into houses and burning any evidence they might leave behind," Tim said.

"Yeah, but," Doug started to say, but Tim interrupted him.

"Doug, think about it. If the old man disappeared or was found dead after the house burned, he might just be the reason the sheriff needs to start really investigating. Right now, they're not giving it much thought. Better to leave best alone.

Doug still didn't like this. The old man saw his truck, not Tim's. His. The old man had to die. Tim was just going to have to understand that.

"Tim, this whole thing is out of control and you should be taking care of it. You're a fool if you think this won't come back and bite us both in the ass. Take care of the situation."

By now Doug was almost screaming as he paced the length of the hotel room he had moved into. He didn't want Tim to know that he'd lost yet another job and had no place to live other than a room at the Days-eze Inn.

"Doug, I'll talk to you later. I'm moving into a dead zone. Calm down and think about I've said. It makes more sense for both of us. Bye," Tim said and closed his cell.

Motherfucker, Doug yelled. He had a room at the end of the motel and no one occupied the room on the other side to hear his outburst.

It was so fucking easy for Tim, living in his own home with his bitch and sons and a job that he could retire from with a pension. He got all the good things and I just get shit, Doug thought.

Doug threw himself onto the old bed and tried to find something to watch on the four or five channels the TV would pick up.

How did he get to such a low point in his life, he asked himself. He was the one with all the promise, the scholarship, the brains. But, no, Tim the idiot, got stuff because he was willing to settle in the Gap.

Doug had decided that the fat bastard at Tom's Printing, who'd owned the print shop, didn't like the fact that the customers liked him better. He refused to see the truth that he was fired because he never showed up for work on time or that the customers he thought who liked him actually started coming in on days when he was off.

His persistent flirting and sexual comments with the younger women had gotten so bad that the women complained to their bosses and asked to go somewhere else. Eventually, that got back to Doug's boss and that ended his run at Tom's Printing.

He would not admit that his own ego had landed him in this motel room with dark fake wood paneling and a broken down bed with sheets that hadn't been changed since the last occupant had left.

When he lost the job, Doug was dead broke. He had had to either sell the contents of his apartment in Kanawha City of just leave the rest for the owner to clean out. He packed his clothes and a few boxes with his old football trophies and some other mementoes he had collected from a victim every so often and put them in his pickup and moved to the Days-eze Inn between Kanawha City and Marmet. He could hear the constant traffic on the turnpike and the blinking Daisy at the front of the motel only lit up in parts. The curtains were so thin that that light from the sign was the most irritating thing about the place.

Of course, he kept the lights and the TV on all the time now and his rage was fueled by his continual intake of caffeine and drugs to keep sleep at bay. Every time he closed his eyes and dozed off, he would immediately start having that same damned dream about the dead people and that fucking woman and the little girl. He would wake up in a cold sweat and would grab his dad's handgun and wave it around the room as if the people in his dream were in the room with him.

All this was that bitch's fault, he decided. If he could sleep, he wouldn't be living in this shithole that stank like urine and beer. He was going to do something and Tim was going to help him or by god, he'd take out Tim's whole family and Tim with them. Then he'd head for Florida and get the fuck away from all of it. Start over. Do anything but what he was doing. He decided that he sure as shit didn't need Tim to hunt with anymore.

If Tim had known how unstable Doug had become, he might have taken things into his hands then and there. He knew he couldn't allow Doug to live much longer. Doug would tell the state troopers about everything they'd done. It would ruin his life. Just like Doug wanting to kill the old man. It was crazy shit. Tim wondered why he had ever agreed to help Doug burn the Taliaferro Farm.

The partnership, their friendship was over. Unknown to either of them, it was the only thing that they both had decided.

Chapter Thirty-Three

At Trey's house that night, after everyone had retired for the evening, they each waited for the sounds of the piano to drift upstairs. They were almost all asleep when they heard the sounds of music from the living room.

Trey decided he would let the others go downstairs first. They had planned to make their way to the room one by one, with Mary going first, followed by Thomas, then Joseph, Diana and finally Trey.

Mary still thought it was a stupid idea, but she saw how desperate Trey was and in an act of pity, had agreed to help. The others felt they had little choice but to follow Mary and Trey's lead on this.

Mary slowly walked down the staircase, but instead of going into the living room, she went to the kitchen first and poured a glass of orange juice to take with her. She quietly entered the room and sat down in the armchair farthest from the piano.

But Pea had seen her reflection in the mirror above the mantel as Mary entered the room and she stopped and turned to her sister.

"Don't stop. I was thirsty and couldn't sleep. The music seems to calm the baby down. Play some more," Mary said.

Pea turned her back to Mary and paused. Mary held her breath, wondering if Pea would start to play again or would leave. To Mary's surprise, she started to play Brahms' Lullabye softly. Mary sipped the juice and smiled as she closed her eyes and listened to her sister play again for her for the first time in years.

When Thomas, Joseph, and Diana entered the room and sat down quietly, Pea still continued to play. They silently sat in the room and listened as Pea went back and forth from classical to more modern pieces, all them having one constant – they were all soothing and soft. Joseph was sitting in the floor in front of Mary with his head lying in her lap next to their unborn child when Trey finally had the courage to leave the landing and come into the room.

And that was when Pea stopped. She turned to them and smiled and said she was sleepy, kissed Trey good night in the doorway and went upstairs.

Once she was out of earshot, they began to whisper together. Mary was thrilled that Pea had allowed them all to hear her play. But, when she looked up at Trey, she saw the disappointment in his eyes. She lifted her hand from Joseph's head and held it up to Trey.

"It's a start, Trey. Really. It was a good start," she said.

"Yeah, until I came into the room," he said and squeezed her hand and released it.

Joseph got up from the floor and moved to the sofa.

"Trey, she's got a lot of baggage. You could say she opened the first suitcase tonight. I'd say that's a major start," he said.

Trey put his hand in his pockets and shrugged.

"I'm just tired of trying to convince her I'm not going to turn into Manley."

Thomas shook his head.

"I don't think she thinks that. I think she's more afraid of failing you than you hurting her," he said.

"Is this the first time she's played for anyone since she was married to him," Diana asked.

Mary nodded, but didn't elaborate.

"Let's just say he was a monster in more ways than one. Now, I'm going up, too. Joseph, come with me?" she asked and they both went upstairs, later followed by Thomas and Diana who tried to console Trey a little more before they left as well.

When Trey entered their bedroom, Pea was already in bed with the lights out. Only the starlight from outside lit the room and he let his eyes adjust to the darkness before he undressed and crawled into bed next to her. Her back was to him and he guessed that she was either asleep or didn't want to talk. So, he was very surprised to hear her voice in the dark room.

"I came up because I was tired. Not because you came down," she said, but she still did not turn to him.

He moved close to her and spooned up next to her, taking her hand in his and kissing her shoulder. Her hair seemed to be the only thing that the starlight lit in the room. She held tightly on to his hand and drifted off into an easy, dreamless sleep. He fell asleep about ten minutes later listening to her even, soft breathing. The last thing he thought before falling asleep was that Mary was right. It was a start, a good start.

Trey was already out in the field cutting the last of the hay for the round bales before Thomas left for work that morning. They all had their tasks to do except for Joseph who was beginning to feel the need to do something to take the burden of worry and boredom from his head.

When he told Mary that he was driving into Staunton that morning to run a few errands, he thought she was going to have one of Pea's infamous panic attacks. She said to him that she didn't understand why he needed to go out. She pleaded with him that it might be too dangerous for him. And then she finally pulled from her deck of excuses what she thought would be her trump card – what if something happened to her and she needed him there?

He was so calm and so resistant to her pleas that she began to lose her temper with him.

"You just don't care. It doesn't matter about the baby or me," she said.

"Guilt will not work, my dear. My Italian grandmother can beat you at that. I've been hearing every single guilt ridden sentence since I was a boy."

"Mary, I can't stand just sitting around here. I'm going to go buy a computer. I've been thinking about starting a new book. I'm going to also buy a printer and whatever other supplies I need. And if you're a sweet wife and try to understand, I might bring you some pastries from the Depot," he said and headed toward the back door.

"That is so condescending, thinking that you can ease my concern with pastries!" she said. As he walked to their car, she ran to the back screen door.

"At least, make sure they're blueberry or apple," she called out. He nodded and smiled as he got in the car and drove off. "Please let him be safe," she whispered and went into the solarium where Pea was potting plants.

"You and Diana should join forces with all these plants," Mary said.

Pea laughed at that. "I think Diana's light years ahead of my little projects. Did you know her dissertation is on western Virginia plant species and that she's found at least four that were previously thought to be extinct?"

Mary stretched out on the wicker sofa.

"I feel so useless. I was supposed to be working or at least doing a clerkship by now. But instead, I'm here watching everyone else. Even Joseph's gone to buy a new computer to start a new book. All I do is housework," she said.

"Well, aren't you a little whiny person this morning," Pea said. "I think this has more to do with your third trimester and what I used to call "the endless wait" than it does with your going back to work."

Mary sat up and leaned her head on her arms on the back of the sofa, watching her sister carefully cutting Iris corms to plant at the back of the house.

"Did you feel this way with Alicia?" she asked.

"You have no idea. It was horrible. Manley was never home. He took my keys. And every time I stood up too fast, I would become faint."

"He also wouldn't eat anything I cooked and always brought food from the hotel home with him in what really looked like doggie bags of whatever he had already eaten there."

"Alicia kicked me constantly. I don't think she ever slept much so I couldn't sleep, either."

She paused a moment and took a deep breath.

"By the last month, Manley made me move into the daybed in her room because he said he couldn't stand having to sleep next to me and my 'fat' belly," Pea said.

Pea now had Mary's full attention. This was more than Pea had told Mary about Manley and her marriage than she had ever said before.

"He really said that?" Mary asked softly.

Pea nodded again.

"I got used to it. I became more absorbed with Alicia and started throwing the leftovers he brought home out. But that's when he started . . ." she stopped for a moment and looked around the room as if afraid to continue.

"When he started what, Pea?"

Pea turned away from her sister and wrapped the cut Iris corms in wet newspapers.

"It was the first time he hit me, Ree," she said and gathered the bundles and went out the back door of the solarium to the prepared bed she had dug for the Irises.

Mary didn't follow her. She didn't quite know what to do. She had always thought that there might have been some kind of physical abuse, but she hadn't thought he would have done it while Pea was pregnant. She wanted to cry for her sister.

No wonder Pea didn't leave Alicia with him. She was surprised that Pea had had the strength to finally offer him the money to get him out of her life. Mary shivered and wondered for the first time if he had tortured her the way he had tortured his victims. Pea had said after Manley died that she realized that Alicia was his 13th victim, but Mary thought that maybe Pea, herself, was also his victim.

Had it not been for meeting Trey that day in the bookstore, she might never have gotten the nerve to leave the farm again. So much weight of so much disappointment had almost crippled her. Mary wondered if she could have made it through it, but shook the thought off immediately. Joseph was nothing like that and would never treat her that way. If she was sure of nothing in this world, she was sure of his love and kindness.

She could see Pea outside the glass windows, kneeling on the ground and every now and then wiping her hand with her gloved hand. The few tears that fell were just enough to streak her face with dirt. She didn't think that Pea would want Trey to see her upset so she went into the downstairs laundry room and grabbed a face cloth from the dryer and moistened it.

She went back to the solarium just as Pea was reentering from the back door.

"Here. Wipe your face. You've got dirt smeared on your cheeks."

Pea looked at her sister in an unspoken moment of understanding and then took the damp cloth and wiped her face clean. Mary knew Pea wasn't going to talk about it anymore, but that was ok. Like the piano last night, it was a start. As Joseph as said then, this was another suitcase opened.

As Mary headed out of the solarium to get the rest of the towels out of the dryer, she heard her sister say, "Ree, thank you."

Mary didn't respond to her sister's soft thank you. She just kept walking and said as she left that the laundry waited for no one.

Trey came in from the field around lunch. Pea had fixed him a salad and had made a fresh pitcher of sweet tea. As he sat at the table, she thought of how he looked now compared to the man in the black suit and Burberry coat.

He felt her stare and looked confused for a moment.

"What do I have something on my face?"

She walked over to him and lowered herself to face him directly.

"No, I was just thinking of how you're nothing like the man I first met and yet exactly like him."

He leaned over and kissed her forehead.

"I yam what I yam," he said and drank half of the glass of iced tea in one swallow.

"That is the worst Popeye imitation."

She started to stand and found her knees had gotten stiff while squatting next to him.

"Help me stand up, please."

"What me? Help?" He looked around the room as if she were talking to someone else.

"Stop that," she said and punched his shoulder.

"Oww. Joseph was right. You and your sister need to stop playing punch buggy with the men who love you."

"Then help me stand up! My knees are locked up. I spent the morning planting irises outside the solarium and now my legs aren't cooperating."

He lifted her up and onto his lap.

"Remember what we talked about yesterday?"

She pursed her lips and pretended to think about what they had said.

"Remind me. Was it your plan to have everyone come down to listen to me playing the piano? Or maybe getting the security guys out of here?

He tilted his head and sighed.

"So you figured it out about the piano?"

"Duh. When everyone in the house comes down at two in the morning, well, let's say I could see what was going on."

"Sorry. It was the only way I could think of to get you to play for other people. You do know you're very good at it, don't you."

"I'm good at a lot of things, but I appreciate what you did. I felt good playing last night. I wasn't embarrassed. But you still haven't reminded me what you were talking about," she said, running her fingertip across his mouth.

"Oh, that. Yeah. But sitting on my lap and doing that is starting to distract me.

"Well, can't do that. You still have a lot of hay making to do," she said as she stood and started to move away from him.

He grabbed her hand and pulled her back onto his lap.

"We can go make hay while the sun shines," he said and kissed her slowly and deeply.

"Okay. I'm going back to the solarium and you're going back to the field. Otherwise, we're liable to get caught by one of the many people you have here in the house now. No making hay when someone could walk in at any moment."

He groaned and stood with her as he drank the rest of the tea.

"You are no fun."

"Try me tonight. I may be more agreeable then."

She laughed as he headed out the door and back to the field, the whole time mumbling under his breath. When she saw that he was far enough away, she frowned. She had known exactly what he was trying to bring up when she had distracted him.

Although she had brought up the subject yesterday, now she asked herself silently if she were really ready to take this next step. She shuddered at the thought of being in a bad marriage again. Trey didn't seem to be able to be cruel, but then Manley hadn't either and he had been so horrible. She realized that only those poor women he had tortured could understand how much he had abused her.

Trey had never shown even the slightest inclination to be that way. And she did want their child to have a real father. She wondered if she were afraid that he would start to turn on her when she started to really show as Mary was showing now.

Joseph was so kind to her sister. Maybe a little overprotective, she thought, but she couldn't imagine him being cruel. But she also knew from her own experience that every marriage had its secrets.

"Yes, I know that better than anyone," she said to herself as she put the lunch dishes in the dishwasher.

She found Mary asleep on the wicker chaise in the solarium when she went back there to work on potting some spider plant babies. Her sister was sleeping well, with one hand resting on her stomach. She noticed that the baby sat low in her sister's belly and she inwardly smiled. A boy, if she believed the old wives' tale.

When she had been pregnant with Alicia, she had carried her high, like a small round basketball shoved up under her shirt. It wasn't till Alicia dropped into position for birth that her body shape had really changed.

Mary, on the other hand, was changing faster every day. Pea wondered if Mary could have gotten the dates wrong as she worked with the baby plants, placing three to each hanging basket.

Mary woke up and sat up slowly.

"How long have I been asleep?"

"I think about an hour and a half."

Mary stretched and then felt her bladder tighten.

"Hell, I can't sleep at night and now I'm always either eating or peeing," she said, standing to go to the downstairs restroom.

As she got to the door into the dining room, she stopped and asked if Joseph had returned.

"I don't think so. I haven't seen his car."

"I knew it was a bad idea his going out alone."

"Ree, he hasn't been gone that long. It takes almost 30 minutes just to drive into Staunton and he's been cooped up here for days. Let him enjoy his time out. He'll be alright and you keep forgetting that he's retired FBI. He'd notice if someone were following him."

"You're right, Pea. Oh, I have got to get to the bathroom," she said and rushed through the dining room toward the north wing of the house.

Chapter Thirty-Four

September passed quickly and by mid October, they had all settled into a routine at Trey's place. They watched as the green Shenandoah Mountains began their spectacular show of color that brought tourists from every direction.

The warm days cooled off and became shorter and sweaters and warmer clothing came out or were purchased in Joseph and Mary's case since they hadn't expected to be here so long. Pea purchased a few things, but knew that she could get by mostly on oversized sweaters and drawstring pants for a while.

Each of them continued their lives much as they had before the house in Greenbrier had burned. Thomas wanted to move back to his apartment, but the others had pled with him to stay and Diana had gotten her project so spread throughout the old nursery that she said she was at a point where she couldn't stop until she had everything ready to write. So, Thomas reluctantly agreed to stay.

Joseph had indeed begun a new book and Mary and Pea had overseen the last of the contents from their home being moved to Trey's empty barn where they slowly began the process of deciding what would be kept for the rebuilt farm house.

They had hired Michael Chalmers, the same architect from Charlottesville who had done the restoration of their home when their parents were living. He met them at the house one September morning after Labor Day.

"Damn shame," he said and shook his head. "And the police definitely determined it was arson?" He removed his camel hair coat and threw it in the open door of his black BMW and removed a pair of old Dickey coveralls, gloves, and boots. As he poked around the downstairs, using a small steel bar to prod at different beams, the women watched from the yard.

"I'm going to go see Alicia," Pea said. "Want to come?"

Mary nodded and slowly followed her sister around the barn. Trey, who was in Fredericksburg for the closing on the property there, had insisted that they bring the great danes with them for protection. The dogs followed the women, their noses alternately sniffing the air and the earth.

When they had first arrived at the farm and the sisters released the dogs from the back of Trey's Celica, the dogs had made a bee line for the back porch, only to suddenly stop at the top of the porch steps. One of them sniffed and then raised his snout and howled like a trapped animal. His sister nuzzled his neck and stared back at the women as if to ask where was home.

The dogs' sad howl brought tears to Mary's eyes and she pulled an old tissue from her navy jacket and daubed at the corner of her eyes.

"Hormones," was all she said and Pea grimaced, but refused to shed a tear over what those men had done to their family home. They would rebuild it and make new memories. I'll be damned if I'm letting anyone take anything from me again, she thought.

The walk back to the small family plot was more difficult for her than looking at the house. She felt like she had failed her parents and her grandparents and even those ancestors who slept under the giant Maples in unmarked graves. For a brief moment, she looked around hoping to see the tiny mop of red curls, but the air was still and cool and all she could hear was Anthony Creek from across the fields.

She took Mary by the arm and leaned her head against her sister's shoulder. Mary could feel Pea's guilt and she silently handed the tissue to her.

"I keep thinking 'if only'," Pea said.

"Don't do that to yourself. Thomas was right. If you hadn't stopped Manley, think of the other women who might have suffered. If you hadn't found the link to those deaths on the New River, well, it's not your fault there are evil men in this world."

"Stop blaming yourself. Mom and Dad wouldn't want it and Alicia wouldn't either."

She hugged Pea and pulled her back towards the house to see what the architect had found.

Chalmers was distressed by what the fire had done to the old house. Fortunately, he had retained the drawings and blueprints from the earlier work. While the work had not included the second storey rooms, Mary and Pea were able to assist him in the layout of the missing areas there from their memories and some photographs they had salvaged.

"I think we can probably completely restore the house since only the one section of it burned, but the 200 year old timbers on the one side are gone. They'll have to be replaced with new wood. The rest of the house is good, mostly smoke damage and superficial problems."

"How long will it take?" Mary asked. She was anxious to come back home. As much as she loved being with Pea, she wanted to bring her child here as soon as possible.

"Probably about eight or nine months if we do it right and I assume you want it back to the way it was."

"That long?" Mary could not hide her disappointment.

Chalmers turned to her and saw her impatience. He had liked her parents and he remembered Mary as a child when the first renovation had taken place, bouncing around the kitchen and asking question after question.

"I'm sorry, Mary, but you want it done right. This is a much bigger job than what we did before. And, trying to push the date forward could cost you in quality. You want this place standing here another 200 years, don't you?"

Mary sighed and nodded her head, but then turned to her sister.

"Do we? I mean, do we want to do this, to spend all this time and money when we're the last Taliaferros left here? You're going to stay in Augusta and Joseph and I could leave. Why not just demolish what's left and sell the property?"

Pea looked in her sister's bright blue eyes and then back at the barn.

"We may be the last ones with that name, but this will always be our home. Later generations might sell it, but I can't. Our family, whether their name is Taliaferro or not, will have this as their legacy."

"You're right," Mary said.

"Ladies, it's going to be expensive," Chalmers said. "If we do use the same quality materials, it could be costly."

He had removed the coveralls and was pulling his coat back on.

"I'll send you an estimate and you can get back to me on it."

As he drove away, the sisters went into the barn to find Mr. Dickson.

"I didn't want to interrupt your conversation with Mr. Chalmers, but I'm glad you stayed. I needed to talk to you about something."

He removed his cap and brushed back a few strands of grey hair on the top of his head.

"A few weeks after the fire, a deputy from Gladstone County showed up here asking questions about meth labs, wanting to know if that's what caused this fire. I told him he needed to talk to the Greenbrier Sheriff's office, that I didn't know much about it."

"Didn't seem right to me, somehow. He seemed a little squirmy and I didn't trust him."

The color drained from Pea's face and Mary sat down hard on the bench in the stable.

"Oh, Pea, this is so bad," she said.

Pea regained her composure and tried to think of the things she would need to do.

"Mr. Dickson, if that man comes round again, call 911 immediately and then find a place to hide from him until the police arrive. Don't take any chances with him. He's very, very dangerous."

Pea looked at Mary. "I cannot believe he came here."

Mr. Dickson looked perplexed.

"Miss, do you think he did this?"

"I can't prove anything, but I believe he could hurt you. Can you hire someone to stay here and help you out? I don't want, we don't want you here by yourself where someone could hurt you."

He put his hat back on and looked a little put out by her request.

"If you don't think I can take care . . ."

Mary stood and took his hand.

"It's not that, Mr. Dickson. We know you can take of things, but the man who was here, he has a friend and we don't want you hurt. You're family to us. We couldn't live with ourselves if those men hurt you. If someone else is here with you, they might not be so quick to do something.

He nodded his head and pushed his cap back for a minute as he thought of who would come out here to work, especially someone he could stand to be around and trust them not to steal.

"The Burton boy from up at Renick. He was working for the quarry, but messed up his leg. He's a good boy and strong and trustworthy. I go to church with his folks."

"That would be great, Mr. Dickson. Offer the job to him at $12 an hour and tell him he has to stay here. He can have one day off a week, but he needs to stay here every night. Once the crews start work on the house, you'll be safer," Pea said.

"And he can help you with the animals, too," Mary added.

"Yes, Miss, I'll give him a call later today. If it doesn't work out, I'll let you know and we can look for someone else."

"Great. And Mr. Dickson, remember, if you see that deputy again or that blue ford truck, call 911. Don't talk to that man again. Promise? Please?"

He smiled at the sisters and saw that they really were more worried about him than replacing him.

"Yes. Absolutely. I promise."

They both hugged him good-bye, which surprised him as neither of them had hugged him since they were little things running around farm.

As they left, he called out to them.

"Your parents would be proud," he said and went back into his rooms.

Pea whistled for the dogs and they started the long drive back to Trey's.

They were almost to Covington before Mary spoke.

"Pea, just when I thought this nightmare was almost over. Damn it. Where the hell is the FBI? The bastard shows up at our house – our house! What if he had done something to Mr. Dickson? Oh god, this just gets worse. We've got to do something. This has to stop."

Pea glanced at her sister and saw how angry she was.

"Ree, there's not a lot that two pregnant women can do. You're about to hatch in a little over a month and by that time I won't exactly be in running condition. And we can't tell Trey and Joseph or even Thomas. We can't have them endanger themselves either."

"What about the 'no secrets' thing you promised Trey?"

Pea shifted gears in the Celica as they headed up into the Alleghenies, grinding the transmission before she finally found the right gear.

"I know. I know. But do you want Joseph going out looking for these men?"

"No, but I have a feeling we're going to hear about this from some very unhappy people."

After that day, they received the estimate from Chalmers by courier, with contracts ready to be signed. They were surprised by the amount, not by how high it was, but by how much lower it was than they had expected. Chalmers had attached a note explaining that the materials cost was much less than he had thought because of the housing bubble. The total cost was less than half of what he had thought it would be.

They showed the papers to Trey and Joseph, but ultimately it was their money and their decision and they signed the contract and had the contract overnighted to Chalmers so he could begin the work as soon as possible.

Their evenings were filled with long suppers, laughter, and once the football season began in earnest, the men took over the living room while the women spent evenings sitting next to the fireplace in the solarium. Mary sat knitting scarves and both Diana and Pea teased her that she should be making baby booties. She frowned at them and then admitted that all she had the patience for was for making quick, long scarves. At the rate she was going, Pea said they'd all have two scarves each by the time the baby came.

"And then you'll be wishing you had slept because sleep will be a rare thing for a while."

"And you'll join me in that come late January," Mary retorted.

Diana laughed at the two of them, bickering over knitting and sleep.

"Oh, don't think you won't go through this, Miss," Mary said to her.

"Wow, you are really grouchy," Diana replied.

"When you feel like a beached whale, you'll be grouchy, too."

Diana sighed. "I have to admit I'm a little jealous, but Thomas wants me to finish my dissertation first, though I wouldn't mind starting a family."

"So you've talked about marriage," Pea asked.

Diana nodded. "Yes, but he's right. If we married before I got my Ph.D., my family would come after both of us. And I still need to get him to meet them. He thinks that they won't approve of him. He forgets that I'm the one he has to get approval from."

"Well, you've got time. You're just 25. Time for plenty of babies."

"I know. I just envy you two sometimes."

Pea laughed this time.

"Envy me? I can't even get Trey to talk about getting married. At first he talked about it all the time. Now, when I mention it, he changes the subject. Sooner or later we're going to have to get our timing right."

Mary giggled. "I think you got it right at least once she said, pointing a long bamboo needle at Pea's swelling belly.

"Tell me something," Diana said. "Why do you guys look so different, you know the way your bellies look?"

Pea frowned. "Can't say. Women carry babies differently."

"I think I read . . ."

Pea shook her head. "Don't say it. Mary doesn't want to know."

"Know what?" Mary said and then cursed under her breath as she had to go back and pick up a dropped stitch.

"Forget it, Ree. It's an old wives tale. If you wanted to know, you would have looked at the ultrasounds."

"Oh that, I don't want to know, so just change the subject."

"How do you know what to buy?" Diana asked. "Don't you need to know whether to buy the right colors and things for whether you're having a boy or girl?"

"I've bought neutrals and things that I can use no matter what. And it's not like I have a baby room to worry about. It looks like that's a decision I'll know the answer to long after the baby comes."

Pea shifted in the chair and laid her hand on her belly.

"I want to know. Actually, I already do know, but since Trey didn't go to the doctor with me, I didn't tell him, either."

"Pea! Tell us, please! Come on, tell!" Diana said excitedly.

"Did you ask Trey to go with you?" Mary asked without looking up at her sister.

"No, but he hasn't even asked how I'm feeling or if I have a doctor's appointment. Sometimes I think he doesn't care much."

"Don't be ridiculous. You spent so much time pushing him away that he's probably afraid to approach you about it," Mary said.

"You should have told him about the ultrasound and taken him with you. You were selfish and afraid of how he might have reacted."

Diana kept her thoughts to herself and watched the sisters. She knew where the disagreement was going, where they always went.

"That's not true! Ree, you've kept Joseph from knowing on purpose. How is that different?"

"It's different because I don't want to know and Joseph is honoring my wishes. You haven't told Trey for a completely different reason. And you've pushed him away. I've seen it. We've all seen it. When the hell are you going to trust him?"

Pea stood up, her face bright red.

"Don't try and tell me what I should or should do with Trey. I should think you would understand and I could say a few things to you right now, but I'm not going to be as cruel as you're being to me."

"Cruel? Since when is speaking the truth being cruel? And don't blame this on my hormones. I can't believe you didn't tell him about the doctor's appointment. He doesn't know about that stuff. He depends on you to tell him. You're just so damn afraid he's going to be like Manley."

"I am not!" Pea yelled.

"You are or you would have married him and told him and trusted him!" Mary was yelling now.

Diana had shrunk into the chair. She had never seen the sisters fight like this before. Pea was starting to act like a cornered animal and Mary's words were like a whip that stung her sister with every word.

By the time the women were yelling, the men had left their football game behind and come to the solarium to see what was going on.

Mary saw them at the door and blushed, embarrassed by losing her temper. She sat back down and picked up the knitting and held her tongue.

"What the hell's going on it here?" Joseph asked.

Mary shook her head and refused to answer.

"Pea," Trey asked. "Are you two okay? We could hear you both yelling over the game."

"We're fine." She glared at Mary and then turned back to Trey.

"Trey, I went to the doctor last week,"

"I know. I saw the appointment card on the dresser."

"Don't interrupt me. Mary seems to think I'm afraid of telling you the truth."

"Is something wrong? Are you and the baby okay?" he asked and moved into the room.

"Nothing is wrong".

"I had an ultrasound. We're having . . . we're having twins. Boys. I should have told you. I'm sorry," she said and pushed past the three men and headed up the stairs.

Mary's face went pale. "Trey, I had no idea. Shit. I should have left well enough alone.

Trey said "Excuse me" and followed Pea upstairs to their room.

Joseph sat down in the chair next to Mary.

"Never a dull moment with this family," he said rubbed his face as if the entire argument had never occurred.

Diana stood and went to Thomas who led her into the living room where they could get away from the couple.

"I think we need to get out of this house more. At least you can go to work and I can hide in the old nursery during the day, but the nights. I feel like we trapped in that old movie, *Who's Afraid of Virginia Woolf*, except that there's not enough liquor in the house. Maybe we should find that whiskey Joseph had. Of course the women have enough hormones on board to replace the whiskey," she said to Thomas.

"Come on," he said. "We'll watch something like Ice Road Truckers."

"Ugh," she replied. "I'd rather watch an old movie. Please? Something funny?"

In the solarium, Mary had set her knitting aside and was staring intently into the fire, wondering why she had chosen to goad her sister. Pea was right. She was being cruel.

"Mary, I don't know what that was just about and it's probably better that I don't, but if this isn't working, we can always leave. I still have my place in Fairfax."

"Leave?" she said, raising her eyebrows. "I'm not leaving my sister. Yeah, I'd rather be back at my house, but I don't want to leave her just because we had a fight."

"I'm only putting the offer out there. I'll stay wherever we're safe. I just don't want to see you so unhappy and you seem miserable lately."

She threw the half-knit scarf, yarn and needles at him.

"You'd be miserable, too, if you were the size of a whale. I'm going to bed, for what good that will do."

The solarium was quiet except for the leaves blowing across the lawn outside. Joseph sat there. He wanted to follow her and make her feel better, but he decided to give her a few moments to cool off first. He could hear Thomas and Diana laughing in the other room and the voices of Gene Wilder and Cleavon Little. He smiled. *Blazing Saddles.* Suddenly, instead of following his wife upstairs, he followed the sound of the TV and joined Thomas and Diana just as the movie's town residents reverently said "Randolph Scott!"

Trey went to their bedroom where Pea was sitting on the bedside. He sat down next to her. He was speechless. He didn't know how to react to the news she had just delivered to the entire house. Twin boys. Jesus, he thought.

"Oh good god, why can't I keep my mouth shut? I wanted to tell you last week. I tried several times, but I couldn't do it. I don't know why," she said.

"Are you and the babies ok?"

She took a deep breath to keep from crying and looked up at the ceiling.

"Yes, healthy as can be."

"You should have told me."

"I know."

"Your next appointment is when? Two weeks?" he asked.

"Yes."

He did not look at her, although she had turned to face him.

"I'm going with you and then we're going to meet Mary and Joseph and Thomas and Diana at the courthouse. We'll marry there. No big party, unless you want one," he said.

"No, no big party."

She looked at his face and wiped a tear from her own cheek.

"Don't I at least get a proposal?"

"Do you want one?"

She shrugged.

"I'm going to shower," he said. "Do you want something from the kitchen before bed?"

She shook her head and he went into the bathroom, turned on the shower and shut the door. She lay down on the bed and held her unborn boys with both her arms. What she couldn't admit to anyone was that Mary was right. She was so afraid that he would treat her as Manley had.

It had started out with slaps and then punches while she was pregnant and had escalated as the baby within her grew larger. It had been as if Manley were trying to get rid of their unborn baby. And he probably had been, she thought now. He had never wanted a child. A child would have meant less money for him and his mother. Why hadn't she seen him for what he was?

After Alicia was born, he showed two different faces to the world – one was happy and celebratory, the good father and husband; the other was the one that only she saw. That face was the one where he never spoke to her or if she tried to talk to him he would look at her as if she were the stupidest creature he had ever seen.

The beatings became worse when Alicia was three months old. He made her sleep in Alicia's bedroom still, but some nights he would drag her into their bedroom and rape her savagely, hitting her the entire time. Sometimes he had inserted foreign objects into her vagina and she was terrified on more than one occasion that he would kill her, pushing the objects as far as he could into her.

That was one reason she was surprised when she had discovered she had become pregnant by Trey. She thought that Manley had damaged her uterus when he had hurt her. So she was afraid to tell Trey that she was scared of losing the babies. She had never told anyone what had been done to her or that she was terrified, not of Trey, but of losing her babies again as punishment for killing the man who had tortured her for six years.

She went to the bathroom door and entered it. Trey was still in the shower, but he turned off the water and looked out at her as she put the lid down sat on the toilet.

"Close the shower curtain," she said, handing him a towel. "I need to tell you something and I can't look at you as I talk."

He took the towel and wrapped it around his waist. He then closed the white shower curtain and leaned against the wall. She began to tell him everything and the last suitcase opened. For one of the few times in his life, he wept as he listened to her voice.

Chapter Thirty-Five

Trey woke the next morning to find Pea almost buried under the covers and holding him tightly. She was mumbling in her sleep.

Sometime during the night the dogs had crept into the room and sat watching them in the bed. As Pea tossed about in the bed, one of the dogs began to whimper and actually put its paw on Trey's leg.

He tried to wave them away and whispered 'shoo' to keep them from waking her. Last night had been one of the longest nights of his life. It had taken every bit of his strength not leave the shower as Pea had told him everything about her torture at Manley's hands. Once she had finished, she left the bathroom, closed the door and had climbed into bed.

He had opened the show curtain and stepped out into the bathroom. He went to the sink and rinsed his face with cold water. Somehow, he didn't think that she would ever speak of what she had told him again to anyone.

And as much as he wanted to cry again for her torture, he was also filled with a murderous rage that had no outlet. Pea had had her revenge when she shot Manley, but even that didn't seem enough to fill the deep hole burning in his gut.

After a while, he opened the bathroom door, shut off the light, dropped the towel beside the bed and lay down next to her. She was still awake and she reached out the trace the lines of his face. He moved closer and began to kiss her shoulders and breasts with kisses as soft as a feather. When he reached her belly, she involuntarily moved her hand there as if to protect them.

He lifted her hand and first kissed her palm and then kissed the taut skin above the babies. He never spoke, but began to make love to her, taking his time and making each stroke within her as gently as he possibly could. She reached climax just he was on the edge of it himself. He had held it back as long as he could if for no other reason than to show her that he would always treasure her and love her.

This morning, they had slept in and he had loved holding her, watching her sleep, and wanting to begin again what they had done for so long last night. Instead of making love to her again, he slowly pulled his arm from under her head and had grabbed his clothes and went into the bathroom to dress. He exited through the other bathroom door into his father's old room and took the steps as fast as he could.

Just as he was grabbing his keys from the card table next to the front door, Joseph emerged from the kitchen with a cup of coffee.

"Care to make a little trip with me? I need to run a very important errand," he said to Joseph.

Joseph shrugged sure. Mary was still grouchy and he didn't feel like working on his book much this morning.

"Where are we going?"

"I'll tell you in the car, but let's get out of here before Pea or Mary comes looking for us. I don't want to be gone for long and you've got to promise not to talk about this afterward."

"Sure," Joseph said as he grabbed his barn coat from the closet and rushed to catch up to Trey.

In the kitchen, Mary saw the two men get in Trey's car and leave. The baby gave her a hard kick and her back was hurting this morning. Now, watching Joseph drive off with Trey, she wished she hadn't been so nasty to him this morning. She had gotten mad because he hadn't come to bed with her last and had chosen to sit and watch a movie with Thomas and Diana. She realized it was a stupid snit and she was afraid she had made him mad when she wasn't really mad at him. She just felt achy and so heavy.

Outside, the last leaves of October were hanging on to the live oaks next to the drive. She could see the sky darkening to the west and walked out the back door and around the house to feel the wind against her face. It had been the last warm spell of autumn and she felt sad that with the darkening sky there would probably be colder weather coming behind it.

As she stood there, her back began to hurt again and she decided to go into the living room with a pint of Breyer's and rest on the overstuffed sofa and watch junk television shows. Maury Povich was declaring "You are not the father!" when Pea joined her in the room. She held out the pint and spoon and Pea took a bite of the rich chocolate fudge ice cream.

Pea put her feet up on the coffee table and handed the ice cream back to her sister. On the TV screen, a man was dancing around the screen laughing as two women were screaming at him and at each other.

"What the hell are you watching?"

"Maury. I'm being lazy. I decided to leave the dishes for someone else to do."

Pea leaned forward to stand and said, "Fine by me, but I think I need to get something to eat other than fudge ice cream."

"Oh, I don't know. It seems to be a good breakfast to me."

Pea snorted at that.

"You are so close to having that baby."

"Well, if I'm as big as a whale, I might as well enjoy eating like one."

"Ree, whales do not eat fudge ice cream. You know that. Now if you'll excuse me, I'm going to get that hidden box of Lucky Charms you stashed in the kitchen."

"Hey, stay out of my Lucky Charms. Besides, I've eaten most of the charms," Mary giggled.

Mary swung her legs off the sofa and started to stand when her back hurt again. She returned to her former position and grimaced as she did so.

"Hey, would you put this up for me, she called out to Pea, who sighed and returned to get the ice cream and spoon.

"Miss Ree, you are getting lazy or are trying to keep me away from your cereal."

"No, Pea, my back is hurting this morning. Must be Braxton Hicks, but they really pinch today.

Pea sat the ice cream down and went over to where her sister sat.

"Stand up," she said.

"Do I have to? My back cramps every time I do."

"Yeah, here, let me help you."

The minute Mary stood, Pea could see that the baby had dropped.

"Where's everyone? It's Saturday. Even Thomas should be here."

"Can I sit back down now?" Mary asked.

Pea nodded and said, "Of course, sorry."

"Well, Thomas and Diana went to their old apartment to turn the water off. And as for my husband and Trey, they took off about an hour ago in Trey's car. Joseph's mad at me because I've been grouchy. I have no idea where they went."

"Ok, well, I'm going to get some cereal," Pea said and picked up the ice cream again and went to the kitchen.

Once she was in there, she dialed Trey's cell from the house phone in the kitchen. No answer. Damn, she thought. If Ree goes into labor, she's going to need her husband.

She had poured her cereal and was about to join Mary in the living room when the phone rang. She grabbed it before it could ring a second time and whispered, "Trey?"

"Yeah, Joseph and I had a few errands to run. Do you need us to pick something up?"

"Yes."

"Why are you whispering?" he asked. She rolled her eyes.

"Because Ree may be going into labor and I need you and her husband to *pick* us up."

"Oh, shit, we're about 15 minutes out. Do you think you need to call an ambulance?"

She could hear Joseph talking in the background.

"No, calm Joseph down. The labor has probably just started and her water hasn't broken yet, but the baby's dropped."

"What do you mean dropped?"

"Oh, Jesus, Trey, just get home and make sure that both of you are calm. She hasn't realized that she's been having back labor. It could be hours or it could be 30 minutes. Either way, you need to make sure he's calm for her."

It was at that point that Mary walked into the kitchen, her dress soaked with her broken water.

"Pea, I think something's happening," and she suddenly bent over with a labor pain.

Pea dropped the phone and ran to her sister to lead her back to the settee in the hallway. As they left the kitchen, she could hear Trey's voice calling her name.

"How long has your back been hurting?" Pea asked.

"Since yesterday. I thought it was just Braxton Hicks. It's two weeks too soon. I'm not ready," she said and grabbed Pea's hands.

"Ree, calm down. Joseph and Trey will be here any minute. How far apart are the contractions?"

Mary thought for a minute and said, "I think about twenty minutes or so. I know my back really hurt at least three times while I was watching Maury. Then about the time *The View* came on, my water broke. Now it seems as if they're a little closer."

Pea stood and looked around.

"Do you have a bag packed?"

Mary looked surprised.

"No, it's not time yet. I was going to do it next week."

"Shit, Ree, you pack the bag at least a month or two before the baby's due."

Mary began to cry.

"Oh, don't do that. Please, I'm sorry I yelled."

"No Pea, it's not that. I'm sorry about last night. I shouldn't have said anything. I didn't want to cause a problem between you and Trey."

Pea wiped the tears from her sister's face and lifted Mary's chin to face her.

"We're fine. Truly," Pea said and smiled.

Pea ran to the laundry room and grabbed a clean dress for Mary. Pea helped her sister into a dry dress and they got their coats on.

"Are you ok?" Mary nodded yes.

Trey and Joseph pulled up. Joseph was out of the car and up the steps before Trey could turn off the engine.

He took Mary in his arms and led her out the door, murmuring to her that it was going to be okay and headed for his car.

Pea yelled out "No!" and they turned.

"Let Trey drive. He knows the roads better and, and we'll get there faster."

The contractions started coming faster as they drove to the hospital and by the time they reached it, Pea was almost afraid that her sister was going to have the baby in the back of Trey's car. But somehow Mary made it up to the labor suites with Joseph and Pea holding her hands as her labor ended.

A few minutes later Joseph was cutting the cord to his newborn daughter, his face glowing. He handed her to Mary to see, before the nurse took her to the warming lamp as she began to squall loudly in the bright light and colder air of the room.

Pea squeezed her sister's hand and kissed her forehead.

"I'm going to go let Trey know everything's fine."

She stopped before leaving the room and saw her new niece, then looked back to her sister.

"What's her name?"

Mary looked at Joseph.

"We don't know yet. We hadn't decided. I see why knowing the sex ahead of time helps."

"Well, you need to think of something other than Baby or she'll be saddled forever with someone saying 'Nobody puts Baby in a corner'," Pea laughed and walked to the waiting room where she was surprised to find Thomas and Diana as well as Trey.

The three of them rose in unison as she entered the waiting room.

"They're both fine, though Joseph got a little pale at one point. They have a beautiful, blue eyed, blonde daughter with all the right number of fingers and toes."

Trey hugged Pea and Thomas and Diana hugged one another and they all laughed in relief.

"I think this is the first time in over a year that I've felt this good," Thomas said.

Trey squeezed Pea's hand when Thomas said that, knowing that no one could possibly know just how much joy this birth had brought to Pea than any of them.

"When can we see them?" Diana asked.

"I think in about a 30 minutes. They've got to get everything cleaned up.

Thomas tilted his head to the ceiling, slapped his forehead and said, "Thank you, lord. Oh we really needed something good after so much."

He then crumpled into the chair and wiped his eyes. Diana stood next to him and he buried his face in her side.

Trey and Pea watched, each with an arm wrapped around the other's waist as Diana comforted Thomas.

"Today, life was good, a gift from god," Thomas said.

An hour later they were gathered in Mary's room. Joseph sat on the edge of her bed as the others gazed down at the soft pink miracle that just by sleeping seemed to give them all great joy.

"I never realized how tiny they are," Diana said, starting to reach down to touch her and then withdrawing her hand.

Joseph went over to the crib and lifted his daughter from the crib. He looked to Mary and then to Diana.

"Would you like to hold her?"

"Are you sure?"

"Just support her head in the crook of your arm, like she's the rarest flower you've ever touched," he said as he handed her to Diana.

Tears welled in Diana's eyes.

"Oh my god, she's so soft and she smells like heaven."

Thomas moved closer and touched the baby's cheek with his large hand. His face lit up as he did so.

Joseph took the baby back into his arms and smiled down at her.

"I'd like everyone here to meet Taylor Sophia Hallett, named for our grandmothers."

Pea walked over to her sister and sat down on the bed next to her. Mary took her hand.

"I never understood until today, just how much happy and afraid you could be at the same time."

Pea tilted her head down and then looked away from everyone so they could not see the tears that threatened to form in her own eyes. Trey walked over to her and knelt in front of her.

"I forgot about this and, Joseph, I hope you'll forgive my doing this now. I wanted to do this tonight when we were all together for supper, but this seems like a much better time."

Joseph laid Taylor back in her crib and went to stand next to his wife.

Trey pulled a small black velvet box from his pocket, opened it and held it out to Pea.

"You asked me if I was going to propose, so Joseph went with me this morning."

"We apologize for being gone, Mary. Our timing could have been a little better."

Trey removed the emerald cut diamond ring and took Pea's left hand in his. Her hand trembled as he slid it on her finger.

"Pearl Taliaferro, will you marry me?"

She stared down at the ring in silence and for a brief second, Trey was afraid she was going to say no. But she took his face in her hands and kissed him, saying, "Yes, yes. I will."

Everyone clapped softly, even though Taylor chose that time to emit a small squeak. Thomas bent down and lifted her from the crib to hand her to her mother.

"Four sisters and five nieces and nephews," he said as he stepped back beside Diana.

"Aha! You are going to come in very handy," Joseph laughed.

"Oh, no, diapers and midnight bottles are not on my agenda right now."

"Right now," Joseph said and raised his eyebrows.

"No, not right now," Thomas replied, but he put his arm around Diana as he said it.

"You get that personal joy, Joseph. Being your best man does not mean I am required to diaper."

Trey walked around the bed to where Thomas stood.

"Speaking of best men, ahem, since you did it for him, would you do the honor for me as well?"

"Damn, don't you guys know anyone else? Sure, I'd be honored," he laughed and shook Trey's hand.

"I thank you."

Pea, who had been holding her ring out to Mary to examine it, spoke up.

"No big wedding. We had talked about the courthouse, but maybe with Taylor's arrival, we should just ask the minister to come out to the house. The solarium would be perfect. Just us and new baby Taylor."

Mary grinned. "At least those boys will have their dad's name on their birth certificates.

"Oh, yes, boys, as in plural. Since you're a Third, what are you going to do about names?" Joseph asked.

Trey shook his head as if he had just realized for the first time the quandary of naming twins.

"The hell if I know."

Pea patted her small belly and smiled at Trey.

"We've got four months to figure it out."

"Right now, let's celebrate Taylor, no longer just 'Baby'" she grinned at her sister.

"Which I also think means we should all leave this new family to be alone. Ree, do you want me to bring some things from home?

"No, I think they're sending us home day after tomorrow so I guess I'm good. Joseph might need his car. Trey, could you and Thomas drive it out in the morning?"

"Sure."

"Okay," Pea said, "then we're out of here. Love you guys."

As they left with grins on their face, not one of them thought of the fact that the men who were supposed to be watching the house hadn't been around in the chaos when they left the house that morning. It wasn't until the next day that Trey thought of it and by then, it was too late.

Chapter Thirty-Six

On the Saturday afternoon that Mary's baby was born, Tim walked into an empty house. He called Tiff's name and then the boys' names and started to walk through the house toward the living room. No answers to his call. Surely, they hadn't left for the stadium already, he thought.

His question was answered when he entered the living room and found Doug sitting in his recliner drinking a Schlitz from his refrigerator.

"What the fuck? How'd you get in here?"

Doug chuckled and tossed a beer to Tim.

"Tiff let me in, you idiot."

Tim felt fear creep into his gut.

"Where's Tiff now?"

Doug shrugged his shoulders.

"Probably with your boys."

Tim threw the can of beer at him.

"Where the hell is my family, you bastard? If you've hurt them . . ."

"If? What're you gonna do? Pull that gun and shoot me? Fuck, if that wouldn't make my life easier, but then, of course, you'd never see them alive again."

Tim sat down on the dark leather sectional sofa he and Tiff had bought last year. He threw his hat down next to himself on the couch and leaned back. He was going to have to play this very cool or he'd lose everything.

"What do you want?"

"What do I want? Fuck, I'd settle for a place to live other than my truck right now, but I'm not going to have anything until we get this mess with those women settled."

Tim expected this. He was surprised about the fact that Doug was living out of his truck, but the part about the women he'd seen coming.

"What happened to your apartment?"

"Got fired. Lost it. Now I can't even afford a motel that charges by the hour."

"What about going out to your mom's?"

Doug spewed beer across the room.

"Hell no, I'm not coming back here. I'd sooner shoot myself than live here. Listen, those bitches have money. We can get it from them and then take care of them at the same time."

"Kidnap them? Are you serious? Do you realize that FBI husband would have more Fed guys down here faster than a flea on a hound? No way."

"Well, I'm sure your little family can get by for at least a few days, though it's gettin' cold out so that might make it shorter."

Tim took a deep breath and tried to think of a way out of this, but he was out of answers.

"Doug, tell me what to do so we can get this over. I want my family back now."

"Well, you're gonna have to wait a day or two, but they are safe. Just not anywhere you can find them."

"Here's what I thought about doing. One of the women is in the hospital. Seems that she just had a baby and her FBI husband is with her. But the other one, the one who started all this, she's over in Augusta County. We grab her, get her family or whoever to pay up, but we go ahead and get rid of her anyway. We take the money. You get your family and I leave here for good."

"If we do this right, we got no worries, especially if her sister and FBI husband don't even know she's gone.

Tim shook his head and sighed.

"And how the hell are we going to do that?"

"I've already started things. They had security people watching the place, but I took care of them, so no one's there to keep us out."

"What do you mean 'took care of them'?" Tim asked.

"What do you think I mean? That I gave them free tickets to Disneyworld? You are so stupid. You know exactly what I mean."

Tim looked down so that Doug could not see the rage in his eyes. Instead he rubbed them to make Doug think that he was upset, which was just part of how he felt, but he couldn't let Doug see that.

"Oh, I've made you sad," Doug said and laughed.

"Fucking get over it. We've got a job to do. Tonight. We've gotta grab that bitch. Just think of it this way - you can have all the fun in the world with her you want. You can do anything you've ever dreamed of."

Doug sat forward in the chair.

"Think about. It's all her fault that all this bad shit has happened. If she hadn't walked into your office, she wouldn't have gotten herself into trouble. If we don't take care of her, we're the ones who're screwed. So think about how you want her to pay for it. Besides she killed her husband. She should die. No woman should be allowed to get away with that shit."

Tim nodded his head, but was raging against Doug's insanity. He knew then that Doug hated women – all women.

"Hand me that beer."

Doug tossed the beer to him.

"Now that's my boy!"

"We'll punch her ticket, get paid, and no one will ever know we did it."

Tim chugged the beer, letting the alcohol empty into his stomach.

"I need another beer before we leave and I need to change."

He got up to go into the kitchen and stopped, but didn't turn to look at Doug.

"Doug, my family. They're really all right?"

"They're happy as a daisy. Get me another beer while you're in there," he said and started laughing. Happy as a daisy. Yeah, trussed up like hogs in his hotel room. And soon, he have them and Tim happy as a daisy, with Tim's service revolver used to kill them and then to shoot him. Happy as a daisy growing on his daddy's grave. Doug killed off the last of his first beer. He had long since decided that no one was coming out of this alive but him.

Three and half hours later, they drove up Trey's road in Tim's wife's Mazda, the lights off and the small car making little sound as it rolled up the road closer to the dark house.

"We go in through the back part of the house. There's a glass room on the back that has dog doors. We can climb through those and not even trip an alarm. We'll go up stairs, grab the bitch, and leave the same way."

"Wait," Tim said. "Did you say dogs? What kind? Dogs are bad business. The dogs will be on us before we get to the stairs."

"I got that covered."

"Grab that chuck roast in the back seat and put those phenobarb pills in it. They'll be gone just like the guards."

As they walked around the house they noticed a light on upstairs. The room had no curtains and a tiny black woman sat at a desk typing.

"Who the fuck is that?" Doug said. "There's not supposed to be anyone here but the bitch and her boyfriend."

"Doug, listen to me. This is a clusterfuck!" Tim whispered.

"We have no idea who's in that house, much less what kind of dogs. We need to watch them for another day or so to see what we're going to have to deal with."

Doug stood up and headed back to the car. When Tim started to follow him, Tim was stopped by the gun Doug had pulled from his jacket.

"No, you stay here and watch the place. I'll be back tomorrow and we'll take care of things then."

"Doug, what about my family? You can't just leave them out somewhere. For god's sake, you've got to let me see them."

Doug continued to the car. "Do what I said and I'll make sure they're happy. Got your phone?"

Tim hissed "Yes."

"I'll take pictures for you so you can see that they're fine and send them to you on your cell. You just do what I told you. If I have to tell you again, I'll make sure one of those boys never goes near another football field."

Tim gritted his teeth, but nodded yes and walked back to the house to find a place to hide and watch.

He was going to kill the bastard the first chance he had, he thought. Hunting was one thing, but he had crossed the line when he took Tim's family.

It was almost dawn when Doug reached the Days-eze Motel. Tim's family was exactly where he had left them. He had dosed them with the phenobarb he had for the dogs. The boys had been easy. They had cut classes that afternoon in order to practice out back. Their mom wasn't home yet and all he had to do was dope a few beers and they were out fast. He took duct tape to wrap them and put strips across their mouths.

He pulled his pick-up around to the back of the house next to the back door and slid each one of them under a tarp he had secured over the back. It went faster than he'd thought, but he was out of shape since he'd gotten fired and had been sitting around just drinking beer.

Tiff came home about 45 minutes after he'd finished loading the boys onto the truck. She was pissed to find him sitting in her living room, but he already had a plan for her.

Before she could reach for the phone to call Tim, he hit her in the head with his dad's old gun. She fell to the floor, but didn't pass out. A trickle of blood was running through her short, blonde streaked hair. She raised a hand to her head and started to touch her scalp, but he put the gun between her eyes and jerked her to her feet.

She tried to pull at him and fought at him the way that so many women had tried and failed. He twisted her arm behind her and put the gun to her head.

"Get in the bedroom, bitch. Say a word and your boys are as good as dead."

She stumbled down the narrow hallway.

"My boys? Doug, what have you done? Tim will kill you."

Doug struck her again with the gun, this time cutting her cheek. He pushed her into the bedroom and stopped for a minute and looked around. Everything was neat and clean and cheap. He thought of Tim sleeping in those clean sheets and having a bitch to take care of him and it made him angrier. He threw Tiff on the bed and climbed up on her, pushing the gun under her chin.

"If you so much as whimper, I'll shoot your brains all over your nice clean bed and then I'll do the same to your boys,"

He pushed up the skirt of her uniform from the Gladstone Diner where she had taken a job to start putting some money back for the boys to go to college. He pulled her hose and underwear down to her knees. He could smell lavender on her.

He rolled her over and tied her hands behind her back with the hose and the rolled her back to face him.

"You're gonna suck my dick and if you even think of biting me, you know what'll happen."

He shoved his penis in her mouth, but it barely was long enough touch the back of her throat. She stared at him in terror. His dick was flaccid and she didn't think anything she could do would get him hard.

"Suck it, bitch," and he cocked the gun.

No matter how much she sucked at it, nothing happened. He became angrier the more he tried to get hard. After five minutes her jaw was aching, but she kept trying.

Finally he pulled his penis from her mouth and spit on her face.

He shoved his hand into her so hard that she thought she would pass out, but again she stayed awake. He began using his hand in her and used his other hand to jerk himself off. For a moment she saw the gun next to her leg and struggled with the hose to free her hand to reach it while he continued to pump his hand into her, but the panty hose were too tight.

He's going to kill me and my boys, she thought and she closed her eyes, repeating the Lord's Prayer in her head over and over as he raped her with his hand.

As he finished, she watched everything as if she weren't in her body. She didn't see him. Instead, she saw the crystal vase on her dresser that Tim had given her for their anniversary, the quilt hanging of the guardian angel watching over children that a friend had made for her, and Doug's cock dripping on her cream wall-to-wall carpet.

The pain of his fist hadn't been as bad a having her boys, but she could feel blood dripping down her leg and onto her comforter from his school ring. She remembered asking Tim why Doug still wore his high school ring when all the other men their age didn't. Tim had said that most of the men their age were married and had probably lost their rings years ago.

"Now be a good girl, there Tiff and I'll be right back and you and your boys will be fresh as a daisy," he said and laughed.

He returned with a plastic cup with water and shoved three pills in her mouth.

"Swallow the pills, Tiff. Here, take a drink to get them down."

It took about 20 minutes for the pills to take effect. She felt as if a freight train was running through her head and then she was gone. Doug bent over her for a moment to make sure she was still breathing and then wrapped her in duct tape the way he had the boys.

He looked at his watch and saw that he was right on schedule. He would have the three of them back at his room at the Days-eze Motel and be back here by the time Tim finished his shift. Wrapping Tiff in the comforter, he tried to lift her and found she was a little to heavy to move alone so he just used more duct tape to secure the comforter and dragged her through the house to the tiny back porch where his truck sat. He grunted as he put her between her sleeping boys. He felt his back start to ache.

But he didn't have time to let his back slow him down. School would be getting out soon and he couldn't risk even a kid seeing his truck there. By the time he reached the motel, his back was on fire.

"Almost done," he whispered to himself. "Then I can take a happy pill and head to palm trees and more pussy than I'll every want."

He had barely made it back to Tim's house when Tim walked in and found him sitting in Tim's massage recliner. It made his aching joints a little less sore. Damned if he wasn't going get one of those in Florida. Just what he needed to help him ease the back pain he'd gotten from bending over printing presses and standing on concrete floors for 30 years.

Yeah, Florida was going to make it all alright. Just these few little details to clean up and he'd be headed south. The police would see the mess at the Days-eze Motel as murder/suicide and no one would even think he was there. He'd registered at the motel with a fake ID with Tim's name and had never left the room until after dark when no one saw him.

He had everything all ready to go, even the meat to poison whatever dogs that Taliaferro bitch had. Everything until he and Tim saw that black bitch sitting in that back room of the house.

So, now he had to go 'check' on Tim's family and send him pictures of them while Tim watched the house and figured out how many people were there. And the fact that he had lifted Tim's badge, was driving Tim's wife's car and had to drive over four hours to the motel and then back to Augusta County were just more things that could go wrong.

He had to remember after they took care of the bitch up on the mountain that when he took Tim to his little family that he had to make sure to shoot Tim in the face and then set fire to the place. There'd be nothing left to identify and he could go back to being himself with all the money from the Taliaferro bitch.

Tim got the pictures on his cell from Doug almost five hours later. He had sat outside the house and watched in the dark for half the night. When he saw the boys, awake but obviously drugged, he felt relief; but when he saw what the bastard had done to his wife, he felt the fire in his gut burn even hotter to kill the bastard. At this point he didn't care if he went to jail forever, he just wanted Doug dead and his family safe. He decided to take the blame for killing Doug for taking his family hostage, but he would never,

ever tell anyone what he and Doug had spent their lives doing to innocent people.

He felt bad that he had ever let Doug get him started in it and he knew in his heart that he was going to hell, not just because he had done it, but because he had enjoyed it. He didn't think even Jesus could forgive him for what he'd done.

But maybe, this time he could stop it, stop Doug and still save his family. He wanted no more of the hunt, the torture and rape, the death. Too much death.

"Ah, who the hell am I fooling," he whispered to the night sky. The woman would tell everything she knew and his family would find out. He felt bad about it, but maybe Doug was right about one thing. She had to die. He didn't want to do it, but he was stuck. He could go to jail for killing Doug, but his boys could never know that their dad was a monster.

And that's what I am, he thought. A monster.

He stared at the pictures of Tiff and the boys again and wiped tears from his eyes. They were so afraid in those pictures and Tiff was hurting bad. Almost thirty years with her and he could read her eyes like reading a perp his rights. She was really hurt.

Yes, he was a monster, but he was also going to be a monster killer.

Chapter Thirty-Seven

Doug was back by dawn and it took everything Tim had in himself not to beat him to death.

"So, partner, what's going on?"

Tim spit to the side and said, "Nothing."

"No one's come or gone from the house. I haven't seen any dogs, either. The black woman went to bed about an hour after you left."

Doug nodded as if he knew exactly what he was doing.

"So we know there are three people in there at least. Since it's Saturday, I doubt if they have anyone working today. So we wait a little longer and then we move in and take her."

Tim didn't answer. He was tired and cold and worried about his family. Meanwhile, he had to sit here next to a demon and pretend as if everything was just fine. He wanted to throw up. He had spent a lot of time studying the pictures of where Doug had his family. He just couldn't tell. It could have been a bedroom just about anywhere – an empty house, a motel, maybe even at Doug's apartment. He wouldn't put it past Doug to lie about losing his apartment.

About an hour after Doug had come back, they saw Pea come onto the portico with a cup of coffee in one hand and two huge dogs standing on each side of her. She was already dressed for the day in a baggy dark blue sweater and jeans. The rising sun focused on her like a spotlight and Tim inhaled, thinking that he had never seen a woman as beautiful as she was. She was smiling as if she were concealing a secret. It was only when she laid her hand upon her stomach that he remembered what her secret was – she was pregnant. Doug saw nothing but the object of his sick game.

"Those aren't dogs. They look like fucking horses," Doug whispered.

"We could take her now if it weren't for those animals. Shit."

The male dane's ears went up and he turned in the direction of Doug's voice. He began his low growl and was joined by his sister after a few seconds. Both dogs moved from a sitting to a standing position and sniffed the air trying to locate what they had heard.

"Shh, dogs, you'll wake everyone," Pea said and reached down to the male nearest the men hiding on the hillside and felt the hackles raised along his back. Something told her she was very close to danger and she backed up to the door, watching the same direction the dogs were facing as she opened the door and called them in with her. They hesitated for a moment and then went with her but not before uttering loud barks.

"Motherfucker," Doug said. "Now what do we do? "Where's that meat we brought?"

Tim nodded in the direction that Doug had left Tiff's car.

"Shit, Tim, if you'd left it out near the house, the dogs might have taken it."

"That would have been easy if you hadn't taken off with it in the car. You know, Doug, this is fucking stupid. Trying to kidnap a woman who's surrounded by guard dogs and other people, probably all the time is just damn stupid.

You're gonna get us killed. Look, it's been five months since she came to the office. Don't you think she would have turned us in if she were going to?"

Doug slapped him hard across the face, hard enough to knock Tim backwards onto his ass from where he had squatted for most of the night.

"Listen, you bastard, I want that money and I want her dead. I'd kill her fucking sister, too, if she hadn't just had a baby and was protected by being in the hospital. So, it's her or your family. Take your pick."

Tim sat on the cold ground and rubbed his jaw.

"The other sister just had a baby?"

"Yes, you moron, I told you that last night. That's why we can't take them both."

Tim looked at the ground. Maybe he could appeal to the man he thought Doug once was, the man who only hunted men and young women – never children and never pregnant women.

"Doug, that woman's pregnant, too, probably about five or six months. Do you really want to kill a pregnant woman and a child who's done you no wrong?"

"How the hell do you know she's pregnant?"

Tim shook his head.

"Doug, Tiff's been pregnant twice. They stand a little different. And that woman," he said pointing at the portico where Pea had stood, "she not only was standing that way, but she patted her belly. She was talking to her baby before the dogs started making noise."

"I've hunted with you for a long, long time, but we never hurt a pregnant woman or a child. It's just not right and I can't do it. You know it's not right."

Doug didn't respond to him at first. He thought of the nightmares he had been having of the black woman and the child. Could that be a sign to back off, he asked himself.

"No. We're gonna take them all up to the mountain. I don't care who's in that house and I don't give a shit if she's pregnant or has children in there. We'll get the money and we'll kill them all. I need the money to get out of that hell hole I'm in. So you got no choice. If you don't help, your family's dead, too."

Doug stood up and moved from the bushes on the hillside and started toward the house.

God damn it to hell, what am I going to do? Tim stood and shook out his cramped legs, before following Doug. He knew he was never gonna see his family again. For all he knew Doug had already killed them.

He aimed his revolver at the back of Doug's head and thought it would be easier if he just shot the bastard right now. If only he knew where Doug had put them, if they were still alive, then shooting Doug would kill them for sure. He holstered the gun under his coat and followed Doug. He suddenly thought of that dream he'd had and he shivered. God help me, he thought.

Doug had Tim stand to the side of the front door as he used the brass knocker on the white paneled door.

"You know this must be a really old house," Doug said looking around the front of it and the columns supporting the portico.

Tim just stared at him as if he had completely lost his mind.

Once Pea had gotten the dogs in, she ran up the stairs to wake Trey and Thomas and Diana. They were all still half asleep and she practically pulled Trey from the bed. He and Thomas had had more than a few drinks with dinner last night and Trey's head was pounding.

"Get dressed, Trey. I think those men are outside and I didn't see the men you hired to watch the house."

Now he was awake and he pulled his jeans on.

"Go wake up Thomas and Diana while I get something on."

She ran down the hall and pounded on the guest room where their friends slept. The dogs were running up and down to hall, never leaving her side.

She woke Thomas and Diana and then ran back downstairs where she stuck her cell phone in her pocket and the .45 in the back of her jeans. She was just dialing 911 on the house phone when the knock came at the door. She told the dispatcher that two men were trying to break in her house, gave directions to the farm, and although the dispatcher told her to stay on the phone, she lay it down on the table next to the staircase.

On the other end of the line, the dispatcher couldn't tell her that the nearest deputies were in the southeastern part of the county. All the dispatcher could do was keep the line open and listen. She patched the call to Dan, the deputy who had come to Trey's house, but she was desperately afraid that he wouldn't get there in time.

By that time, Trey, Thomas and Diana had come downstairs and stared at the door with her.

"Did you call 911?" Trey whispered.

She nodded and he put her behind him as Thomas did the same thing with Diana. The dogs stood between the women and the men and were barking madly, but never left Pea's side.

Outside, Doug looked over at Tim.

"Fuck this shit," he said and started to kick at the door.

"Girls, go hide upstairs. Thomas, come with me. I've got a couple of rifles in the gun safe," Trey said.

When Pea didn't move, he grabbed her arm and pushed her towards the staircase.

"For god's sake, Pea, for our sons, go hide. You know this house as well as I do. Find a safe place for yourself and Diana. Go, now!"

Pea grabbed Diana's hand and ran up the stairs. She led her to one of the smaller bedrooms and opened the door to an empty closet. She grabbed an old stool and stood on it to push against a panel in the back of the closet.

Diana couldn't see what she was doing and she looked up to see if there was a light in the closet, but she saw nothing but darkness. She went to the bedroom door and opened it a tiny bit to try to hear what was happening downstairs. All she could hear was the pounding at the door and then what sounded like the panels splintering. She closed the bedroom door and ran back to the closet.

Pea had managed to dislodge the panel and pulled a rope ladder down. She began to climb it and had barely gotten through the hole in the closet ceiling when she heard one of the dogs screaming, then the second one and then all sound stopped.

"Hand me the stool and shut the closet door," she whispered.

Pea hoisted the stool into the attic crawlspace as Diana climbed the ladder towards her voice in the dark. Once Diana had joined her there, she pulled the ladder up and put the panel almost seamlessly back in place. Both women knelt across from one another, staring at the panel and not speaking.

Pea was crying. Her puppies were gone. The bastards had killed her dogs. She bit her hand to keep from making a sound as she thought of Trey and Thomas downstairs.

Before Doug had gotten into the house, he gave up on kicking and pounding at the door and grabbed an axe from a wood pile at the side of the house. He handed it to Tim and pointed at the door. Tim took the axe to the door and after a few minutes working at the panel nearest the lock, managed to break through it and reach in and unlock the door.

As he opened the door the great danes charged down the front staircase, but never made it past the bottom step. Doug shot one and then the other without missing. The two dogs lay in a bloody huddle on the floor, their black and white bodies empty of life.

Doug walked into the foyer and listened to see if any sounds were coming from within the house. He pointed at the door next to the fireplace in the living room that led to the small wing where Trey and Thomas were getting guns.

Trey and Thomas had heard the shots and the dogs scream and stopped and stood absolutely still, hoping that the men had not heard them.

They hadn't had time to get the guns from the safe when Doug opened the door and pointed the gun at them. Only a few seconds more and they would have been armed, if not safe.

Doug pushed the gun at Thomas's head.

"Where's the bitch?"

Tim had come up behind him and they recognized him as the deputy.

"At the hospital," Thomas said.

Doug hit him hard in the head with the butt of the gun.

"Liar. We saw her come in the house. Now where is she?"

Blood was streaming from the laceration on Thomas's scalp. Shit, he thought, I'm going to get shot again.

Just as Doug was about to hit Thomas again, Trey spoke up.

"She's gone. She went out into the field through the back of the house. She's probably halfway to Old Stone by now.

"Bullshit," Doug said and hit Trey this time. He hit Trey hard enough to knock him down.

"Both of you get to the stairs. She's still in the house. Those dogs wouldn't have left her here and they're still, well, they were still here, he said and laughed.

He pushed the men through the house and into the fancy foyer with Tim following him.

"You people sure have it sweet here," Doug laughed.

Trey saw the dogs lying next to one another at the base of the stairs and thought about how much they had given to save Pea and Diana.

"Sorry about your dogs. Don't generally like to hurt dogs, but they were in my way and nothing's getting in my way," Doug said.

Tim still said nothing. He hated that Doug had shot the dogs, but the only thing he could think of was getting to his family.

"Now, where is she? Oh, and that black girl. Guess she's yours," Doug said to Thomas. "So both women must be in here somewhere."

"You got about 10 seconds to start talking or I start shooting."

"They're not here," Trey said.

"Oh, yeah, they are. And whether you're still alive or thrown on that pile of dog meat is up to you. Now you get them or we do, but we are going to find them."

"Kneel down put your hands behind your back."

Doug pulled the roll of duck tape from his jacket pocket and threw it to Tim.

"Tape 'em up," he was saying just as he heard a car pull up to the front of the house. He looked panicked for a moment and then heard the car stop. Not the cops yet, but they had to hurry.

Trey saw through the panel Joseph's head of thinning straw colored hair bobbing up the stairs and he yelled out.

"Joseph, run. Run!!"

Doug kicked Trey in the face and ran to the door and jerked it open. Joseph stood there in shock with the gun pointed in his face.

"We've got another member of the party," Doug said kicking Joseph to the floor next to Trey. "Tape him up, too."

"Now I know your bitch is in the hospital, but she can get the money we want and as soon as we have the other bitch, you get the money to us, we let her go, and we'll have ourselves a little fairy tale ending."

"Money?" Trey asked. "Is that what you want? I can get you more money than the women can. If we leave the women and the others here, I can get you whatever you want. Just take me."

Doug paced in front of them, and then headed up the stairs as Tim held the revolver on the men on the floor.

They could hear Doug's voice calling upstairs, but couldn't make out the words.

But in the crawlspace, Pea and Diana heard his threat to kill Trey, Thomas, and Joseph unless they came out.

"How did Joseph get here?" Diana whispered.

Pea shrugged. She knew she couldn't let him kill the men and she began to pull the panel up. Diana said nothing. She was terrified, but she knew she couldn't live with herself if she hid while Thomas died for her.

Diana climbed down the ladder first and then Pea followed. They walked through the bedroom and into the hall where they saw Doug standing with his back to them. Just as Pea was about reach for the gun in the back of her pants, he turned and saw them standing there.

"Ladies, exactly who I wanted to see!" he exclaimed. He aimed the gun at them and pointed at the staircase with his other arm.

"Please join the gentlemen downstairs."

As Pea descended the steps first, she saw her dogs lying in a heap with Joseph, Trey and Thomas kneeling in front of them with their arms trussed up with duct tape.

Trey saw Pea and his heart sank. Why hadn't she stayed hidden? God, didn't she realize these bastards wanted them all dead. Trey knew it when the man had ignored his offer of money. He had no doubt that the man wanted money, but he also knew in his heart that the man wanted them dead, too.

Doug looked to Tim.

"Tape the women up, too."

Tim shook his head. "The roll's empty. The guns will keep them from misbehaving. They don't want their men dead."

Doug looked at the women and said to Tim, "Guess you're right. We'll take their cars to the mountain. Put the women in the Audi and make the white bitch drive. You sit in the back seat. I'll put the men in the Toyota, though the new guy might have to go in the trunk."

He kicked Joseph in the back of the head and Joseph's face landed hard on the edge of the table where the phone was lying with the dispatcher still recording the call.

Doug picked up the phone and saw that it was still on. He threw it against the front wall where it shattered. The police are close, he thought.

"Hurry up, idiot. The police are probably minutes away."

He jerked Joseph up and shoved him toward the door, then kicked Trey in the kidney to get him moving. He just pointed the gun at Diana to get Thomas on his feet. Thomas glanced at Diana and could barely see her with his eyes almost swollen shut from the hits that Doug had rained down on him.

Tim put the women in the front seats of the Audi and climbed in behind Pea.

"Drive now, as fast as you can without getting attention. Head to the New River exit in Gladstone and I'll give you the directions from there."

They headed out and were passing Augusta Military Academy just as three sheriff's deputies passed them on the road. Diana closed her eyes and began to pray. All she could think of was Thomas in the other car. It was all so unfair, hadn't he suffered enough?

Tim sat back in the seat and stared out the window. He wanted to say something to the women, but he couldn't think of anything.

In the Toyota, Doug could not stop talking, at times almost ranting incoherently. Most of what Trey could get out of it was something about hunting and money and how stupid his partner was. Trey didn't speak. Although Doug had put the gun between his legs on the seat, there was nothing Trey could do with his hands taped. And in the back seat, Thomas was in bad shape. His head was still bleeding and every now and then he said Shawnette's name. Trey only hoped that Joseph was faring better in the trunk.

He decided to try one more time to talk to this man about the money he said he wanted.

"Listen, those women don't have any money, but I do. Seriously, if you'll just leave us somewhere, you can get the money and be long gone before anyone would find you. I even have a boat outside of D.C. You could take it wherever you wanted and nobody would every find you," he said, lying about the last part about the boat. He'd never had a boat or even been to the Chesapeake Bay area.

Doug didn't say a word for a minute and then reached over with the gun and hit Trey in the head again. Fresh blood began to roll down his face.

"Will you just shut the fuck up? We'll get to the money part in time."

In the Audi, Pea glanced in the rear view mirror and saw Tim almost nodding off. She thought of driving the car into a tree or bridge abutment, but was afraid that she would not only hurt herself and her unborn boys, but also hurt Diana, not to mention the problem of the Toyota following them. Who knows what that bastard will do, she thought.

Diana looked at her and her eyes were full of tears. She reached out to Pea and started to pull a cobweb from Pea's hair when Tim knocked her hand away.

"Keep your hands to yourselves."

"I was just trying to get something out her hair."

Tim grunted and then said, "Okay, but don't try anything," and turned to look back to see how far away the Toyota was from them.

Pea looked sideways at Diana in surprise. This man is different, she thought. Maybe he can be reasoned with.

"Mister, please don't do this. We don't have anything and I'm pregnant. Please don't hurt my babies."

Tim turned back to stare at Pea's eyes in the mirror.

"Did you say babies?"

Pea started to cry and said "Yes."

"I'm having twin boys. Please don't kill them. I'll give you whatever you want, just let us go. Give my boys a chance to live."

Tim thought of his own boys trussed up in that room with Tiff. His head hurt bad. No, no, no, he thought. My boys have to come first. He was sorry for this woman, but his boys had to be saved.

"Shut up and drive. We're almost to the exit."

They took the exit to Gladstone Gap but he directed them to take an old mine road before they reached the Gap. The road went from a roughly paved and abandoned two lane road to a narrow single dirt lane that wound its way up and around the mountain. A few times Pea thought the car was about to go over the edge and tumble down toward the river, but she managed to keep it on the road and keep it from losing traction on the road.

When they reached the top of the mountain, he made them get out and sit down with their backs to a tree. As he walked to see the progress of the Toyota up the mountain, Pea stuck her hand in her pocket, dialed 911 and put the phone back in her pocket. She hoped the police were already looking for them and would notice the cell signal from the mountain top. She could see a cell tower on a mountain on the other side of the valley.

Diana buried her face in her arms and continued to pray, asking for forgiveness and help for Thomas.

Pea put her arm around Diana and pulled her close to her and whispered, "Don't be afraid. Be brave. Believe."

The Toyota Celica pulled up behind her Audi and Tim walked to it as Doug exited it.

"Listen, Doug. I'm not killing a pregnant woman."

Doug laughed and walked toward the women, pulled his gun up and shot Diana. Diana screamed from the pain, but the bullet had passed through her shoulder. She slumped over into Pea's lap as she passed out from the pain.

"Oops, missed," Doug said and laughed again.

The blood from Diana's shoulder poured into Pea's lap and Pea took her and held her, saying, "No, no, Diana, please, no!"

In the Toyota, Trey watched the entire thing. He could not believe that the man had shot Diana. Thomas heard Pea screaming and he began to kick at the window, trying to get out of the car any way possible.

Tim stood in shock at what Doug had done. Doug was burning all his bridges and Tim knew now for sure that Doug was going to kill all of them, including his family.

"What the fuck? Have you lost your mind?" Tim said.

Doug looked at Tim as if he were looking at an animal he'd never encountered before. And then he raised the gun and shot Tim in the head before Tim could even react. As Tim fell to the ground he saw the flash of a child in red behind Doug and then he closed his eyes and saw nothing. His last thoughts were that he had failed his family.

Doug felt as if someone ran behind him and he quickly turned to see who was there, but he saw nothing but Pea holding Diana in her arms and weeping for her friend who had done nothing but be her friend.

Everything I touch turns to dust, she thought.

Doug got Trey and Thomas out of the car and put them over at a tree across from Pea and Diana. He hit Thomas over and over trying to control the man. He feared the black man more than the others because of his size. Thomas and Trey slumped against the tree and Thomas could not clearly see Pea holding Diana, but he could tell that something was wrong about the way Diana was lying against Pea.

Doug went back to the car and pulled Joseph out of the trunk and walked him over to where the men sat. It wasn't until Joseph sat down that he saw Pea holding Diana. Oh, god, he thought. There was so much blood on Pea that he couldn't tell if she was shot too.

Doug stood in front of all of them and started to recite "Eenie, meenie, miney, mo, catch . . ."

He never finished the rhyme as Thomas screamed and ran at him knocking him down and beating his own bloody head over and over against Doug's head. In his surprise,

Doug had almost dropped the gun and he struggled to bring it up as Thomas continued pounding his head against his. It took a few seconds but he finally had the gun against Thomas's side and pulled the trigger. Thomas fell away from him, the blood coming out from his left side.

While Thomas was rushing Doug, Trey turned his back to Joseph and tried to remove the duct tape from Joseph's hands as Joseph did the same for him. They had almost freed themselves when the gun shots started.

When the first gun shot echoed through the valley, they stopped and turned to watch Thomas fall away from Doug. Doug stood and looked around. There was fear on his face and he was whirling in a circle as if trying to escape something. What they did not see was Doug's nightmare coming to life before his eyes. He began to shoot wildly and they flattened themselves against the ground to avoid the bullets.

But Pea saw what he was seeing.

Dozens of men and women were surrounding him and moving closer to him. He fell backward and she saw a skeletal hand reach out from a sinkhole and grab his leg, tripping him. He was screaming a high pitched wail as he scrambled to get away from the hand.

And that was when Alicia and Shawnette appeared, standing in the middle of the victims, all unseen by Trey and Joseph. Just as in his dream, they pointed to him, except this time, the child spoke. She turned to Pea.

"Now, Mommy, now."

Pea pushed Diana away from her and pulled the .45 from her waistband. She had never been so grateful in her life that Tim had not searched her or Diana. She aimed the gun at Doug's hand holding the gun and shot. The gun flew from his shattered hand and he tried to get to his feet and try to run, but he was surrounded by his victims.

Pea stood and walked next to Shawnette and Alicia. She took aim at Doug's leg and shot him in the shin. He fell against the limestone ridge. She walked over to him, but Alicia's hand touched hers and stopped her.

"It's okay, Mommy. You're okay now."

Doug laid on the ground cringing from the shadows gathered around him. He had curled his body into a fetal position, covering his head with his arms. The blood from his hand that Pea had shot was smeared on his shaved scalp and face.

Pea turned away from Doug to watch as Shawnette walked over to where Thomas lay bleeding. She whispered something to him and then walked back to take Alicia's hand. Then just as quickly as they and the others had appeared, they were gone.

Pea kicked the gun away from Doug and then went over to free Trey and Joseph. Joseph ran first to Thomas and found that he was still breathing. He saw that the bullet had passed through mostly muscle and had exited through Thomas's back.

"Diana," Thomas whispered and Joseph ran to her, but she was unconscious. Her fainting had been mercifully swift and unexpected. Joseph went to Tim's body and picked up the gun.

Pea was sitting on the ground next to Trey who was holding her the way she had held Diana.

"Are you shot, Pea?" Joseph asked.

"No. This is Diana's blood," she said and stared at Diana's broken body, like a doll thrown on the forest floor.

"I've got to get her bleeding stopped."

She pulled the cell phone and tossed it to Trey.

"Dial *69 to get the West Virginia state police. Tell them we need medical help."

"What the hell happened?" Joseph said and looked around. "I thought for sure we were next."

"You didn't see them?" Pea asked.

"See who?"

Pea shook her head and walked over to Diana to tend to her shoulder and attempt to staunch the bleeding as Joseph did the same for Thomas.

Chapter Thirty-Eight

Thomas left the hospital within the week. This time he helped Diana as she slowly recovered from her shattered shoulder. Her family had driven from Baltimore and it was not the best of circumstances for him to meet them.

Once their initial fears were eased, they directed their angry at Thomas and the others. They could not understand why Diana had involved herself with someone so dangerous. It would take them a long time to even acknowledge Thomas, but Diana finally made them.

Instead of going home, Thomas stayed at Trey's for over a month before he went back home, taking Diana with him. Her parents were furious, but she would not leave him.

Joseph and Mary took their new daughter to Trey's and put her in a bedroom adjoining theirs while the Taliaferro home was being rebuilt.

Trey and Pea married in January, almost a month before the boys were born. Thomas stood next to Trey and Mary next to her sister while Joseph, standing next to Diana, held Taylor.

Those were solemn months for them. Thanksgiving was spent at the hospital with Diana. They refused to allow Thomas and Diana to spend the day alone among strangers in the hospital. Since the hospital cafeteria was closed, Mary prepared almost a full dinner for them to share in Diana's room.

Christmas was not much different. No trees were raised nor decorations placed in Trey's home. A few presents were shared, mostly for young Taylor. Their physical wounds were mostly superficial, but their emotional wounds were deep and raw.

The FBI and the West Virginia State Police recovered the bodies of over 40 people from the ridge above the New River; most of the bodies were stuffed in sinkholes, small caves, or old mine shafts.

Many of the bodies could not be identified immediately and it would take almost two years before they could match many remains with people who had gone missing along the river. Families supplied whatever they could to help the task along, but the two men had been killing for so long that some of the victims had no living relatives left.

Mr. Harrison, their first victim was found in a sink hole and his DNA was matched to that of the great-grandchild born the week he had died, who was now over 30 years old. In Harrison's skeletal hand he was still clutching his dead wife's faded Lucite key ring shaped like a broken rainbow when he was found.

Other victims were never found. The FBI posited that the two men had been two of the most prolific serial killers in the last one hundred years. The families blamed the FBI for their lack of action when the news was leaked that they had known for almost a decade that they had known the identity of at least one of the men. But, in truth there was nothing they could have done without evidence and they would never have found that evidence had Pea not picked up the wrong newspaper the day after her sister's wedding.

Pea never told Trey or Joseph or Mary about what had happened on that ridge when they were dodging the bullets from Doug's frantic attempts to escape from the ghosts of his victims.

Tim's sons, once completely awake had rolled over to the door of Doug's room at the Days-eze Motel and had kicked at the door until someone had finally found them. They and their mother had buried their father, changed their names, and moved to Florida, living in the place that Doug had wanted to live, but forever hiding their and their father's past for the rest of their lives. They never went to college and never played football again. They eventually took jobs working in the orange groves, and when asked about their parents, they said they had been raised by a single mother. No one ever found them again and they spent the rest of their lives taking care of their fragile and broken mother.

Doug, who might have been considered legally insane by that time, was not allowed the luxury of pleading insanity as a defense by an angry Federal judge. He was convicted on five counts of kidnapping, one count of attempted murder, and 40 counts of homicide He was sentenced to 40 consecutive life sentences. Each night a different ghost of one of his victims crawled into bed with him and tortured him until he would start to scream. When the lights were turned off, he clung to the wall next to his cot trying to escape the corpses whom he could feel and smell lying next to him. His cellmates, who at first beat him for his nightly screams, began to fear his insanity and would each request transfer. Eventually, the prison administrators had to place him in a single cell. His screams were then muffled by the closed door between his cell and the rest of the general population.

He would live to be 102, each day tormented by the victims he had killed since he was 17 years old. And no matter how many times he was given a mental health status evaluation, the mental health commissioners decided each time that he was pretending insanity to escape his punishment.

One day in late January, Pea went to visit Thomas after he had left her home. She chose a day when Diana was not there. She did not want to hurt Diana anymore than she had been hurt by the ordeal on the ridge.

She believed in her heart that while he may not have seen everything she had, he had heard Shawnette. That afternoon she had one simple question for him – what had

Shawnette whispered to him after Alicia had stopped her from killing Doug.

Thomas paced the living room and stopped to stare out the window of the apartment at the traffic and the people entering and exiting the dry cleaners below. He did not want to remember that day, but he also knew that what had happened on that ridge, at least part of it, was one thing he shared only with Pea. No one else had seen what they had seen, heard what they had heard.

He turned to her, said one sentence, and then turned back to the window.

"She said 'It's not time, yet. It's not time yet'," he said.

Pea pushed her very pregnant body up from his sofa, walked to him and hugged him. She saw that they were constant North Stars in one another's lives. Their lives would always be connected, no matter what else happened to them.

She left without another word. She drove herself from there to the hospital and called her husband and family to join her. Her labor had begun as she descended the steps from Thomas's apartment and her water broke just as she sat down in Trey's Celica.

She realized as she drove that she was wrong on that ridge when she had been holding Diana's bleeding body. Everything she touched did not turn to dust. Things were and never would be easy. It was just life, neither fair nor unfair, and she smiled as she drove to the hospital to bring her boys into the world. She knew that no matter what happened to her that, she could survive – without guilt. Redemption was as much a matter of forgiving oneself as it was asking the forgiveness of others.

Reneé Porter

ABOUT THE AUTHOR

Reneé Porter is the author of the series of novels, The Taliaferro Chronicles, including *The 13th Victim* and *Redemption Ridge*, as well as the novel, *Bell Park*.